ON SHAKY GROUND

OTHER TITLES IN THE SERIES

On Shaky Ground

V. Domontovych

Translated by
Oksana Rosenblum

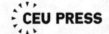

Central European University Press

Budapest–Vienna–New York

English translation copyright © 2024 Oksana Rosenblum

Published in 2024 by

Central European University Press

Nádor utca 9, H-1051 Budapest, Hungary
Tel: +36-1-327-3138 or 327-3000
E-mail: ceupress@press.ceu.edu
Website: www.ceupress.com

On the cover: Konstantin Bogaevsky (1872–1943), "The Dnieper Power Plant"

MOVING FORWARD
TOGETHER

The translation and publication of this book is
supported by the European Union under
the House of Europe programme.

ISBN 978-963-386-757-0 (paperback)
ISBN 978-963-386-758-7 (ebook)
ISSN 1418-0162

Library of Congress Cataloging-in-Publication Data

Names: Domontovych, Viktor, 1894-1969, author. | Rosenblum, Oksana, 1976-
translator.
Title: On shaky ground / V. Domontovych ; translated by Oksana Rosenblum.
Other titles: Bez gruntu. English
Description: Budapest ; New York : Central European University Press, 2024.
| Series: CEU Press classics, 1418-0162
Identifiers: LCCN 2024025350 (print) | LCCN 2024025351 (ebook) | ISBN
9789633867570 (paperback) | ISBN 9789633867587 (ebook)
Subjects: BISAC: FICTION / Classics
Classification: LCC PG3948.P42 B413 2024 (print) | LCC PG3948.P42 (ebook)
| DDC 891.7/9334--dc23/eng/20240730
LC record available at https://lccn.loc.gov/2024025350
LC ebook record available at https://lccn.loc.gov/2024025351

Translator's Preface

*O*n *Shaky Ground* (Ukrainian: *Bez hruntu*) by Viktor
Petrov (the pseudonym of V. Domontovych;
1894–1969) is a modernist novel written in the
late 1930s–early 1940s. It was first published in the literary journal *Ukrainskyi zasiv*, issue No. 4, in Nazi-
occupied Kharkiv in 1942. One of the best examples of
Ukrainian intellectual fiction of its time, the work sum-
marizes the struggles of the Ukrainian intelligentsia in
the late 1920s–early 1930s, when totalitarian reality, together with rampant industrialization, began affecting
everyday life.

Much has been written about the complex personality of the author: his impressive academic background,
which included a doctorate in archeology and leading
positions at the Ukrainian academic institutions in the
1920s–1930s; his association with the group of Ukrainian poets-Neoclassicists; his parallel life as a double So-
viet/Nazi agent; fleeing with the retreating Nazi army to
the West, followed by teaching jobs in Berlin and Mu-
nich; his mysterious reappearance in the Soviet Union;
and, finally, Petrov's life-long romantic relationship with
Sofia Zerov, the wife of the purged neoclassicist Mykola

Zerov. For further information on these and other twists of Petrov's unconventional life, I recommend the works by Vira Aheyeva, Andrii Portnov, Myroslav Shkandrij, Solomiia Pavlychko, and, of course, the novel *Amadoka* by Sofia Andrukhovych, which contains a long chapter focusing on Petrov's history of relationship with the Zerov family.

Strictly speaking, my translation of *Bez hruntu* is not the first one. The novel was translated by the late Dr. George Luckyj and Moira Luckyj, with assistance from Halyna Hryn, in the mid-1990s. However, this translation has never been published. Two manuscripts of the English translation (*No Ground Under Us*; *Rootless*) are kept in the University of Toronto Archives collection.

Domontovych's novels attracted me from my time at a high school in Kyiv, when I would to spend hours sitting on various benches in the city's historic Podil neighborhood, engrossed in reading the modestly published volumes issued by *Krytyka* in the early 1990s.

Back then, *Bez hruntu* piqued my interest with its lengthy descriptions of nature, recreation of the landscape from the Scythian times to the years of NEP,[1] and a vibrant gallery of characters.

Now, however, having spent months with Domontovych's characters, having studied them almost intimately, I can finally fully appreciate what I had missed before: the slightly condescending humor of the main

---

[1] A policy that was announced by the Bolsheviks in 1921, after the disastrous period of the War Communism. The goal of NEP was to stabilize the economy and improve living standards.

protagonist, Rostyslav Mykhailovych; his obsession with the minute details of his internal landscape; a tendency to escape into the dream world in the least appropriate moments (when presenting at an important meeting or leaning out of a window).

The novel unfolds against the backdrop of Katerynoslav (present-day Dnipro), a city whose history, from its humble beginnings as a provincial town in the south of Ukraine, until it caught the attention of Catherine II and Grigorii Potemkin, reflected the ebbs and flows of Ukrainian history and statehood. It was therefore important to reflect creatively on the historical terms Domontovych used to describe what Andrii Portnov calls the "Greek Project": from the Varangians and Princess Olha's Christianity, to Byzantium and the Rus, the Greco-Rus, and Russia-as-Byzantium.[2]

The translator's experience is never one-sided. Moments of high energy and being in sync with the text alternate with feelings of resentment. *Bez hruntu* presents a number of challenges in terms of its abundant archeological and historical terminology, which at times make the narrative read like an academic text. One paragraph in chapter 13 mentions an exhaustive list of furs, skins, and fabrics from the Byzantine era. In other instances, the narrator shares his opinions in fields of knowledge as diverse as the history of art, politics, literature, theatre, music, food, women, and even the theory of perception. He comes across as an expert in all of them, but to keep

---

[2] Andrii Portnov, *Dnipro: An Entangled History of a European City* (Boston: Academic Studies Press, 2022), 29–30.

the reader afloat, I decided to add what may seem like an extravagant number of footnotes. I hope that they will prove helpful for students of Ukrainian history and literature.

In terms of an overarching structure, a curious feature of the novel is the presence of a few metanarrative elements, which reference the author's literary sources and, at the same time, make the reader wonder about the chronology of events. In chapter 10, Domontovych provides the author's digression with an extensive quote from Mykola Hohol/Nikolai Gogol's *The Government Inspector*. The excerpt from Hohol is echoed in chapter 38, where Arsen Petrovych Vytvytskyi, the director of the local art museum, shows Rostyslav Mykhailovych around his art-filled house. Even more enigmatically, in chapter 21 the narrator references an event that would have taken place in 1961, while the novel itself was first published in 1942. The time-warping experiments create an illusion of time and space being non-linear.

A note on transliteration: I have followed the Library of Congress Ukrainian romanization rules, giving preference to Ukrainian spelling of names and geographical locations. In those parts of the novel that are set in Saint Petersburg and make reference to a number of Russian artists and literary figures, I follow the Russian romanization rules. I believe that the effort to distinguish between the two contributes to the project of the decolonization of Ukrainian culture.

And finally—this book would have been impossible without the editorial input of Graeme McGuire and John Puckett. Graeme brought his profound knowledge of stylistic nuances of the English language, as well as creativity and a sense of adventure to this project Without his support, the long hours of grappling with Domontovych's rollercoaster would have felt so much longer. John, with his vast knowledge of Eastern European history and culture and intuitive understanding of the text, helped to untangle some of the most challenging fragments of the novel. Many thanks to Andrea Talaber, Production Coordinator at CEU Press for her kind support with all the administrative matters.

Oksana Rosenblum

On Shaky Ground

I

At the Committee for the Protection of Monuments of Antiquity and Art, where I was working part-time as a consultant, the secretary, Petro Ivanovych Stryzhyus, rose to greet me. Extending his hand, he said in his languid, unhurried voice,

"Here we are, Rostyslav Mykhailovych, eagerly awaiting you! It's been a while since you were kind enough to visit us. Quite a while! Nearly four days, if not more! We even considered sending a courier to your home... So much work!"

I shook the hand extended to me, and as always, from its cold and moist touch, I was left with the impression of having touched a corpse that had lain in the morgue for a long time... ugh, how wretched! A separate decree should be issued to prohibit the appointment of secretaries with such palms to institutions.

I pulled my hand behind my back and held it so as not to touch anything with it before I could wipe it with a handkerchief.

We stood opposite each other. Me—hefty and portly in a blue jacket; gold glasses; respectable and self-

1

assured. Him—pale, no eyebrows; thin, prickly hair; layers of fat deposited on his back; wide pelvis, like that of a woman; and short, scrawny legs with helplessly sagging pants that he occasionally pulled up. A stinking pedant with the shrill, screeching voice of a eunuch. All soft and bloated, like dough that oozes from a mixing bowl.

He was petty, persnickety, and vindictive. Like all pedants, he forgot nothing: neither off-handed complaints against him, nor any fleeting grievance or jibe, nor any accidentally hurled reprimand that he could take as an offense. He would let this be felt on occasion, clinging to trifling matters to an annoying and painful extent.

He was highly valued, however, and I was criticized for being unfair in my attitude towards him. Perhaps! I could not stand him, in any case, and he felt the same about me. I got on his nerves. He got on mine. Our dislike was mutual. We couldn't talk to each other calmly. When we did talk, we always ended up squabbling.

My negligent attitude towards my official duties, the fact that I never remained until the end of the working day at my government post, and seldom appeared at the committee meetings—he took all of this as a personal insult. Also, the fact that I signed the attendance timesheet every day, even those days when I didn't show up at all, irritated him. He suffered, he felt outraged. He was furious. But he didn't show it.

He always remained inconspicuous. Quiet, diligent, careful. Throughout the entire work day, he almost never rose from his chair at his desk. A neat and modest worker whose meticulousness and attention to detail were assets. He would come to the institute first and leave last, if he went home at all. Maybe he only left to sleep… After hours, after dinner, he returned to the institute to fiddle with papers. He sorted them silently. Through numbering, filing, sequencing them in folders, designing meticulous systems for the arrangement of office papers, he created the illusion of some sort of work, activity, and complete order in the institute.

To think they would assign vital matters to this dead clerk! He was incapable of separating the essential from the non-essential. He gave equal weight to the significant and insignificant. He did not disregard trivialities. He was too conscientious for that, and he would be outraged when advised to do so. With the shrill voice of a crone at the market, he would convince you that, in affairs of state, there could be nothing trivial or insignificant.

As a result of this, despite all his conscientious attitude towards work, despite all his persistence and stubborn fastidiousness, and precisely because of this, he was utterly incapable of taking care of things. Unorganized piles of papers kept multiplying on his desk and accumulating in the drawers. Important and urgent matters were postponed from day to day, for they too had to wait their turn. And ultimately, chaos and utter disorder reigned in the affairs of the committee.

"Here you go!" he said, handing me a folder with cases that I was meant to review and consult upon.

"Understood," I replied.

I took the folder of papers he gave me and, greeting our girls at the typewriters as I passed, went to my small desk, above which a neat black-lettered sign was solemnly nailed to the wall, "Consultant. Office hours daily from 12:00 to 15:00."

Someone had added a sarcastic "NO" before the "Office hours" in tiny handwritten letters. Only Allah knows who did that! I didn't snoop around and I didn't erase the word either. The amendment, unofficially made to the official text of the sign, was not inconsistent with reality. I have always held the view that accuracy in official matters is essential to their successful outcome.

I sat down. I pulled a handkerchief from my pocket and wiped my hand. Doing so brought me a sense of relief.

The girls, noticing this, burst into laughter and, bent over their typewriters, clicked away with renewed zeal.

I opened the folder. In it, several renumbered papers were neatly filed.

A petition from the Art Museum in Dnipropetrovsk to the Committee for the Protection of Monuments, requesting to declare the church built from Lynnyk's blueprint in 1908 as a cultural and artistic reserve.

A copy of the Regional Executive Committee's resolution on removing a tenement house from the possession of a parish council.

A 12-page-long report of densely typed text, arguing the artistic value of the church as a highly valuable architectural monument, and the need to preserve it as a separate cultural and artistic institution by reorganizing it into a new branch of the Museum.

I didn't expect to find anything new in that document and therefore flipped through its pages without reading.

I yawned.

Why should I care about any of this? Is there anything more tedious than clerical weekdays? I languished in despair!

There were more papers in the folder, each under a consecutive number. Announcements stating that the Department of Arts of the Regional Executive Committee and the Museum Directorate were convening a meeting with representatives of interested institutions and experts to discuss the matter of transforming the church built by Lynnyk into a branch of the Art Museum. The daily program of work. The agenda for the first meeting.

On all those papers and the report, in red pencil, someone wrote the resolution of our committee's chairman, "Consult Rost. Mykh. for the final decision," and on the invitation, "Suggest Rost. Mykh. to attend the meeting."

I fulfilled my duty. I had reviewed the papers. What more could be expected of a consultant? I suffered from fatigue, exhaustion, and boredom. I was nobody and nothing here. I sought salvation for myself. My eyes wandered around the room. Collecting impressions, as others collect postage stamps, I strove to save myself from defeat.

Two long rays of silk stocking unexpectedly enticed me with a promise of liberation. The black body of the typewriter put a distance between the carmine pair of lips and the black shine of polished shoes. A burnt-out cigarette lay at the edge of the desk.

Symochka caught my gaze and lifted her auburn-dyed head. Her smile betrayed anticipation. Encouragingly, I smiled back at her. With a gesture, she indicated that she needed matches.

"Catch!"

A flat copper lighter made a curve in the air and landed in her hands, firm like a monkey's.

She lit a cigarette. Her eyes were filled with permissiveness. The smoke wafted upwards, mimicking the Egyptian exoticism of the drawing on the cigarette carton. She crossed her legs in a show of defiance.

Who can tell me whence, from what unknown expanses emerges this regret that a man feels when he is looking at a woman?

With a decisive gesture, I closed the folder and went to the desk where the secretary sat. Quietly and carefully, I placed the folder in front of him and said,

"I'm not going!"

Bewildered, he lifted his narrow head of thinning hair, looked at me as if he had just woken up, and asked:

"How do you mean, Rostyslav Mykhailovych, that you aren't going? The chairman has decided it must be you!"

In disarray, he blinked his blond lashes. He hated me.

I felt uplifted and free. In response, I stated emphatically:

"I will not go!"

"So that's that?"

"That's that. I will not!"

He gasped for air. He was breathing heavily, with an asthmatic wheeze. He clutched the arms of the chair with his fingers.

"But why, exactly, do tell me, please, why do you refuse to go?" he asked, and there was fury in his voice.

The girls at their typewriters listened in on our argument. They were accustomed to me speaking to our secretary with a swagger, in a manner that irritated him, amused me, and entertained them. They stopped clicking. Hiding behind the typewriters as if behind a shield, leaning over the manuscripts they were transcribing, they pretended to be engrossed in their work, trying to decipher the unclear handwriting of the documents.

"Why?" I pondered aloud.

Why? To be honest, I had no precise reason I could articulate as to why I refused. I searched for the first plausible argument and it appeared that I'd found one. It was, or at least seemed to be, the most convincing of all possible reasons.

"I will not go because I will not go. Why should I go when I can just as well not?!"

He looked at me with his clouded, fish-like gaze. I was mocking him. He understood that. Surely, he would have liked to respond with something biting and brutal. He muttered to himself; I thought I heard him whisper *the audacity*, but restrained himself from speaking aloud. For him, office rules and formal subordination were paramount.

He nervously adjusted his tie, fumbled with his shirt collar, stretched out his hand, and grabbed a ruler from the table. And though the ruler trembled in his fingers, he replied as gently as possible:

"Of course, Rostyslav Mykhailovych, you are right. No one would dare to insist or demand anything from you. From the chairman's side, it was more of a suggestion, so to say, a proposal, as I understand. Nothing more.

Merely out of respect for you. The weather is nice, so to speak, springtime and all, and you enjoy traveling. So..."

"Very well," I said, "the weather is nice, and I do enjoy traveling, all of that is true. But why, if they wanted me to come down, wouldn't they approach me directly and invite me in person?"

The secretary helplessly shrugged his shoulders. What could he do?

"I suppose," he said submissively, "they were certain that the Committee would suggest you go, and no one else!" He caught his breath and then added,

"To approach the Committee for Architectural Monuments is to approach you, first and foremost. You are the sole authority in all of Ukraine!"

He had to squeeze this tasteless compliment out. A glob of red paint, wrung from a tin tube, coiling like a worm.

Of course, nobody intended on bypassing me, much less offending me. And generally, it would be ludicrous to be agitated by some missing piece of official paper. I made no demands of anybody. As for the Director of the Art Museum, Arsen Petrovych Vytvytskyi, I had true respect and regard for him. He was a cultured, kind, and friendly fellow.

But I continued my resistance.

"No, I won't go. And don't you say a word; I simply won't. Look, ask Sofron Vikentovych or Panas Karpovych. Anyway, what does all of this have to do with me?"

Irritation appeared in my voice. Until now I had been enjoying myself; I was starting to get angry.

The secretary nervously shook his little head and lifted his ruler imploringly. Both he and I knew very well that for a meeting like this, where the fate of this little architectural masterpiece, Lynnyk's famed Varangian Church, hung in the balance, it was I who should go, and no one else.

He shifted the conversation to the plane of material calculations.

"They will cover all expenses. Provide accommodation. Pay a travel allowance."

"A travel allowance, you say!" I shrugged my shoulders dismissively. "Well, isn't that simply marvelous! Did they expect me to go otherwise? What is this travel allowance, anyway? Pure nonsense! It wouldn't cover even a single dinner in good company at a fine restaurant. Good grief..."

I turned, intending to leave. I looked around for the folder that I absentmindedly placed somewhere upon arrival. I cast a friendly glance at the typists, and particularly at Symochka.

The secretary could not stand it. He came out from behind the desk—an extraordinary event—and blocked my path.

"Don't worry. We'll take care of everything. We'll request they pay not only your travel allowance but also your consultation fees."

"They'll never agree to that!" I said.

The secretary was bewildered.

"If we write to them and ask? On the contrary! Shall we arrange for your travel authorization, then?"

I was weary of Kharkiv. The weather was impeccable. A selfish desire for travel awakened within me. I said,

"Go ahead, arrange what you will. Might as well take a trip. What am I to do with you? You keep saying that I do nothing in the Committee anyway."

"Do I say such things? Heavens, Rostyslav Mykhailovych, how can you even fathom such a thing, let alone say it? Seriously! Do you think I don't get it? The Committee is you, and you are the Committee! What would the Committee be without you?"

"Very well, very well. Leave it. I'll go. Just don't forget to send a telegram to book a hotel room for me, for the day after tomorrow. Otherwise, this and that, one way or another, cunning as you are, you'll end up not sending it!"

The secretary frowned, blinking his blond lashes, and nearly choked on a cough.

I turned back, just to catch Symochka's admiring gaze lighting up towards me. She could not stand the boss any more than I.

II

I stood by the open window, and I imagined I could smell the scent of flowers, the aroma of grain and steppe grasses. The train rushed past the red buildings of a small station. From the high plateau, the Dnipro sparkled in the distance. Behind it, the massive ridges and the sprawling city spread beneath the hill. My curious gaze, seeking the unknown, wandered greedily through the morning mist which lightly enveloped the endless expanses of the steppe wilderness beyond the river.

It was stronger than me, this feeling of inner turmoil that arose from the depths of my solitude—it flooded me unexpectedly. It had awakened somewhere in the vast, unspeakable depths of my being.

Weary from destitute wandering, impossible to up-root and never attempted to be uprooted, these dormant, powerful instincts of connection with place, with land, and with soil, inherent in humanity since its inception, suddenly overtook me with renewed strength.

Modern humans have developed the habit of flying their nests. They have severed the umbilical cord that connected them to the womb of their world. They have renounced the feeling of communion with the land. They have forsaken the consciousness of oneness with the country. Above all, they have lost the memory of kinship with their homeland. A birthplace has become a certificate issued by the Registry Office, another entry on the list of forms to complete.

In their habit of constant roaming, humans sought to defend themselves from the power of primal instincts. And yet, these instincts could never be completely es-caped; at the first opportunity, they broke through these artificial barriers, as a river floods in springtime.

And here I am, standing by the window, the wind blowing in my face. I am looking at the distant city, where I have not been since childhood, and I feel pain in my heart, as if it has been pricked with a needle, and a dull anxiety envelopes me. I feel that something is for-ever lost, and nothing has been recovered in return.

The train thunders across the bridge over the Samara River[1]. In vain, I look for the large green willows that

---

[1] A tributary of Dnipro River, near the city of Dnipro in Ukraine.

once grew on its banks. I cannot find them; instead, a naked river flows between barren shores. Flat and colorless. The tedious and tortured invention of a Dadaist poet. An abstract formula of a mechanistic theory. Scarcely a river! No river, only a corpse of a river. The dead flow of immobile liquid. A schematized sketch from a hydrography textbook.

I could not bear it. I turned away from the window, feeling empty and disillusioned, in silent dejection. I longed for sympathy. I lamented. I protested. Addressing no one in particular, I said,

"Just imagine, not a single tree!"

A cry burst forth from inside me. A silent cry, and wordless.

People looked at me, surprised, but no one responded.

We pass the bridge, and what suddenly unfolds before my eyes, just beyond it, unexpectedly strikes me. The same boundless expanse of space and sky that was there before, but is no longer the steppe's vastness, but that of rails, slag, and switches, boxcars and flatcars— red and green rail wagons, white wagons carrying ice, open platforms, tankers. Not a trace remained of the former steppe; across this colossal expanse, countless parallel rows of railway tracks stretched out; a railway park sprawled for dozens of kilometers. No trace of fertile land any longer, only a surface slick with oil, shimmering black from greasy pools of petroleum, covered with a layer of fine coal, slag, refuse, and dirt.

Steel, cast iron, coal, petroleum coke, cement, and brick transformed the steppe into a black graveyard. The green-gray unplowed fallows disappeared, and the train rushed through spaces filled with tracks, wagons, brick buildings of power stations, factories, and mills.

I was approaching a city that was yet unknown to me.

At the station, I was greeted with a bombastic ceremony. I had not yet stepped off the train when Ivan Vasylovych Hulia, beaming with excitement, hurried to snatch my suitcase and coat from my hands. Arsen Petrovych Vytvytskyi made his way through the crowd to me. Giving me a triple kiss, he let his hieratically lavish beard touch my chest. I shook hands with somebody, someone else handed me flowers. I walked through the enfilade of unfamiliar faces. The pageant of greetings reminded me that I was in the south.

It was touching.

At the square in front of the station, I took a few steps towards the tram, but I was already being led to a car, with Hulia standing on the running board, waving my suitcase like a flag.

In the finest of hotels, a large, comfortable room had been booked for me. Everything looked quite imposing. Ivan Vasylovych Hulia showed the utmost zeal. I had nothing to worry about. He took care of everything. He never left my side. He stayed in the room while I took a bath. He sat beside me while I dined. He accompanied me on a walk when I went out to explore the city after lunch.

Hulia! He seethed and effervesced, this emphatic, excited, disconcerted little man with a portly belly. He had been my student at the Art Institute. Now he worked at the Museum as a researcher and, concurrently, served as a delegate of the Committee for the Protection of Monuments. I liked him for the almost childlike sincerity and naive spontaneity, the enthusiasm, that keen and turbulent enthusiasm with which he reacted to everything that directly affected him and also to matters that did not concern him, that had actually nothing at all to do with him. Mailing letters at the post office. Fixing the fuse box. Trimming the white-cedar bushes in the palisade in front of the Museum building. Intervening in the way a janitor sweeps the sidewalks.

It would have been alright, this heightened sensitivity of his, this constant readiness to react to everything around him, relevant or irrelevant, if only he possessed two basic, essential qualities: mental equilibrium and at least the slightest sense of self-restraint! For him, there were no shades, nuances, gradients, intermediate links that connected extremes.

He thought in dichotomies: night and day, darkness and light, good and evil, white and black, yes or no. Anything in between, anything that could not be described as a contrast or something that arose from the combination of opposites, did not exist for him. He either did not perceive it at all or dismissed it with contemptuous disdain.

Instead of connecting, he separated. He did not seek to reconcile anything. There was no peace for him. In his hand, he held the naked blade of a sword, always ready to duel with any opponent.

He was capable only of grasping rigid truths—grandiose, cumbersome, heavy, cast in iron or chiseled from granite; truth-monuments, truth-epitaphs erected over truth itself. Truths that had been established and recognized with a memorial plaque nailed to their facade. Only a gold-lettered inscription on the pediment convinced him that any given truth was deserving of respect.

While demanding an answer from a conversant on a matter of interest to him, Hulia required a categorical response. Anything else did not satisfy him. He could not fathom that between yes and no, between black and white, between the dichotomies of good and evil there could be colors or values worthy of respect. He crushed the shaky and unstable with disgust, like an insect. This was his approach to people, too. He divided people into two categories—good angels and wicked demons. The former descended from heaven, the latter were emissaries of hell. Hulia either idolized a person, proclaiming them a vessel of all virtues, or he scorned them, becoming their implacable enemy. He was easily agitated and quickly reached a state of frenzy. Raging, he knew no path to conciliation. He vilified his adversary, disgraced them, attributing them with the most loathsome flaws and the worst intentions against humanity in general and against himself in particular.

Was he capable of behaving moderately, gently, and calmly, speaking without exaltation? I could hardly imagine it! I only ever saw him in two states: either filled with indignation and anger or captivated by someone, something, a work of art, a cause.

In those moments when he felt sentimental and sensitive, he would start pontificating; in those moments he did not speak but rather sang with abandon. Flustered,

15

he spoke in fragments, tossing out individual words and exclamations.

Visitors to the Museum were profoundly impacted by Hulia when he, acting as their guide, led them through the exhibition halls showing paintings, furniture, and porcelains, brandishing his long walking cane like a sword. The spiciest of dishes, an over-peppered Hungarian goulash meant for a connoisseur, was offered to the visitors after the tour.

His expression, the dramatic nature of his presentation, overwhelmed the visitors. Every chair, cabinet, terracotta statuette, landscape sketch, or drawing of a *kobzar*[2] turned into an occasion, a cause for reverence or an outburst of anger. The way he moved and spoke, each gesture and word were akin to a solemn and ceremonial rite, the emergence of the Sun King, a vivid theatrical performance, a fragment of ancient Greek tragedy in chamber rendition.

The paintings, the porcelain, and the furniture merely served as decorations. Against their backdrop stood Hulia, the centerpiece. Everything else was merely an addition, accessories that highlighted his presence in an improved, more distinct way. To remain entirely in character, Hulia only lacked two things: a pair of buskins and a tragic hero's mask.

After the tour, having finished accompanying visitors through the Museum's halls, he stood leaning on his walking cane, pale and exhausted, brushing strands of

---

[2] An itinerant Ukrainian bard, often blind, who played a string lute-like instrument and sang to his own accompaniment.

black hair from his forehead. Pulling out a handkerchief, he wiped sweat from his face.

Workers from the metallurgical plant visiting the Museum as part of a cultural program; cleaners from the *Oblvykonkom*[3] or another large institution; elderly women brought by a female organizer who addressed them as "girls," with gray hair wrapped in red headscarves—all of them approached Hulia to personally express their gratitude. They were in awe of him. They shook Hulia's hand. They wrote extensive comments in the museum guestbook.

Hulia was a man of a single thought, a singular idea: art above all. Art was untouchable. Art of the Middle Ages and the Renaissance, icons and portraits from the times of the Cossack Baroque, Byzantium, and Holland were for him milestones of eternity.[4] States appear and disappear, peoples emerge and vanish, wars and revolutions erupt, the course of history fundamentally changes, but what remains unchanged is a shard of clay with lacquered ornament, a fragment of brick from a building, a scrap of lime with faint traces of pinkish paint, a miniature on parchment, the canvas of a painting. Everything disappears; only the work of art remains immutable.

Hulia believed that his mission as an authorized representative of the Committee for the Protection of Monuments was to ensure the preservation of artistic works. He saw his official profession, the nomenclature

---

[3] Ukrainian: *Oblasnyi vykonavchyi komitet*, or Regional Executive Committee.

[4] Cossack Baroque: a distinct style of art that emerged in Ukraine in the late 17th–early 18th century and was characterized by the simplicity of forms and ornamentation.

of his positions, and the signing of the payroll for his salary as necessary components of this lofty calling, his messianic destiny to protect art monuments from destruction.

Patiently, fanatically, with the stubbornness of a bull, he continued to perform his duties.

The fate of the Varangian Church, built in 1908 according to the blueprints of the renowned Stepan Lynnyk, was a matter that directly concerned Hulia as an authorized representative of the Committee for the Protection of Ancient Monuments and Art. It was, for him, a personal matter of great urgency.

III

The door to the room kept opening and closing. People entered in single file—acquaintances, semi-acquaintances, and people whom I had never met in my life. Mostly the latter.

They knocked on the door, and Hulia responded, "Come in." He greeted them, welcomed them, and found places for them to sit. Some, at his discretion, were brought to me, others were not. I shook hands and expressed my pleasure.

One of the first to arrive was Arsen Petrovych Vytvytskyi, a long-bearded man, dignified and imposing. A gray, spacious jacket hung off of him with tremendous elegance. I was genuinely happy to see him and speak with him, but we had hardly exchanged a few words before he was pushed aside.

The Director of the Historical Museum, Danylo Ivanovych Krynytskyi—an old professor in gold-rimmed glasses and black frock coat, a connoisseur of Zaporizhian antiquities. He had arrived with his deputy, the head of the Ethnographic Department, the well-known Petro Petrovych Piven, who was wearing the embroidered shirt of a *chumak*[5] and sported long chumak-style mustaches. His rosy, round cheeks shone, his eyebrows bristled like brushes.

In a lightweight blue jacket and white trousers appeared the civil engineer Stanislav Byrskyi, who led the Zaporizhia project—a new city that grew around the Dnipro dam. So too did the editor of the local literary journal *Zoria*, the bulky, bald, and bespectacled poet Semen Ocheretianyi.

The room gradually filled up, and soon there were no more seats available. Hulia called the concierge. Extra chairs were brought in but even this, as it turned out, was insufficient. Some sat on the bed, some on the armrests of the sofa, some on the windowsill. Others stood leaning against the wall. Those who came later on could hardly tell who the host was.

As for me, I receded into the background. In the foreground, Ivan Vasylovych Hulia dominated. People gathered to meet and speak with me but I remained silent; it was Hulia who spoke.

The case of the Varangian Church had overwhelmed him, especially today, on the eve of the council meeting

---

[5] A traditional occupation in late-Medieval and Early Modern Ukraine. *Chumaks* were long-distance merchants engaged in trading salt, fish, and other products.

that would be convened to decide its fate. So much so that he could not even contain himself, he could not stay silent. So he kept talking.

Agitated, rising up on his tiptoes again and again, as if trying to appear taller, he spoke, flustered and excited, addressing everybody and nobody in particular,

"Hand over the church built by Lynnyk to the *Miskkomungosp*[6]... Huh? How do you like that? To treat a work of high art as an ordinary building, as premises with so many square meters of usable area that could be used more efficiently than before! Shall we just convert it into a warehouse for flour, oil, kerosene, herring, and other essential products within the general system of consumer cooperation, so as to supply the surrounding small shops?"

He turned to me. He grabbed my hands and squeezed my palms. Tears glistened in his eyes.

"What are you going to say, Rostyslav Mykhailovych? You must have your say. They will listen to you. They cannot help but listen to you!"

He demanded an answer from me, a definitive one. He was not capable of demanding anything else. It was a summons; it was time for me to act.

He stood before me, relentless and stern, his magnificent strands of black hair rising like rays above his head, the head of an angry prophet with a short nose and sparse freckles scattered across his face. He hoped that the words I would soon utter would resound in this hotel room like the trumpet of an archangel announcing the day of judgment.

---

[6] Ukrainian: *Miske komunalne gospodarstvo*, or Municipal Economic Council.

There was in fact something biblical in his overly exalted pathos. A tiny Samson, prepared to seize the pillars supporting the ceiling, to shift them such that the roof and the stones of the walls would fall on the heads of the blasphemers who would dare disrespect a heavenly work of fine art.

"Such a renowned, such a genius work of art," he exclaimed, "and they intend to turn it into a commercial warehouse. It's sacrilege! It's blasphemy. It's, it's—"

He grasped for words that could convey and embody the depth of his despair. He was wanting both for language and breath. He was gasping. He groaned, agonized, aware of his helplessness.

He sounded like a broken record. He repeated the same things over and over again. He would circle back to what had already been said. He delivered a long speech in which he praised the significance of the Varangian Church as an architectural monument, the creativity of Lynnyk, the splendor of his mosaics.

"The mosaics of Kyiv's Saint Sophia Cathedral from the eleventh and twelfth centuries and Lynnyk's mosaics are the first and the final links in a great chain, defining the consummate perfection of our national art in the last millennium."

He called for action.

"We must not be indifferent. We bear responsibility in the face of eternity!"

Stanislav Byrskyi, sitting in an armchair with one leg crossed over the other, listening to Hulia, frigidly raised his narrow head, bisected by the white line of a middle part. With a calmness in utter contrast to Hulia's frenzy, he declared,

"But you, dear comrade, have neglected to mention that there is another project. You have somehow failed to address it, despite it perhaps deserving our greatest attention in this case."

Perhaps Byrskyi was amused by Hulia's exuberance and wanted to fan the embers. Perhaps he intended to draw attention to himself.

The sparks caught. Dry grass blazed in a flash. Hulia erupted.

"Of course, there is," Hulia asserted emphatically, turning to the man who made the insinuation. Then, turning to me, he said with bitter frustration,

"Can you even fathom this, Rostyslav Mykhailovych? The genius creation of Lynnyk might cease to exist entirely, be demolished, turned into a pile of ruins, leveled to the ground!"

Hulia clenched his fists. His face turned red, blood rushing to his cheeks. He implored. He almost jumped, this short, squat Hulia.

"There is a plan under consideration," he continued, "to demolish all the houses along this entire stretch of the Dnipro, from the county hospital all the way to the cemetery, and build one massive industrial complex in its place. And to demolish the Varangian Church, to end this whole Lynnyk story."

His voice trembled and trailed off. Thrusting forward his corpulent tummy, he flitted around the room, from one guest to another. It was hot and stuffy. He was sweating, collar skewed, shirt untucked between his vest and trousers—this he noticed and hurriedly, blindly stuffed it back under his belt.

"This," he shouted, "cannot be allowed. Under no circumstances! We must intervene in this matter. It's our moral duty."

He called for action. He demanded that all present stand up and fight. Then, seized by doubts about the possibility of achieving anything, succumbing to a sense of hopelessness, he suddenly transformed. He lost all his color; pale and despairing, wringing his cold fingers, he paced around the room.

Dear me, this Hulia could never restrain himself in expressing his emotions. Completely lost in thought, he paced back and forth, as far as it was possible in a space crowded with so many people. He no longer believed in victory. He shook as if in a fever, tormented by the thought of what might become of a tenement house associated with the name of Lynnyk.

I have never met a prophet in my life. I have no idea how the biblical prophets looked, what kind of collars and ties they wore. Perhaps they didn't wear them at all, or maybe their shirts slipped from under their vests, or they hopped like sparrows when agitated, passionately delivering their fiery speeches. I am equally uninformed as to whether any of them had a freckle on the tip of their sunburnt nose. But I have no doubt that Ivan Vasyliovych Hulia had in him something akin to the abounding ecstasy of a prophet.

Of course, any such statement requires certain limitations, covering up some promising ideas—after all, there is a difference between a modest representative of the

Committee for the Protection of Monuments and a barefoot, bearded Jeremiah or Ezekiel. But then again, is the spirit truly something you can measure?

In Hulia, spiritual zeal reached its highest degree. It reached the ultimate human limit, crossing the final boundary. This zeal led him to self-denial, I dare say—to a denial of anything terrestrial.

Prophets were stoned in the streets. Nobody threw stones at Hulia when he walked down by, and no police officer would have allowed it anyhow, but Hulia's frenzy, his excess in feelings, behavior, and actions evoked a smile in some and astonishment in others.

He suffered greatly.

He was burdened by the awareness of his responsibility to humanity, history, and the Committee for the Protection of Antiquities. To anyone who valued art. Those who did not were entirely beneath his notice.

IV

Stanislav Byrskyi rose from the deep armchair where he sat, one leg over the other.

Our paths had crossed before; I had met him several times at conferences and meetings in Kharkiv and Moscow. A calculating man involved in internal politics, he brought a sense of impatience and persistence into achieving his predetermined goals: Lermontov's Pechorin reincarnated. He combined an animal ferocity and a flexible stride with an outward display of indifference. He was unshakably confident of himself, confident of his service to history. Or rather, the service that history provided *for* him. He did not distinguish between himself and history. He viewed history, everything that had come before, as a pedestal to stand on, or steps he had to climb to reach a higher level of personal recognition and success. He nurtured a certainty that beyond him, history did not exist. For him, all phenomena were clear, decided, calculated, and expected: the movement and trajectory of history, its laws, and the logical underlying principles of these laws. No discussion was alien to him. He knew no hesitation. He preemptively accused anyone who dared to oppose any premise he put forward. Accusation and thus destruction. He was convinced that he was the one who embodied the ironcast logic of the revolution. He placed himself above all.

He straightened up. He stood, thin, sharpened like a guillotine's blade.

He started by invoking the industrialization slogan[7] and the leap over the abyss that the country was making. He repeated clichés. He proclaimed principles from on high, imbuing them with his own personal interpretation, shades of meaning uniquely his own.

"The industrialization slogan," he said, "the slogan on the liquidation of the New Economic Policy was thrust out, to the masses, as a rallying cry to make this great leap, into a planned, foreseeable doom, into a grand denial which will reveal itself either as salvation or

---

[7] The industrialization slogans were brief statements regarding the five-year plans that were supposed to propel the Soviet people to embrace the shift to industrialization policies starting around 1927. They were printed in newspapers, posted on billboards, etc.

catastrophe, the scope and limits of which are hard to predict. In any case, they are measured by the figures that lie at the basis of the five-year plan."

He pulled out a white handkerchief and carefully wiped his thin, dark fingers. He continued,

"The edges of the chasm we must cross are lost in the dim twilight of a day that has yet to arrive. But already, in advance, the sacrificial hecatombs, the masses in their millions who will not withstand the superhuman excess of this forced leap from the realm of necessity into the realm of freedom, have been calculated."

He paused. He was not in a hurry. He had the confidence of an experienced orator who took the attention of his audience for granted. I could not deny it—he was a fine speaker.

"Everything must be collectivized, everything must be subordinated to the iron will of the party: the person, her personal disposition, her morals, her views, her relationships with people, her daily life, her home. Nothing can remain in private isolation, be it ideology, labor, personality. Everything is subject to unification and centralization: the thinking of the village chairman and that of the president of the Academy of Sciences. Cultivation of the land and the construction of steam engines, higher mathematics and the production of washbasins... The work of funeral parlors must be carried out according to the principles of Marxism-Leninism, just as the treatment of acne must be interpreted in the light of Marxist-Leninist science."

Was he a party member? I wasn't certain. But I doubted it somehow. More than likely he wasn't, but he was well-connected in some party circles and enjoyed unfailing support from their side.

He took a breath and continued.

"This must be done today because tomorrow may be too late. We must not stop halfway. The deeper the rupture between the two worlds, between the past and the future, the better. Our heads spin at the precipice. Straining your muscles, closing your eyes, you leap across the chasm, hoping you might cling to the opposite edge. The sensation of flight, where everything, body and consciousness, loses its weight, takes over. The feeling of finality can be shaded differently, but in its essence, it is always about the same thing."

Where was all of this coming from? From arrogance, a desire to shock, from true conviction? Was he speaking because he could not help it? The room was hot and stuffy on this vast, sunny evening. But now the horizon darkened, a low sky hung over the wasteland, a piercing wind blew, carrying an icy snow. A blizzard approached.

Anticipating the calculated impact of his words, he continued,

"Some of us harbor the hope that they will be lucky enough not to jump, to linger on this shore, escaping the cataclysm and riding out the storm. They think that all this concerns everyone else, but not them. Vain illusions. Futile hopes. Senseless, unfounded dreams. Their names too are inscribed in the book of fate. Only written on a different page, one that will be turned not today, but tomorrow."

He spoke loudly. He was incredibly calm and utterly confident. This was the blunt inflection of a person who feels his superiority intimately. There could be no objection he would care to consider, no refutation he would welcome.

He was not defending, but accusing. He didn't speak as much as pontificate. It seemed that he was never in any doubt. The verdict he pronounced was incontestable. On the blackboard, he wrote mathematical formulae pristine in their accuracy. That is how he was: lean, taut, dry, deliberately cold and articulate. The impeccable parting, straight as an arrow, split his black, glossy-looking hair. He wore a jacket made of the same cheap blue cloth used for the worker's clothes, cut by the city's most expensive tailor.

"The apartment building, the sum of the arithmetic sequences of its private residents; the private estate with its own garden and yard, intended as an individual household, have become a thing of the past. Housing must become communal, like everything else. Here on the slopes of the Dnipro, we will build a grand housing complex, a commune that will take the place of private residences of the capitalist past."

Where did this certainty come from? The meetings wouldn't even begin until tomorrow. The *Oblvykonkom* was to make its decision based on the resolutions of the Council, but Byrskyi spoke about everything as if it were predetermined! Was he bluffing?

"No individual residences," he said with a didactic intonation, as if reporting to the Little Rada of the *Radnarkom*,[8] "will exist in the future housing complex. We must end the era of small apartments. So far, the struc-

[8] Ukrainian: Mala rada Rady narodnykh komisariv, or Little Council of the People's Commissars' Council.

tural unit of the capitalist era's urban housing was the individual room. We will make a hall, not a room, the constructive component of modern architecture. Massive restaurant halls, enormous common bedrooms are destined to replace the obscure nooks, the closed cells of family dens where eating and sleeping take place."

He was proud of his ability to think on a massive scale. He had cultivated the habit of gliding along the highways of life. He believed that the future was awaiting him. He believed he had a keen ear and could hear the footsteps of what was to come. Indeed, he recognized the echo of his own strides in the steps of the future: the familiar and beloved sound of clicking heels; not rushing nor delicate, but the brisk, confident steps of his bouncy gait.

I turned my head to see the impression Stanislav Byrskyi and his speech had made on our two elders, the honorable local advocates sitting in the foreground by my side, each in armchairs. Both were clean-shaven, with mustaches; Danylo Ivanovych, a lean man in gold glasses, a black frock coat, a yellowed white tie, and a similarly weathered standing collar that had not been in style for half a century. The Zaporizhian elder looked like an old beekeeper, a former friend of Kostomarov and Repin.[9] The walls of his home were painted with

<hr />

[9] Mykola Kostomarov (1817–1885): Ukrainian historian and writer, member of the Cyril and Methodius Brotherhood that supported the ideas of Pan-Slavism and Ukrainian national renaissance. Ilia Repin (1844–1930): a Russian painter of Ukrainian descent, who spent most of his life in St. Petersburg. Professor of the Academy of Arts. Repin became well-known for his paintings demonstrating attachment to Ukrainian history and culture, particularly his large-scale piece *The Zaporozhian Cossacks Write a Letter to the Turkish Sultan* (1880–1891).

murals of Taras Bulba and his sons, the bridles of their horses inlaid with sparkling pieces of colored glass.

The other elder, Petro Petrovych Piven, was the younger of the two. Robust and ruddy, with the round, closely cropped head of a steppe fisherman, he was wearing an embroidered shirt and *tserabkop*[10] trousers tucked into his scuffed, rust-colored boots. He was an ethnographer and writer, temperamental and impetuous. As Mykhailo Kotsiubynskyi[11] mentioned in one of his letters, "Piven has sent me a piece of his writing. He reads nothing because, as he noted in his accompanying letter, he does not want to corrupt his own style!"

Together with Danylo Ivanovych, Petro Petrovych considered himself a true defender of Zaporizhian antiquity, the sole bearer and embodiment of the Sich[12] spirit, a friend and supporter to Kashchenko.[13] For him, Kashchenko embodied the limit of imagination for both Ukraine's past and its future. In 1917 in Sicheslav,[14] it was he, Petro Petrovych, who had published Kashchenko's historical novels on flimsy newsprint.

---

[10] Ukrainian: Tsentralnyi robochyi kooperatyv, or Central Workers' Cooperative. In the 1920s–1930s, these cooperatives provided goods for the consumers of a certain district or a region through a chain of shops.

[11] Mykhailo Kotsiubynskyi (1864–1913): Ukrainian modernist writer known for his lyrical, impressionistic style.

[12] Zaporizka Sich: several centers of the Zaporizhia Cossacks on the Dnipro River. The first Sich was established ca 1552 near present-day Zaporizhia. The last Sich near present-day Nikopol in Dnipro oblast, was destroyed by the Russian army in 1775.

[13] Adriian Kashchenko (1858–1921): Ukrainian writer known for his mediocre prose on Ukrainian history of the Cossack period.

[14] Former unofficial name of Dnipro (city in Ukraine) in 1918–1919.

I could tell how utterly frightened Byrskyi's tirades made him feel. The soft collar of his embroidered shirt was tightening like a noose. His nose, already beet-like, was reddening. The old man was clearly anxious. He kept glancing at the door, seeking an escape.

I could see Danylo Ivanovych's yellowed cheeks turning pale. He sat motionless, frozen in the rigid pose of a statue in a wax museum.

I sensed they were reminiscing about the leaves of the poplars, trembling tenderly in the evening air of their gardens; about the warm wind from the Dnipro caressing their faces as they walked, tapping their canes along the brick wall on their way home from the museum. But they did not ponder the fate of their houses, the fate of their books, manuscripts, archives, and ethnographic collections. They pondered their own fate.

I sensed they were experiencing tragedy in its refined, pure form. Inside them, the process of its crystallization was unfolding. Fragments of poison settled at the bottom of the glass and melted slowly, saturating with death the liquid glowing through the bluish reflections of the vessel.

They recognized the danger that loomed over them, felt in every statement and word of the present speaker.

V

I looked away from them. I continued listening to Stanislav Byrskyi's confident declarations,

"Public communal dining will liberate women from the chains of household chores. It will eliminate the need for a separate kitchen and a separate bedroom. Nurseries for children should perform a similar function regarding structural changes in the building principles of the modern construction of proletarian communal dwellings."

"I am certain," proclaimed Byrskyi relentlessly, "that the motto of familial demise must become the slogan of the nearest future, ultimately, even of today. And why shouldn't it? After all, the family is a mere historical construct. There was a time when it did not exist, and there will come a time when it will disappear again."

The man did not shy away from definitive conclusions. He wanted to be at least five minutes ahead of his time, to outpace the era he lived in, to preemptively declare what the party would offer as tomorrow's next mandatory slogan. A singular combination of Pechorin and Gogol's Bobchinskii, of predation and prudence.

The statement about liquidating the family astonished all present. It descended like news of a catastrophe. Some might have been gasping for air. Mouths agape. Hoarse breath. Spasmodic efforts to swallow amidst the crushing air pressure.

Some attempted, dutifully and cheerfully, to support Byrskyi.

"Exactly. This is absolutely the case! I've been saying this for a long time."

Someone tried to clarify the situation.

"It seems to me, however, that the party's decision on this matter has not yet been announced!"

Some were more interested in the details.

"In that case, there should be a provision for the living conditions facilitating population growth."

With his refined courtesy, Byrskyi hastened to meet all inquiries.

"Everything has been anticipated, everything has been thought out in advance. Do not fear, comrades. All human biological needs will be satisfied. Special rooms—let us call them matrimonial—will be provided in the residential complex, and a key to those will be kept in the hallway, with the concierge. In response to the corresponding applications, approved by the residential building administrator, the keys to these rooms will be issued to married couples."

He continued.

"Bourgeois architecture is marked by a rift between function and form, between form and content. We eliminate this rift: architecture shall be grounded in technology."

Byrskyi went on to illustrate the logic of the new, functionally-oriented and yet aesthetically pleasing style.

Planes of infinite width are stacked on top of one another. Complete subordination between material, function, and form. The functional expediency of the structure is revealed and affirmed by the unity of material and form. The bare visibility of a brick square. Cube joined with cube, free from any externally imposed adornments. Beauty is born from the combination of geometric forms, planes, and cubes; that is, if one must at all use such an outdated and worthless word in a situation where the purposefulness of function and structural necessity should define the features of an architectural style.

I listened to him and wondered whether this speech of his was a real weapon in his hands, or just a plywood model? The threats, the arrogance, the persistence— were they genuine, or were they just a model of a threat, a diagram of conditional anger, a schematic of a gesture that would never come to be?

In those days, Stanislav Byrskyi and the school of thought he represented claimed complete monopoly in matters of architecture.

In time, all of the following would be declared leftist deviations: the brigade-communes where workers' earnings were divided equally; communal housing and dormitories for workers, and the subsequent newspaper polemics as to who exactly—porter, building administrator, doctor—should keep the keys to the matrimonial rooms; and all these ideas about the demise of the family.

Since then, the names of those who headed these projects have sunk into oblivion, but at the beginning of the thirties, these ventures sparked fervent passion. One had to think deeply, ponder fitfully, strain the gnat and swallow the camel before daring to vote for or against.

Later on, I ran into Byrskyi on a few more occasions in Kharkiv. He flew past me, once, in the hall of some congress in Leningrad. The last time I came across him was in a list of surnames mentioned in connection with the sensational political trial of the Trotskyist right in 1937. After that, he ceased to exist.

VI

Strangely, at this moment, Byrskyi was making far less of an impression on these local provincials than one might have expected, considering the refined self-assurance he so insistently passed off as the genuine party line.

A few minutes passed and the audience managed to recover. They shook off the bewitching haze of astonishment. Noise erupted in the room.

The one in the frock coat—Krynytskyi—was the first to stand up. With a cracked, aging voice, clearly irritated, he spoke out against the concrete buildings typical of the modern style. Having denounced these monstrous, industrial boxes, he began to bubble expansively about the old Zaporizhian church in Novomoskovsk.

"The most precious expression of the Sich creative spirit in architecture! The true creativity of the Zaporizhians. This church should be vaunted as a model, a touchstone for all architectural standards!"

It was childish. He did not comprehend the danger of such backward statements. Had he somehow forgotten that this was not a meeting of the provincial Archival Research Commission, transpiring twenty-five years ago in the presence of the Most Reverend Agapetus, Archbishop of Katerynoslav and Taurida?[15] Nor, in fact, was he attending the Archaeological Congress under the

---

[15] Archbishop Agapetus (Vishnevsky, 1867–1923), Ukrainian Orthodox authority, archbishop of Katerynoslav and Mariupol. One of a very few Orthodox church leaders who supported Ukrainian independence in 1918-1919. Taurida: historical name of the parts of Crimea, Kherson, and Zaporizhia oblast of Ukraine.

chairmanship of Countess Uvarova.[16] This was taking place during the socialist revolution, when words ought to be zooming by, searing and crackling, subordinated to the strict discipline of social upheavals.

Fearful, I glanced at Piven, unrestrained and noisy, styled like Falstaff in ethnographic Ukrainian wear. What would he blurt out next, this boisterous hoarder of pipes, carpets, textiles, traditional skirts, chumak wagons, *Cossack-Mamai* figurines, anecdotes?[17] My fears were confirmed. As one elder wound down, the other started up again. They acted as a united front. One adhered to the tradition of Cossack church architecture, while the other, as one might have guessed, championed the traditions of the peasant hut—wood, straw, and reed.

I sighed bitterly. Why did I have to carry this cross? All these speeches and statements of today would be recorded in my book of life! I was nervous. I kept rising, then sitting back down, pulling my handkerchief from my pocket and then putting it back. I shifted from seat to seat, from the sofa to the bed, from the bed to the armrest of a chair. I felt restless. The room was overheated, cramped, chaotic; it was muddle and nonsense, all of it.

Why on earth had I come here? What ill fate drove me to this backward town? And all because of that wicked secretary of ours, that snake Stryzhyus. It was

---

[16] Countess Praskovya Uvarova (1840–1934): Russian archeologist and historian, a Chairman of the Moscow Archeological Society in 1885–1917.

[17] Cossack-Mamai: a popular hero of Ukrainian folk paintings in the 17th to 20th centuries.

he who had persuaded me to come here. I had no actual desire to go anywhere. Surely, he knew all that; he anticipated that my coming here would result in this dire predicament. I was seized by anxiety and boredom. The tips of my fingers grew cold. My heart froze, snapping feebly, and sank into the abyss. Who knew what unpleasant rumors would spread through town tomorrow concerning a meeting in my hotel room!

Did I really travel here so as to, from the very start, take a plunge into this tense atmosphere of disputes, protests, and complaints? Each of those, for everyone present, could turn into the most catastrophic accusation, the consequences of which could hardly be foreseen. Who could guarantee that tomorrow they wouldn't say—look, this fellow came here, gathered all sorts of people in his hotel room, greeted them, shook their hands, cordially invited each one to sit down and… Much more of this and that will be said. And how, then, would you justify yourself?

Better to neither listen nor think. I got up and went to the window, leaning my elbows on the marble sill, feeling the coolness of the stone with my sweaty palms, and looked out on the street. Greenish dusk swallowed the dark leaves of the evening trees. The wires flickered electric blue and lilac. A tram rumbled down the boulevard. What carefree tranquility! But even leaning out of the window, I could hear the conversation in the room. I grabbed my handkerchief and bit through it; I tore at it with my teeth in blind fury. Then I threw the shredded rag out of the window.

Our honorable Petro Petrovych Piven was the noisiest of them all. He had already lost the feeling of concern that had briefly captured him.

He leapt up and rolled, round and sturdy, from his chair. He shouted and yelled. He shook his fists in Byrskyi's face.

"Why, who the hell needs this what's-his-face, this Shmarbusier fellow, when we Ukrainians have a beautiful, neat hut whitewashed with clay, covered with straw or reeds, which, certainly, has existed since time immemorial, since the day God created the first man, the first Ukrainian with a pipe, a forelock, and wide trousers with a waistband!" The old man blathered on, round and rosy as a watermelon, an ethnographic model of a simpleton.

What concern did this rotund fisherman from the Samara swamps have for RAPP,[18] for the dictatorship of Averbakh's[19] followers who, with the relentlessness of little popes, were pigeonholing all styles and epochs, all works and artists according to their social class, as if they themselves were not fed on ideological pottage of questionable quality? These helpless dilettantes issue boisterous statements of left-bourgeois snobbery from Paris and Berlin, imagining them the ultimate slogans of proletarian doctrine.

The old man, tanned by the Dnipropetrovsk sun, waved a hairy fist. Proclaiming the hut as the source of all folk virtues, he bent his will with the idyllic bluntness

[18] Ukrainian: Rosiyska asotsiatsiya proletarskykh pysmennykiv, or Russian Association of Proletarian Writers.

[19] Leopold Averbakh (1903–1937): Soviet literary critic, member of the RAPP, senior editor of the *Na postu* magazine.

of a provincial, the naive simplicity of Chateaubriand's Iroquois, the sincere clarity of some abstract Rousseauist.

He defended the necessity of the rapids.

"We have survived up until now without this dam— we will manage without it. Our fathers lit the tallow candle, and we will light it too. But how are we to live without the rapids, without the steppe, without the hut and a loaf of bread placed by the altar?"

Rage overpowered him. He brought his crimson face close to Byrskyi's and, forming his fingers into a well-known ethnographic combination,[20] thrust them right at him, saying:

"You want us to give up our hut for that Mister Karbusier? How about you try...*this*!!"

A burst of cackles shook the room.

Victorious, Petro Petrovych triumphantly returned to his seat, plunged into the soft depths of the chair and wiped his broad, sweaty forehead with a handkerchief.

Byrskyi stood in the corner, leaning over the back of a chair with his hands, indifferent and motionless, acting as though nothing was bothering him. The reality that he subscribed to existed beyond the reach of ordinary people. He felt like a stern guardian of a country to which no uninitiated would be granted entry.

I moved away from the window where I had been standing. I paused in front of the vanity and sank into the deeper waters of its mirror. I gazed into the cold, ambiguous gleam of the glass, where everything was repeated identically, inverted and doubled: my anxious self,

---

[20] A rude gesture with one's fingers that conveys the idea of refusal.

the embroidered collar ribbon of Piven's shirt, the black strand of Hulia's hair, the yellowed wax of Danylo Ivanovych's face, the blue undulation of tobacco smoke, the dusk of summer cornices under the ceiling, the upper semicircles of high evening windows.

The illusory structure of the mirror reflection opened up a non-existing space before my eyes. In its estrangement, the space resembled a dream phantom. I was dreaming.

Then I awoke from my dreams. Someone was calling my name. They addressed me demanding that I speak up and clarify the matter. Were the architectural slogans of *Na Postu*[21] to be accepted as final, as directive decisions from the government and the party?

I expressed my opinion with utmost caution. I offered neither yes nor no. I smoothed out the rough edges, I avoided the darkness and shadows. I walked on the bright side of the street. I attacked the tasteless architectural inclinations of the bourgeoisie. I spoke of capitalism, that is to say, degeneracy, which brings with it the decay and distortion of style, a rupture between content and form.

As I spoke, with my shoe I was toeing at the edge between solid ground and the abyss. I stood on sand, and the rapid water of the stream was swirling, rushing past me, tearing, wresting the sand from under my feet. What an odd feeling of impermanence! The last, feeble stroke

---

[21] Russian: *Na postu* / *On Duty* (1923–1926). Soviet literary magazine of the radically left, communist orientation. The literary critics who united around the magazine were called *napostovtsy*.

of the arms before the waves engulf me, and the hope borne of despair: "But perhaps I will be saved! Perhaps I will make it to shore!"

I was done. I spoke eloquently but I had said nothing!

The abyss beckoned me. Waves rocked the walls of the brick enclosure. Bonds unclasped. Noise erupted from the solitude of the room. Everyone was screaming. Everyone wanted to express their "for" or "against," to defend or attack, grab someone by the collar, throw him on the ground, press with their knee, choke him out. Destroy the other in order to save himself. Only himself.

All of them were worried about the fate of their houses, poplars, the cherry trees in the gardens. Their fate? And what of my own? They were hoping to save their property at the last moment, when the world, tossed in the maelstrom, was going to hell.

It was necessary to immediately end this type of senseless and dangerous chaos, to break off this mad helplessness. The best way was to suggest dinner at a restaurant. But I was the host, and it was awkward for me to say—my good fellows, let's make our way out of here! I glanced about, forlorn. So many people and yet nobody of use. Except for, perhaps, Hulia. But where was he? I looked around the room, searching for him.

There he was, sitting astride a chair, gloomy and concentrated, elbows on its back, chin resting on his hands. Brimming with his own anxieties, he was silently considering the black semicircle of the evening sky, cut off by the window frame. How lucky that our wild Hulia had not joined the conversation. No doubt he would have turned the fragile chaos of the discussion into a catastrophe.

I made my way through the maze of knees, chairs, elbows, shoes, and lit cigarettes. I approached him, leaning over, and speaking confidentially, I asked for his help.

"My fellow, you have to help me—I'm sinking here!"

His face lit up, full of joy. He beamed. He would do anything for me. He was devoted to me utterly, now and always.

"Anything you want from me, Rostyslav Mykhailovych!"

VII

Flat steps of wide stone tiles led us deep underground to a cellar, where, as I was assured by local restaurant connoisseurs, we would find not only genuine, high-quality *shashlyk*[22] but also the most exquisite wines.

We descended slowly, and my attention was drawn to the unpretentious paintings by an amateur artist on the walls of the stairs—varied drawings, flamboyant landscapes, random everyday scenes. I paused to examine them.

Before my eyes, a swift stream was flowing down from snowy, blue-white peaks perched among gray rocks into the depths of a narrow valley.

Peasants wearing *beşmets* in vivid colors,[23] with knives shining like lightning, were at work cutting heavy clusters of green and blue grapes.

---

[22] Same as shish kebab.
[23] An outer garment worn by men in Turkic cultures.

Gray donkeys, one after another, crept along a narrow footpath between mountain and river in the pink, flaming haze of a sunlit day.

Against the orange background of a bazaar square, under the wide branches of a large sycamore painted in hot lime, stood a small *dukhan*[24] made of purple stone.

On the vermillion fire of a furnace, an ultramarine cook was frying shashlyk into shades of carmine.

Peasants who had come to the city for the market sat at the dukhan's long tables, the color of golden ochre, drinking wine and coffee. Red and dark brown.

Right there, with their legs neatly tucked underneath, sporting sheepskin hats, sat a group of musicians; they were blowing into their pipes, bulging their eyes, puffing their cheeks like frogs.

The next one was a wedding. The groom's cheeks were youthful and rose-puffed; his calf-like raisin eyes were calm and thoughtless; a long merchant's frock coat and a high *karakul*[25] hat completed this ideal sample of a standard groom.

There was more: scenes, figures, events. Among the plentiful beşmets, grapes, shashlyk, ruby drops of tomato juice mixed with onions, there was also a painting of Cossack-Mamai. A horse was tied to an oak tree. Pistols peeked out from his chumak-style belt. His saber hung from a branch, the mustachioed Cossack with a

---

[24] A small store or a restaurant in the Caucasus or Crimea.
[25] A hat made from the fur of the Qarakul sheep, typically worn by men in Central and South Asia.

forelock played the *kobza*. [26] A tribute by a simple-minded local artisan to this Ukrainian motif, innocent and pure-hearted.

Ivan Vasylovych Hulia and I stood on the steps, examining this mural and exchanging thoughts. Rather, I spoke as Hulia listened.

"What can an artist do," I said, "when he must paint both a searing sky and frigid snow of distant peaks, the slippery fish scales and the silver shimmering tremble of the river's surface, all with the same white paint? Have you," I asked Hulia, "ever thought much about realism?" He turned to me, surprised. What did I want from him, really? What kind of answer was I expecting from him? He did not understand me.

I placed my hand on his shoulder, gazing into his eyes through the lenses of my glasses. I wanted us to rid ourselves of the anxiety that had settled in. To break free from the fear that engulfed us, that leached the color from our vision of the world, the fear of looming catastrophe.

Bon courage! Let us uncover the secrets of creativity yet unknown to us. Let us find within ourselves gentle peace and inner silence, and do so while looking upon these kind-hearted and naïve drawings.

"We must," I said, "appreciate this master's experience. Somewhere in the depths of his memory, perhaps unknowingly, he preserved memories of the ancient traditions of the Persian miniature, its canonical characters, gestures, and colors. As a naïve artist, he combined a millennia-old archaism with his own lack of experience.

---

[26] A Ukrainian folk string instrument from the lute family.

By way of courage, which he certainly did not lack, this unschooled painter managed to overcome his artistic helplessness."

"See," I turned to Hulia, "he never spared paint to impress the viewer. He did not limit himself in the choice of colors. He was generous and sincere. He used the paint that he liked. He followed his own inclinations, evoked by the simplicity of his unpretentious heart, when he decided what and how to paint, what colors to use."

"Every artist," I went on, "also represents his people. The millenary, many-eyed, manifold memory of the people nurtures and feeds the memory of the artist. Realism is," I continued, "a phenomenon more complex and profound than it seems upon the first, often superficial glance."

I savored listening to myself, to my own hastily expressed thoughts. Within my own words, uttered only to entertain myself, I kept discovering truths that dawned on me unexpectedly but, for the time being, were not binding.

Hulia did not contradict me. He listened with an endearing, even touching gratitude. Perhaps this is how the students had listened to their teacher in the workshops of Quattrocento or Cinquecento—solemnly and with reverence, with a kind of trust containing no trace of ambiguity or darkness.

"What is especially valuable in the creative work of this master," I expanded, "is that he entirely eschews the traditions of the contrived realism that we inherited from the artists of the nineteenth century. An artist of

45

this contrived realism paints a sunset as he sees it, never as he *knows* it. He paints a red-yellow sun setting on the horizon, although from his school days he knows that, in fact, it is the earth that moves while the sun remains motionless. Our master does otherwise. He paints what he sees and what he knows simultaneously. For instance, consider this drawing of the river, if you will. Here is the river's surface, shining in the sun, brilliant rays reflected and blinding to the eye. But the master is not satisfied with this depiction. He does not want to be accused of being untruthful in his art and failing to paint what he knows best—that every river in this fertile and blooming country swarms with good, hearty fish. Therefore, he paints what he sees—the dazzling surface of the river, and in addition, what he knows—the river full of fish with meticulously painted semicircles of scales."

I gave Hulia a dreamy smile. I wanted the two of us, standing here in front of the dukhan's entryway, to fantasize about art that did not exist.

"That's how art should be: not only externally accurate but also, first and foremost, honest, depicting what the master sees and what he knows, not hiding his intentions to influence, agitate, compel, move. Isn't it true," I insisted, "that modern art strives to combine these three instances, these three formulas: *I see, I know, I want?*"

I took Hulia by his shoulders, squeezing them firmly, spreading them apart, pushing him forward, as if trying to force him to straighten up.

On the door leading to the restaurant, there was a painting of a pan with three fish frying. They were generously sized and sizzling; golden droplets of oil scattered in all directions like fireworks.

"Look," I said to Hulia, pointing to the painting, "how these trout are depicted. The master did not take into account the laws of perspective. He did that consciously and deliberately. The laws of perspective contradicted his intentions. He aimed to show everyone who crossed the threshold of this restaurant, just how massive are the fish being fried, how appealing and tasty; how the cook spared no oil to fry this delectable fish. The artist was commissioned for this, and everything he painted was intended to attract the visitor, arouse a sense of hunger, compel him to enter the cellar, convince him that he would be welcomed with warmth and hospitality, generously and at scale. No, he did not hide or obscure his intentions. This art had a purpose. The master truly understood the purpose of genuine art and his vocation as an artist. Is that not," I asked, "where the egalitarian art of the Dutch Masters came from?"

And I turned the handle, stepping over the threshold.

VIII

The chubby, squat host met us at the door of his establishment with cordial greetings and a bow. Hulia introduced me.

"Our professor, just arrived from Kharkiv, has traveled through Armenia. Studied the local, ancient architecture. A deep connoisseur of its native wines, shashlyk, and ancient temples."

We greeted each other warmly. I shook this satyr's wide, firm palm. Magnificent flesh, filled with warmth and blood, gently touching my fragile, nervous hand.

I hastened to express my astonishment at the artistry of the painter who had decorated the walls of the eastern corridor.

Smacking his tongue, he savored our praises with a sweetened, cat-eyed squint. As both the establishment's host and the one who commissioned the paintings, he took complete credit. He thanked us with an air of self-assurance,

"Let me tell you, a great master painted it. Very great. An outstanding talent he had. Where, in what other dukhan could you find such a thing? How much wine the man could drink! And he cooked shashlyk wonderfully!"

He was choking with pleasure. Then he added, with bitter sadness,

"But he drank himself to death! I did not spare the wine. It's your business to drink as much as you want if you have such talent from God. Go on, drink!"

Undoubtedly, the host was right to conflate the things that, at first glance, seemed to have no connecting thread—the ability to cook shashlyk, the art of painting, and the capacity to drink a tremendous quantity of wine.

The host led us to a separate room in the depths of the cellar. He personally rearranged the tables. He called the boys to bring a clean tablecloth. We sat. Leaning on the backs of the chairs, he bent his body over us—Sabaoth, the Lord of Hosts, blessing the descendants of Noah. The scene followed the biblical style; he directed

our choices as we passionately and chaotically deliber-
ated on what wine to order.

After lengthy conversation and lively debate, seeing that
we could not decide for ourselves, he gave an indulgent
smile and suggested we settle on a barrel of red wine that
he had apparently been saving for a special occasion.

Everything was done with a touch of dignified ritual.
There was no hurry whatsoever.

The host received us as though he was performing a
sacred rite. It left an impression that we were not merely
chance visitors who had stumbled in from the street, but
stewards of a ritual, his dearest and most amiable com-
panions. To serve people shashlyk and regale them with
wine was a lofty calling from above, bestowed only
upon select individuals.

In this manner, the vital and important matters found
their expression. Eating and drinking were not just
physiological acts of satiation, but affirmations of a
community, a joyful and sincere human friendship.

Nothing was portioned or measured. Drinks flowed
without limit, and food was consumed without restraint.
What use were calculations among friends and family? A
cook emerged in a white apron, tall and slender, with
arched black eyebrows and a petit goatee, his Adam's
apple forming a right angle with his throat. He greeted
us, shaking our hands in turn. He inquired whether the
dishes he had prepared were to our satisfaction.

Our praise was effusive. We complimented him
unanimously and enthusiastically, perhaps a touch too
loud for this low-ceilinged room. He thanked us for our
kind comments on his labors. Upon our invitation, he

raised a glass with the rest of us; his sharp Adam's apple moved and bulged, spasmodically twitching on his dry, sinewy neck.

Tapping the glass, he placed it on the table and wiped his lips and mustache with the edge of his apron. Then, clearly touched, he promised to prepare excellent *chebureks* for us.[27]

"Fine folks like you must indulge in something delicious!" he proclaimed solemnly.

And he kept his promise. He served us golden, speckled, succulent chebureks. They were impeccable. It was an unparalleled culinary masterpiece. I couldn't resist asking him if he also painted, like his predecessor.

Modest and dignified, he responded that he had not yet had the opportunity to test himself in that field.

I ardently advised him to do so, assuring him that a master in the art of making chebureks had every reason to aspire to equally high achievements in the art of painting.

"I regret," I said, "that I did not have the chance to appreciate the artistry of your predecessor in grilling shashlyks, but I believe you will paint just as exquisitely as he did. The way you prepared those chebureks attest to your artistic abilities."

He stood there, lost in his thoughts. It seemed he was dreaming of something distant and wondrous.

He thanked me for my kind remarks and promised to ponder my advice and give me an answer after some thought.

---

[27] A deep-fried turnover filled with minced meat and onions, originating from Crimea.

The chef left, head bowed, the burden of deliberation resting upon his shoulders.

I felt that my conscience was out of balance. I had disrupted this man's inner peace, causing uncertainty. And for what?

On the way home after dinner, I walked together with Hulia. His mood was lyrical and uplifting. He didn't speak; he hummed. He claimed to be a happy man because he had the opportunity to walk with me.

Hulia tried to embrace me. But because he was considerably shorter than me and his hands weren't cooperative after drinking, his legs swayed stubbornly sideways. He kept grabbing at my jacket, tugging, so I eventually had to hold his hands and ask him to leave my jacket alone, lest I end up without my outerwear.

My pleas were in vain. His promises were worthless! He immediately forgot what he had agreed to and repeatedly attempted to wrap his arms around my waist, pulling at my jacket once more, insisting that today he was the happiest person in the whole world.

His recitation transitioned into an expansive, melodramatic speech. Stirred and exalted, he assured me that I was an extraordinary person, and owing only to my innate modesty did I not draw attention to this fact in the slightest.

Struggling against gravity, taking somewhat uncertain steps, we finally reached the hotel. In the lobby, palm trees emerged from oblivion, a vague memory of a journey that never happened. Did we have to order banana salads and monkey steaks for ourselves? At any rate, Hulia didn't seem to object. The tropical wind blew him to parts unknown.

As I emerged at that moment from the chasm of forgetfulness, Hulia suddenly appeared before me. I realized that I didn't actually know what I was supposed to do with him now. I knew that abandoning him to his own fate would be too cruel on my part. Conscience did not allow me to do so. I knew I had to escort him home. I was willing to undertake such self-sacrifice, although I was at the brink of exhaustion after a whole day of traveling, commotion, meetings, and meals… I wanted to sleep. I yawned with no reservation, not even trying to conceal it.

The porter saved me. He managed to arrange for a carriage. The clattering of wheels resolved the situation. But Hulia resisted—he protested. He was outraged. He energetically declared that he was not going anywhere. And certainly not home. He had a good deal more to tell me and, foremost, to prove to me that he was very happy to have become better acquainted with me.

"You cannot imagine, Rostyslav Mykhailovych," he declared, "how endlessly happy I am, speaking with you so sincerely and openly, like friends."

He was completely overwhelmed with happiness. The porter cautiously took Hulia by the shoulders. I assisted with getting him into the phaeton, and the coachman raced the horses. Leaning over the back of the carriage and reaching out to me, Hulia continued shouting for quite some time. Cries for help, pleas to save a dying man, assurances of his unwavering devotion echoed in the dark of night.

The scene was right out of Dickens, and I fell asleep like a true Pickwick, with a pleasant sense of optimism in the future of humanity. Fundamentally, people were good, and a society built on the principles of universal harmony and happiness was still possible in this world.

IX

A brief but profound slumber, and the next morning I woke up lively and refreshed, as always after an evening of libations in good company.

On such mornings, work flowed well. Life seemed cloudless and joyful; all complexities had already been resolved in advance. The anxieties and troubles that only yesterday loomed threateningly, with catastrophic inevitability, seemed immeasurably distant now, trivial and senseless formalities. Everything was clear, assured, and perfectly fine. In this utter tranquility, creative certainty grew without effort.

I felt the urge to sit at the desk that very moment, lay out pen and paper before me, and forget the existing world and everything around by immersing myself in the blueprint of an illusory reality crafted by my hand alone. I would have worked, without fatigue or interruption, until the evening, until night, perhaps even into the blissful hours of the morning.

On the green, grass-like fabric of the writing desk, silent and still, stood the wide marble slab of the inkstand. The squat, capacious inkwell, filled to the brim, revealed the unsullied virtue of its glossy black, slightly convex surface. The quill, resembling a bayonet or lance, glistened inside the pen.

There was not a trace of bitterness in me. No sense of burden or obligation. Complete clarity, perhaps tinged with a hint of sorrow and satisfaction, for I knew all too well that one ought not think of private projects on a business trip. You haven't taken with you, not even for the sake of decency or to appease your conscience, a single sheet of white paper, a fragment of a manuscript still in work, not even an unfinished book! The best dreams are always those you don't have to tend to in order to fulfill, isn't that so?

It was time for breakfast, and then I would be off. Let us press the button three times and summon the waiter.

There he stood before me, a slender young man in white with a nickel badge beneath his left-side breast pocket, ready to jot down my order. The sun reflected off the polished tips of his boots. A white cone-fold napkin hung from his bent left arm. He waited.

"What would you like for breakfast?"

I became quite pensive.

"Oh, something very light! But before anything else, black coffee. But make it," I cautioned him, "strong and boiling hot, my friend! Some butter sprinkled with silver droplets of brine. Radishes, cold and fresh. Some pink ham."

"Is that all?"

"Perhaps! Or..."

A momentary pause, brief hesitation, lengthy contemplation.

"Alright, here's what we will do! Would you put in an order for a sweet omelette with jam for me as well, please?"

After breakfast, lighting a cigarette, I stepped out of the hotel and paused on the veranda.

What a humid morning—not scorching hot, but wonderfully warm! Such mornings in the Ukrainian steppe occurred only in springtime. The water level in the Dnipro had already dropped. Copious rain fell every day. The black soil retained its springtime moisture.

The entire city around me was draped in green. Acacia trees bloomed. White clusters of flowers weighed down the trees lining the sidewalks, densely crowding the boulevard, stretching across the middle of the avenue and forming a continuous green-and-white canvas into the nearby gardens. The morning air was saturated with the sweet, faint scent of the white blossoms.

I crushed a cigarette with disgust and tossed it into a metal bin. Smoking a cigarette on a morning like this borders on blasphemy!

Intoxicated with the aromas, I stood on the veranda. Did any other city in Ukraine possess such a fragrant charm? Kharkiv, Hlukhiv, Kyiv? I envisioned the city of Kyiv, a city atop hills cross-hatched with deep ravines. In my imagination, I recreated the greenery of its streets and gardens, and decisively declared, "No!"

Kyiv was official, ceremonial; one might say restrained. It was polished, almost arrogant. The chestnut trees lining its streets bloomed with opulent chic but lacked any fragrance. Everything was quite proper and decent, devoid of enthusiasm. The linden trees in the old town, their soft, delicate aroma, remained a mere memory in the former, though not entirely forgotten, name of the district of Lypky.

Only here, in this city on the southern steppe, did scent reign supreme. And one's heart, filled with memories of the lush blossoming, preserves forever the recollection of a world that is no longer the same.

X

I took a seat in a small open-air tram car, its tracks running for kilometers down the road between the two boulevard lanes. The conductor, wearing a red head scarf and flats, hurried along the footboard of the car. Her thick, tanned legs flickered past. Colorful paper ribbons slithered from a leather bag slung over her shoulder. She blew her whistle. The tram started moving.

The steel vibrated and sang, chains jangled, the car swayed. I leaned my elbow on the yellow railing of the seat. The warm, humid steppe wind rushed in from the Dnipro, swaying leaves, softly caressing my face, tenderly touching my forehead, ruffling my hair. Having grazed my lips with the barest touch, it whispered playfully in my ear.

I squinted my eyes, fully immersing myself in the sensuousness of the wind, filled with the scents of sunlight.

Perhaps I dozed off. When I opened my eyes, the tram was at a halt. We had already climbed uphill. On the empty expanse of the hillside, exposed to the wind, dust, and sun, between the slender trunks of freshly planted trees, goats were grazing on the yellow mounds of freshly-turned soil.

Against the gray-green background emerged the gloomy silhouette of an unfinished tenement house. I saw the black hollows of the windows, the dark brick skeleton of the walls, the rusty tin roof draped atop the exposed ribs of the ceiling beams. Construction of this tenement house, intended to be part of the city museum, was commenced before the First World War and abandoned shortly thereafter; and here it stood, a forlorn and senseless ruin. A whimsical reminder of unrealized visions, a black and abandoned void. A latrine for passersby; a den for pimps, beggars, vagabonds, and the homeless amidst the uneven piles of garbage.

The squealing tram traced a semi-circle with its body and turned left.

On a hillock above the gentle slope, beyond a green clump of trees, rose the plain, slender shape of a cathedral—a Potemkinesque monument to the fantasy of Russia-as-Byzantium.

Only the brick wall surrounding the cathedral, sized to the regulations set by the governorate, defined the contours of this grandiose, fantastical construction. This "Greek" project was conceived to surpass Saint Peter's Basilica in Rome upon its completion. With St. Petersburg condemned to rot in the swamps of the twilit north, the steppe city of Katerynoslav was destined to be the new capital of the old Greco-Rus empire.[28]

---

[28] The incorporation of southern territories with their ancient monuments into the Russian Empire inspired the idea of a historical succession between Byzantium and Russia.

Such was the whim of one of Catherine the Great magnates,[29] further nurtured by the illusions of Ukrainian "universalists."[30] Among the contenders for the seat and crown of the Third Rome, there was this unfinished steppe city sprawled about a hill,[31] broad and curved like a woman's fertile womb.

At the next tram stop, passengers disembarked. A yellow clay path, trodden amid the weeds, led my eye to the white brick wall surrounding the cathedral which was intended to be grander than Saint Peter's.

A tangle of thoughts floated through my mind.

To start something and leave it unfinished. To design but not complete. To exert oneself so thoroughly, strain one's muscles until they tear, only to fail.

This theme had occupied Gogol. Images and quotations from his works appeared in front of my eyes.

The tram passed the white structures of this venerable institution. Was it not here that Gogol's Zemlianika[32] once governed a century ago? After all this time, Gogol's work still sounded contemporary.

A sense of time's arbitrary nature awakened within me. Time became transparent. Resistance to it dissipated.

---

[29] Count Grigorii Potemkin (1739–1791). The expression "Potemkin village" came to signify a fake facade that conceals an undesirable reality.

[30] Church leaders and philosophers who adhered to the ideas of the Enlightenment, and for whom the creation of Katerynoslav symbolized the victory of reason over the forces of nature.

[31] Ukrainian: *Soborna hora*, or Cathedral Hill: a centrally located hill in Dnipro (formerly Katerynoslav), a place where the Transfiguration Cathedral was erected between 1787 and 1835.

[32] Artemii Filippovich Zemlianika, one of the characters of Mykola Hohol/Nikolai Gogol's play *The Government Inspector.*

Events were shifting. Deeds and people depicted by Gogol became untethered from their times.

I felt anxious. It was the fear one would feel standing at the edge of an abyss. A chill ran down my spine. The tips of my fingers grew cold and motionless, pressing the faceted glass warm from the sun. I thought about the entire social classes executed during the revolution. Why hadn't their "psychology" been executed instead?

Author's Digression

Rostyslav Mykhailovych debates. He argues. He ponders this theme of Gogol as it reflects in, and intertwines with, the present.

He recalls excerpts from Gogol's works—the watermill on Nozdrev's estate which failed to function for want of a single missing component: "[it] lacked the spindle-socket wherein the upper stone ought to have been revolving."[33] Or perhaps, as in Manilov's house,

> "...*something seemed to be wanting in the establishment. For instance, although the drawing-room was filled with beautiful furniture, and upholstered in some fine silken material which clearly had cost no inconsiderable sum, two of the chairs lacked any covering but bast, and for some years past the master had been accustomed to warn his guests with the words, 'Do not sit upon these chairs; they are not yet ready for use.' Another room contained no furniture at all, although, a few days after the marriage, it had*

[33] Nikolai Gogol, *Dead Souls*, trans. D. J. Hogarth (London: J. M. Dent, 1916), 72.

been said: 'My dear, tomorrow let us set about procuring at least some temporary furniture for this room.' Also, every evening would see placed upon the drawing-room table a fine bronze candelabrum, a statuette representative of the Three Graces, a tray inlaid with mother-of-pearl, and a rickety, lop-sided copper invalid. Yet of the fact that all four articles were thickly coated with grease neither the master of the house nor the mistress nor the servants seemed to entertain the least suspicion."[34]

The examples were abundant, countless. The images that arose in Rostyslav Mykhailovych's inner vision, fleeting and unstable, could have been elucidated. But then what had been transient would cease to be so. It was not like that.

For the Author, determining the scope of visual impressions, ideas, and thoughts through which his character passed during his journey, was of importance. The abandoned museum building; the incomplete project of the grandest cathedral in the world; the recollection of the unfinished mill at the estate of a Gogol character; the chairs that are yet to be upholstered; the unfurnished rooms; the luxurious chandeliers and the unpolished copper candlestick, beneath the notice of master, mistress and servant.

To escape the thought of the social classes executed during the revolution, Rostyslav Mykhailovych deviated into psychologism. And this shift into psychologism, even abstraction, has come to characterize his distinct perception of reality.

---

[34] Gogol, *Dead Souls*, trans. D. J. Hogarth, 24.

XI

I disembarked at the last tram stop. A welcoming, quiet street, lined with single-story buildings, led me down a slope to the square where Stepan Lynnyk's Varangian Church stood.

The small brick houses still bore marks of the cosmic storms that swept over the city in the early years of the revolution. The unpainted roofs were rusting away; half-broken gutters hung loosely over boarded up entrance doors. Neglected porches overgrown with grass and weeds; bricks fallen from the steps and strewn about. Barbed wire stood in place of fences that had been converted into firewood. Through the wire, I saw lonely trees of bygone apple orchards.

The new residents lacked the desire or initiative to repair the porches or tend to the orchards or restore the fences or patch up the holes left in the brick walls—bullets from the barrels of Makhno's men.[35] People had lost a sense of constancy. They adapted to living in ruins as if awaiting the next catastrophe, something even more terrible and destructive than the last. They turned their homes into transient shelters, huts into caves or dens, cities into transitional camps.

The former governorate town of single-story buildings, constructed by secondary-school teachers, clergy, staff captains, and collegiate assessors on saved-up

[35] Nestor Makhno (1889–1934): anarchist leader from Katerynoslav governorate, who organized peasant bands for redistribution of the possessions of the local nobility. For a few months in 1919, his troops counted some 40,000 people and controlled a large chunk of Southern Ukraine.

change and paid off through bank loans, had perished. It was struck down during the early years of the revolution, absorbed into a new way of life, and now was marked for final demolition such that a new center could be erected among the ruins, bathing in the light of a new industrial sun.

And here I was, passing through the remnants of a bygone way of life. I reminisced about the city that existed in my childhood years. The idyll of cherry orchards, the bluish-green leaves of apple trees; the shining, almost varnished, upright trunks of apricot. I remembered the dense rows of currants and gooseberries along the darkened fence boards. I relived walking along the paths, black-blue like oil slicks, stretching between the garden beds; the tea sipped in the evening garden, with crickets chirping and the distant tram murmuring as it turned the boulevard; the air heavy with the scent of night flowers.

Walking along the quiet, empty street of the vast steppe city, I surrendered to the comforting embrace of past memories. Those decadent dishes, drowned in cream and butter! Or finely chopped, juicy tomatoes, pepper-dusted and mixed with onion. Even better—the fluffy loaves of bread, or the enormous green-black watermelons that crunched with each slice.

At the turn of the century, life under the steppe's sunlit sky was cheap and carefree, with few days of hardship or unforeseen anxieties. Sheep grazed on uncultivated land across the plains. Peasants did not manure the fields, saying that it would burn the grain. Houses were lit with candles made of dried dung. A bucket of cherries, hauled by *haraba*[36] to the city, sold for a kopeck at *Ozerka*, the city's largest market. And because a bucket of cherries cost so little, a pair of trousers sewn from factory-produced fabric remained an unattainable dream for begging children who clung to their mothers' skirts,

"Please, mama, please get me those *tess-tile* pants!"

Back in the day, very few city dwellers bought cherries at the market. People hadn't yet become tenants renting accommodations and living in other people's houses. Each person lived in their own hut, each with its own little garden. Urban estates were boundless in their vastness, with beehives, vegetable patches, orchards.

Trams were already tearing down the boulevards, but water was still being fetched from the Dnipro in barrels. Water sloshed in the darkness through the top opening. In the hallways, in a dark corner by the door, the barrel would be covered with a lid made of nailed planks. And a brass pitcher placed on top gleamed dimly, a murky gold, in the chilly twilight of the porch entrance.

XII

I walked slowly. I was not in a hurry. Did it really matter whether I turned down that side street or just continued straight ahead? Whether I'll make it to the conference meetings or not? I was lost in memories. The distant eve-

---

[36] Turkish: *araba*. A high four-wheeled carriage drawn by oxen or horses, which was widely used for agricultural and commercial purposes in the South of Ukraine in the 18th and 19th centuries.

ning gleam of the brass vessel, the scent of the hoary stock preserved the mystery of singular experiences for me.

And then suddenly, right where the side street ended at the edge of the hill, on a small square paved with broad granite slabs, against the backdrop of the blue sky so vast it defied description, appeared the Varangian Church—all white, bathed completely in the radiance of the sun.

Following the tradition of cities located along the water route "from the Varangians to the Greeks,"—Novgorod, Kyiv, Tsargorod[37]—the church was consecrated in the name of Sophia, the Wisdom of God.

I stopped walking. I just stood and gazed at the church, without stepping onto the square. I wanted to preserve the fullness and entirety of the sudden impression in my memory: the blue abyss of the sky, the gray sheen of granite, the white radiance of the church, and the green-and-white of flowering trees in the distance.

This tenement house on the cliff above the Dnipro embodied a small architectural masterpiece. It contained a trace of the Church of the Savior on Nereditsa Hill,[38] a touch of its ancient wooden construction. But most of all, it carried the mark of Stepan Lynnyk's creative vision of the imperial grandeur of Byzantium, of Olha's[39] pre-

---

[37] The Slavic name of Constantinople.

[38] A 12th-century Orthodox church near Novgorod, Russia. It was destroyed in 1941 and rebuilt in 2004.

[39] Princess Olha (Helga; ca 890–969): the first ruler of Kyivan Rus who was baptized. According to the chronicles, she was of Varangian origin. During Olha's reign, the religious landscape of Kyivan Rus still contained many traits of polytheism.

Volodymyr Christianity, of the Varangian origins of Christianity in Ukraine-Rus.[40]

I stood there, away from the square, and I was surprised to see no one in the cemetery in front of the Church. No Hulia, no Arsen Petrovych Vytvytskyi, no one at all. Weren't we supposed to start the conference with an inspection of the Varangian Church, under the guidance of the knowledgeable Arsen Petrovych?

What was going on? Was I perhaps confused? Wasn't the meeting supposed to be here? Perhaps I missed an addendum? I pulled a handful of papers, notes and memos, messages on the meeting from my coat pocket. I went through them one by one until I found what I was looking for. Right. The meeting was scheduled for eleven in the morning, and now... The green arrow against the matte background of the steel watch face indicated it was just a little past nine. I had arrived much too early.

I pondered what to do. Return to the hotel? But what would I do there? That would make no sense. Head to the Museum? But again, why? Alright, so be it! I set about to find a peaceful place in the cemetery near the church and sit by the cliff.

I walked around the cemetery. In a circle, outlined by dark-green white-cedar bushes resembling stamped plastic, I found a stone bench by the edge. On this

---

[40] The term was first introduced in the 19th century by the Polish-Ukrainian writer Paulin Święcicki to describe the descent of modern Ukraine, especially its territories around the Dnipro River, from the traditions of Kyivan Rus, through the Galician-Volhynian kingdom, Polish-Lithuanian Commonwealth, and so on.

squat bench, as if hewn in a rock, I settled myself comfortably. I took off my jacket, loosened my tie, unbuttoned my shirt to expose my chest to the rays of the spring sun. I rolled up my sleeves, took out cigarettes and a lighter.

Splendid! How wonderful that things turned out this way. I enjoyed inhaling the air, saturated with the scent of young greenery and blossoming trees. I surrendered to a voracious, joyful tremor, an aimless sense of animalistic, purely carnal satisfaction from the sunlight and the warmth of spring.

The stone slabs of the courtyard appeared white in the sun. Below me was a chasm, a desert of space, a blue infinity: myself and nothingness! The splendor of depopulated solitude!

The edge of the cliff obscured the tops of the willows growing along the Mandrykivka riverbank.[41] Beyond them, I saw a strip of golden sand, then the wide expanse of the river. And across the Dnipro, in a bluish haze, as if in a cloud of incense, the distant Samara meadows.

Have a smoke? Why not! I took out a cigarette and pressed the lighter's lid, in vain. The lid flicked, the wheel caught on the flint, but the wick did not light. Is it out of fuel? Fortunately I had matches. I stroked the green tip of a red match against the rough black side of the box, on the yellow paper of which was drawn an airplane with an obscene hand gesture instead of a pro-

[41] A Cossack settlement, now part of Dnipro (city). Mandrykivska St. runs along the right bank of the Dnipro River.

peller, and the two eloquent inscriptions—*Ultimatum* and *Our Response to Chamberlain.*[42]

The cigarette was lit. A thin stream of gray smoke rose imperceptibly and melted into the air. Once, humanity amused itself by telling tales; now it preferred cigarettes. An illusory source of fleeting whims, a provisional attempt to opt out of reality!

I had sufficient time, the best opportunity to contemplate the content of my presentation at the conference today. With sudden enthusiasm, I seized this moment—placed the box of cigarettes on my knee, opened the lid to jot down a few points, and took out a pencil. But the impulse to work, having flaring up, immediately faded away. I became listless and drained. Faced with the prospect of having to act, I was enveloped with a sense of boredom.

I could never contend with these bouts of boredom. Editing, writing letters, deliberating on the content of replies, drafting speeches, keeping minutes at meetings—no, all of this was beyond me.

Should I ponder over the proper text of an official speech? I'll just say what comes to mind! Improvised speeches always fared much better for me than premeditated and prepared ones. What people considered the result of hard work in my speeches never cost me the slightest effort. I accepted my successes solely as the complementary gifts of a capricious fate.

---

[42] Sir Austen Chamberlain: British Foreign Minister in 1924–1929. In February 1927, he sent a diplomatic note to the Soviet Union demanding it discontinue its support of Communist China. The refusal led Great Britain to break off diplomatic relations with the USSR until 1929.

Was it not more pleasant to think about nothing, the non-essential things that had no bearing on official matters?

XIII

I surrendered to the flow of fleeting thoughts, immersing myself in the stream of random impressions, succumbing to the allure of unexpected associations. Not quite falling asleep, I dozed off in the sweet twilight of this rainbow-hued, sunlit morning!

I pushed through boundaries. I uncovered new frontiers. I acquainted myself with the foreign horizons of distant territories. In my imagination, shapes from millennia past emerged.

Not far from here, my ancestors dwelled even before the end of the first millennium. Boats with triangular sails navigated the river. Before venturing across the rapids, on these steep shores, a gloomy, iron-clad chieftain—a prince, or *konung*—stayed with his captives. Prince—plunderer—slave trader—merchant—guest.

Along the shore, he drove robust, broad-shouldered lads and graceful maiden slaves skilled in housework. The slaves were pillaged from scorched settlements along desolate rivers, amidst untamed depths of dense forests. On his longships, he carried bundles of fur: silvery black, smoky blue, vermilion-colored pelts destined to adorn the shoulders of Byzantine beauties, princesses, and circus acrobats. Bundles of soft thin skins, thick oily skins, colorful goat skins; finely-curried green, red, black, and blue skins, meticulously bound with burlap and bast.

The pungent scent of sheepskin was pervasive. A faint aroma of honey wafted from large lindenwood barrels. Coarse, round discs of vermilion wax and dried white-grayish fish, strung together, filled the longboat's interior.

Returning from Byzantium, the lord konung brought precious gold-threaded fabrics, *pavoloka* cloth and velvet, sheer vibrant silk and heavy brocade. He carried yellow amphorae, narrow-necked and conical, filled with strong, sweet wine; golden and silver chokers for his women; *kolts* depicting the mythical creature Sirin.[43] Simultaneously, he introduced hitherto unknown concepts of walled cities, palaces, and churches, religion and the state—of the divine authority of the Church and the royal authority of the king. The konung dreamed of becoming *basileus*, an emperor. Olaf and Ingvar would become Basil.

As for the Varangians-Rus, who time and again attacked the capital of the Romans, the Byzantine Patriarch Photius once said, "Something severe, unyielding, and perilous blew upon us!"[44]

---

[43] *Kolt*: a piece of women's headgear, hanging from both temples, which was popular in Kyivan Rus in the 11th-13th centuries. *Sirin*: a mythological creature with the head of a beautiful woman and the body of a bird; it appears in the Kyivan Rus legends.

[44] A paraphrased fragment of a sermon by Saint Photius, a Patriarch of Constantinople, allegedly describing his reaction to the siege of Constantinople by the Rus ships in 860.

I recalled this characterization by Patriarch Photius of the savage conquerors who, in their frenzy, perished while destroying and ravaging the Empire. His words brought Stepan Lynnyk to mind. It was the aptest way to capture the whimsical image of the master who built this Varangian Sophia above the Dnipro. He was precisely as Photius described—severe, firm, perilous. This is how he was in his disposition, appearance, the themes of his paintings, his artistic style, his chaotic life, and the circumstances of his tragic destiny.

My personal acquaintance with the artist dates back to my student years, when I had studied at Saint Petersburg University and concurrently attended classes at the Academy of Arts. Stepan Trokhymovych Lynnyk was my instructor. It is possible that I did not benefit as much as I possibly could have from his instruction. But that was my fault, not his.

He held the title of academician[45] but possessed the appearance of an artisan. People addressed him informally, and upon seeing his paint-splattered clothing mistook him for a whitewasher, someone who could have been hired to paint the floors in their residence.

He was not tall, but robust and squat; introverted, moody, heavy in disposition and generally unfriendly. According to the prevailing tradition among artists, he wore a tobacco-colored cape and a wide-brimmed, sunfaded hat. His loose jacket resembled a frock, and the trousers, saggy at the knees, were frayed at the bottom.

---

[45] An honorific title given to influential scientists or scholars in the field of liberal arts, particularly in Europe.

His worn shoes, never once polished, were long overdue for the trash. I cannot deny that among the artists of his generation, it was considered rather chic to resemble a garden scarecrow.

Following an ancient peasant custom, he cropped his hair in a bowl cut, shaving the back of his head and temples. His reddish petit-goatee protruded forward like a wedge.

He lived as a solitary recluse. He could not stand visitors. It was not possible to simply pay him a visit; you had to intrude upon him. If someone was at the door knocking or shouting, Lynnyk would not respond. But if someone persistently and ardently demanded his attention, testing his patience, he would open the door and appear on the threshold in his work clothes, palette and brushes in hand, or in his long johns, nightshirt, and slippers as if he had just gotten out of bed, and stare, silently and gloomily, at the unwanted guest. Then, with a hint of outrage, he would demand, "Just what *is* the matter?" He would slam the door loudly, as if threatening someone, and turn the key in the lock, twice, rattling the chain, emphasizing with his entire demeanor and behavior that he categorically did not wish to be disturbed at home.

He had been born in a village, studied in a rural parish school, and then at the Kyiv Art School. That was before this aloof fellow was granted a scholarship at the Academy of Arts in Saint Petersburg.

For most of his life, after moving from Ukraine and entering the Academy, he resided in Saint Petersburg, this majestic, twilight city, where the pale, colorless sky stretched low over the marshy shores of the Gulf of

Finland. The ursine grimness of his nature harmonized perfectly with the inhospitality of the local landscape. Here, the division of twenty-four hours into morning, evening, afternoon, and night has no meaning; it is a mere convention. The boundaries separating day and night disappear. There is no real day in winter, just as there is no true night in summer.

He spent his autumns and winters in solitude, brimming with emptiness and chill. Left to his own devices, Lynnyk developed an eccentric habit of living beyond time, beyond the movements of the sun and the moon, the count of days and weeks. The rhythm of his life had nothing in common with nature. He lived within himself, beyond nature.

One could easily succumb to drink living like this. The fact that this did not happen to Lynnyk was due solely to his artistic gift, a calling that he carried around as a communion wafer, akin to a mortal carrying a cross, bending under its weight, preparing for the crucifixion.

Friedrich Nietzsche signed his letters as "The Cruci-fied." Could we not say the same of Lynnyk even more so? Both Nietzsche and Lynnyk were crucified on the cross of their prophetic mission! One was a philosopher, the other an artist, yet their lives and creative destinies were equally tragic, resembling the fate of Oedipus himself.

Lynnyk's complete solitude did not allow for fixed hours designated for work, sleep, or leisure. His house lacked a proper clock. Disarrayed clutter filled the large rooms of his dwelling. He had an inexplicable passion for purchasing all kinds of junk from antique shops and flea markets: porcelain, trinkets, vintage ladies' garments, old weaponry, furniture, ancient manuscripts, and books bound in heavy leather. Alongside an empty parrot cage, a collection of painted eggs, a rustic ceramic bowl, a cavalry saddle, he also owned precious antique watches, including some rare pocket models; none of them were functional. He never wound them.

"For my own purposes," Lynnyk would say, "I see absolutely no need for it."

He didn't need a clock to know the time. He lived beyond it, and yet never failed to appear punctually when teaching a class.

He regarded clocks as an unnecessary development, as superfluous as cleaning one's shoes, clothing, or teeth. It wasn't only clocks—he had no toothbrush either. Humanity had managed without these things for so many centuries... Even now, millions of people survived with neither toothbrushes nor clocks. He appealed to the practical experience of the ethnic groups who felt no need to measure their work time by hours or any special mechanical instruments. Despite becoming an academician, he remained in essence a provincial fellow.

"A clock," he insisted, "is a pure ideological construct, an abstraction, a product of theoretical reasoning. It's nothing more than an ideological category directly linked to the paradigm of seventeenth-century mechanistic thinking."

Lynnyk would unfold these observations further.

"No doubt," he said, "watches can be masterpieces of art. I value them as such, and buy them. However, in doing so, I do not seek any practical outcome, because what benefit could possibly be gained out of a work of art?"

He never worked by the clock and never segmented his day into hourly sessions. He worked to the point of complete exhaustion, until he collapsed. He stopped working only when spasms contracted his hand, and he could no longer physically hold the brush in his cramped fingers. Then he would leave home or, utterly spent, lie down to sleep.

Can one work without feeling any joy from their labors? Can one work solely out of despair, hopelessness, self-hatred, and a sense of self-denial? Obviously, the answer is yes, because that is how Stepan Lynnyk worked.

XIV

One could encounter Lynnyk on the street at the most ungodly hour. It might be very late at night, when the heavy fog of darkness lay still on the slippery asphalt of wet streets, only the drunken yelling of the tardy tramps and the hysterical crying of stray cats disrupting the night's empty silence. Or sometime very early, at dawn, when the city was still in deep sleep, and only the big, bearded janitors sporting aprons and metal chest-plates began to sweep away the night's refuse from the vomit-spattered pavement.

What could he be doing on the streets at such hours? What visions was he pursuing? What harpies, with gaping canine muzzles, were chasing this modern Oedipus through the deserted corners of town? Or perhaps, left to fend for himself, he was wandering in an attempt to escape both inner and outer emptiness?

From time to time, oblivious to the hour on one of his ventures, Lynnyk would remember inadvertently that he had business elsewhere and needed to make his way there. The man who never glanced at his watch would hail a coachman at the nearest corner and bid him to "hurry." He rode on empty cobblestone streets in a bouncing carriage, cursing the person he had to meet. He cursed them and all others who, he claimed, imposed themselves on him, disturbed him, never left him in peace with all these matters that were of the least possible concern to him. Never mind that these matters concerned Lynnyk solely. They would involve his participation in the next exhibition of *Mir iskusstva*,[46] choosing a place for his paintings in the exhibition hall, discussing set design for a play by Maeterlinck or Ibsen with the project director, receiving payment for his painting purchased by the Museum, or something else along those lines.

He could stop by someone's place at any hour, simply because that person had the misfortune of having business with him. At three in the morning, just as at six or seven in the morning; when people were already getting ready for bed, were already sleeping, or hadn't even started getting dressed yet. What did it matter to Lynnyk?

---

[46] From Russian: World of Art. An artistic movement and an art magazine in Russia at the turn of the century that aimed to educate the Russian public about the trends and issues in Western art.

He imagined others in his own image: one had to force oneself upon him. Just as forcibly, he would force his way into the life of the person he wanted to see. He probably could not surmise that it was possible to call on someone in a calm, agreeable fashion.

The person became a victim of his visit. Lynnyk's visitations were feared as much as encounters with him on the street. For the owners of the apartments he visited, his arrival bordered on a natural catastrophe—something resembling a flood, an earthquake, a landslide, or a hurricane: all could be destroyed, turned upside-down, shattered, pulverized, torn away!

He appeared at the entrance, looking cruel and relentless. He started making noise even before that—"Open up!" You were already imagining the worst. With his foot in the door, he burst into the apartment, without asking whether he was allowed to or not, whether he would be received or not. He was full of mischief. The following exclamation—"The ladies and gentlemen are sleeping!"—made no impression on him. He pushed aside a maid, herself in slumber, and asked, "Where the hell are the lights over here?" He bossed everyone about, as if he were in his own house. He asked, "Where is your living room?" Then he fumbled around the electric switch by the door, lit up the room, and demanded that the host be awakened.

If he encountered resistance, the doors were not opened immediately, or upon letting him into the drawing-room, he was compelled to wait for a host for some time, Lynnyk took offense. In full voice, he muttered "The nerve!" and then, unwilling to wait any longer, having woken up everyone in the house with his steps, yelling, and general clatter, he exclaimed,

"Feel free to close the doors, I am off!"

He could spend eight, ten, twelve or more hours at someone's place, unaware of how much time had passed. Bidding farewell to the hosts, he left them exhausted, yellowed, agitated, off-balance.

In part, the egotistical naivete of a lonely and pessimistic artist, detached from the ground and completely immersed in his work, found its manifestation in Lynnyk. Nothing existed beyond his art, and the world consisted of nothing except for that art. Even knowing that, I never doubted that somewhere, in the midst of his naivete, there was an intentional and conscious desire to do everything contrariwise, a proclivity toward play for its own sake.

XV

Lynnyk preferred to account for himself, to consider only his person, his own preferences, and nothing more. For him, the external world existed only as it pertained to his desires, habits, ideas, and whims. Tangible reality, as such, did not exist for him. He could not accept anything that would oppose him. He ignored reality insofar as it might exist independently of him.

He was a ruiner; he demolished reality. He composed it in his own image, deformed it according to his imagination, molded it in his own likeness.

Should I define this as impressionistic subjectivism? Perhaps! In the early years of the twentieth century, this trend achieved a leading position in art and prevailed in social ideology. People adapted their art style, beliefs, way of feeling, thinking, experiencing, and living to it. The individual was exalted, and the "self" was nurtured. However, perhaps it was something more, something fundamentally different. It was individualism that transitioned into its opposite, giving rise to the cultivation of the super-individual.

Lynnyk had a streak of the social reformer, the politician, the party leader in him. He was someone who transformed reality, shaping it according to the sections and points of his worldview.

In a nutshell—reality could not continue as it had up until then. Neither could people. Lynnyk rebelled against human ordinariness and against reality.

Was he human? At the very least, he was unlike all other human beings. He renounced his biological essence. He fashioned himself from within his own being—a visionary, a mentor, and a ruiner. A product of his own externally-manifested imagination and will, a mental construction, an idea projected into the world of things against which he struggled.

His extravagant tastes, his distraught and maniacal outlook likened him to the hazy, misty landscape of Petersburg. Imagine you were walking, and suddenly in front of you—from the mist, from behind a street corner or someone's back—emerged the phantom Lynnyk, a concentrated clot of twilight, a nebula endowed with form, conventionally and artificially adorned in human attire, in shapeless clothes picked up at some incidental store.

Out on the street, he walked as if he were the only human being on the bustling avenue of the capital. He walked down Nevskii Prospekt as if forging his path through the jungle. His left hand was tucked behind his back, and in his right he held a large cane—a typical peasant stick that he had pulled out from some fence in the Ukrainian countryside to fend off village dogs.

He carried the cane in front of him, thrusting it forward.

He walked like a blind man—or at least it seemed as if he walked with his eyes closed. Or perhaps it seemed he was hallucinating. It seemed as if ghosts and nightmares, dreadful and odd specters had taken possession of his tired, poisoned brain. As if he could not free himself from their heavy and oppressive captivity.

He walked, and to anyone who saw him, it seemed as if a great misfortune had just befallen the man, from which he could not recover. Enveloped in despair, shattered by catastrophe, overwhelmed by an affliction that surpassed human strength, he no longer reacted to anything, saw and noticed nothing around him.

But he saw, and did so with the vigilance of a steppe raptor! Burdened with solitude, he wandered the city streets. Upon meeting an acquaintance, he stood firmly in front of them. He blocked their path. He held onto them tightly by the sleeve or the hem, so that they could not walk away. He clung to them as a traveler clings to a rock after being tossed by a storm onto a remote island.

You could not leave him, even if you wanted to, even if you apologized and said that you were in a hurry. He did not pay any attention to your words. You begged him to let you go but he pretended not to hear, holding onto the sleeve of your coat even tighter.

He could stand there and chat with you for hours, paying no heed to the world around, to the fact that you were blocking people's way, that people were cursing and pushing past. As if all of this were not happening on Nevskii, at the corner of Sadovaia Street or Liteinii Prospekt, but somewhere beyond time and place, within the confines of a staged production.

You would suggest to him, "Stepan Trokhymovych, shall we step out of the way?"

He would reply, "Oh no, why bother?"

And you would keep on standing in the crowd of human traffic.

And although he spoke all the time, and you remained silent, not daring to get in even a few words (he would not have listened to you anyway), he sounded irritated, as if he were scolding you. It felt as if he had stopped you with the sole purpose of telling you something unpleasant or picking a fight with you. Rest assured that he was neither friendly nor polite when conversing.

He would abruptly break off the conversation, out of the blue, halfway through an unfinished thought.

He would take leave without saying goodbye or extending his hand. And then, having already walked away, he would turn back around.

He would exclaim,

"Wait, my good fellow, I have something else to tell you!"

He would pause for another instant. Essentially, at the very end he would bring forward what he could have started with. He would accuse his interlocutor of keeping him and wasting his time when he had so many matters of great importance to attend to, and he was in such a hurry, and, really, he could not waste his time on just anyone he ran into on the street, on any scrap of nonsense.

And he would keep walking, paying attention to no one, elbowing his way through as if at a country fair, left hand tucked behind his back, right hand wielding his dog-beating stick and thrusting it forward.

I stood there, bewildered and offended, not understanding what had happened. I could not figure out what I had done wrong since, actually, I had not said anything whatsoever to him. It was he who had stopped me on the street. I merely bowed to him with all the courtesy of a student, expressing respect to a professor and a distinguished master. I was certain that now, God knows why, we had forever fallen out.

"Just anyone I run into on the street..." I repeated the remark that Lynnyk casually tossed at me.

I decided then never to greet him, and to bow my head in the most restrained and formal manner.

Upon our next encounter, as unexpected and sudden as the previous one, having noticed Lynnyk in advance, I did my best to disappear at any cost. I hoped he would not spot me. I made every effort to avoid the meeting, to slip away unnoticed, to vanish behind people's backs. I raised my collar and pulled my cap down tightly; I averted my gaze. I hastily crossed to the other side of the street. I tried to flee.

All in vain! He had already seen me. He was already following. Already giving chase, shouting, waving his stick.

I confess that the scene that followed was terrible, almost disgusting; the memory of it still makes me feel embarrassed and ashamed.

I quickened my pace. I started to run. Faster and faster.

People started chasing me; someone hit me, someone grabbed me by the collar, another by the chest. I was stopped. I resisted. They twisted my arms. I protested indignantly. They scolded me. I stood there without my cap, which I had lost while fleeing.

A crowd, hungry for street scandals, formed around us. People were asking one another,

"What happened? Whom did they catch?"

Human imagination is limitless. Some claimed they had caught a pickpocket who had jumped off a moving tram. Others assured that they had detained a bank official who had embezzled money and wanted to escape to America. Still others related, in great detail, that it was a dissolute son who had robbed his parents in order to carouse through the restaurants and indulge in women. The one who was holding me knew all the details. He swore that he saw a gold pocket watch in my hands.

The scent of a lynching was in the air. A well-dressed gentleman already raised his hand to strike me in the face with all his strength.

"All students," he exclaimed, "are revolutionaries! Thrash them!"

At the very last moment, Lynnyk appeared in the role of my savior. He ran like an experienced athlete. In haste, he took me by the hand. He rescued me from the enraged crowd at the final moment when they were about to descend upon me.

Handing me my cap, which he had managed to pick up along the way, he sarcastically observed,

"Well, you see, you didn't escape from me after all!"

He generously reminded me that I ought to be grateful to him for saving me from the vengeful crowd.

I was to blame for everything. Lynnyk played the role of an innocent angel.

Even this encounter, which started with escape and pursuit, ended in an insult—saved for the last moment as always. Everything repeated itself from beginning to end, the same as it ever was.

In the end, I grew accustomed to Lynnyk's behavior. I accepted him as he was, and during all my student years in Petersburg, he treated me with camaraderie the way he alone understood it.

XVI

Such was Lynnyk's way of dealing with people—rude, harsh, always with a touch of mischief.

He treated them with distrust. He believed that man was wolf to man.

"A man," he used to say, "must be grabbed by the collar, seized by the throat, knocked down, strangled with a knee. And only then is there any hope that he will either become who he truly is, or you will make him into who you want him to be."

I have already mentioned that Lynnyk occupied a large multi-room apartment near the Academy of Arts, on one of the cross streets of Vasilievsky Island. He lived alone. An aide from the Academy stopped by once a week to tidy up the living space, change the bedding, sweep the floor, and take the laundry for washing.

Lynnyk ate whatever, whenever, and wherever he could. He paid no attention to food. When he was working, he did not eat. He could go days without eating. If asked whether he already had lunch that day, he would always reply,

"But I had lunch yesterday! Regular daily meals are harmful to one's health."

He would not eat at home; he dined in eateries and cafeterias exclusively. He would only eat when he went out. In his imagination, being away from home meant eating, and eating meant not being at home. He could not stand to eat alone.

So he went out. He would drop the keys from his apartment into the pocket of his worn-out jacket, where there was less risk of losing them—that pocket was in slightly better condition than the other. He wanted to see people, talk, and eat. He needed company, but he didn't care who exactly it was. He would drag with him the first person he met on the street, someone he at least vaguely knew or had seen before. It was better not to argue with him. He forced them to come along. It was better to agree than to resist; it was the lesser evil.

He was equally indifferent on where to go as with whom. It could be the most expensive restaurant— *Medved, Dominique, Astoria,* or *Palkin*—or the most wretched hole in the wall. Whatever he happened to pass by on the way. One was not supposed to argue or choose as he did. Nor was one supposed to refuse in either case, unless one was prepared to face public scandal or Lynnyk's brazen insolence.

It was always Lynnyk who paid.

"It was my suggestion to go out to eat, so I'll pay," he declared categorically.

He tipped generously. No trace of stinginess nor frugality.

I recall one incident that took place sometime in the spring of 1910.

It was May, the time when the White Nights would normally begin in Petersburg.[47] Bushes of blooming lilac reflected in the transparent canals of the old gardens. Marble statues gazed into cold, greenish pond water. The sky shone with a clear light that scattered into unbelievable, unimaginable silence.

I walked briskly through the motionless, deserted emptiness of silent streets. I turned from Gorokhova Street onto the Moika River. Large tenement houses painted green, gray, and lemon shade; anemic willows, pale green things growing along the canal grates, were reflected over and over in the stagnant, dirty water.

It was well past midnight. It was not night, and it was not day either. Neither evening nor morning. Neither

---

[47] The period from mid-May to mid-July when the sun does not set at night in Saint Petersburg.

darkness nor light. There was something precarious about the double life of this ghost city. I was in a hurry. I had an exam scheduled for the next morning.

I collided with somebody in the twilight; I noticed only the glint of a top hat. Without looking, I uttered a curt "Excuse me, sorry!" and strode onward. It was Lynnyk, and he had already gripped my sleeve; he held me tightly.

Skipping the greeting, he said, addressing himself more than me, "So be it! I was already losing hope that I would meet anyone. Where shall we go to eat?"

And even though I hadn't the slightest desire to eat, and the prospect of spending the rest of the night sitting sleepless at a table with an exam the next day held no appeal for me, I could not escape Lynnyk's vise-like grip. He looked at me sternly and gloomily, as if one or both of us were mysterious conspirators in the dead of the night-day, colluding to commit some shameful, vile, cruel crime.

We set off. We ended up on a side street, between the Moika and Morskaia Street, at a filthy basement tavern. We went down the battered steps. The hall: low vaults, damp walls, and a dirty, rotten, spittle-smeared floor. The smells: kitchen soot, tobacco smoke, alcohol stench, and human vapors. In the gray murkiness of the dim twilight, yellow patches of light from large gas lamps spread under wide tin shades. Dicey and dubious personalities, tentative shadows of human beings, pitiful urban outcasts, drunkards with rabbit-like red eyes, thieves sick with consumption, and drunken prostitutes sat at the tables. Signs crowded the walls, "Shoe removal is prohibited at the tables!" or "Using foul language is prohibited!" These were not just empty hyperboles. I saw a cabman in a heavy cotton quilt unraveling his stinking foot wraps.

A feeling of despair engulfed me. Fear mixing with sorrow and pain. I looked at Lynnyk, at his elegant top hat, his red wedge-shaped goatee. He seemed not to care.

Like everyone else, we drank vodka from chipped glasses and chased it with beer. We ate a suspicious concoction called *solianka*.[48] A server wearing a wide and long bright-red caftan, belted with a narrow strap, placed one plate of sausage and another with flat, vinegar-soaked purple herring in front of us. Pickles completed the modest menu of this den that remained open through the night. I picked up a piece of sausage with my fork. I hesitated. I had the courage to put it in my mouth, but I could not bring myself to swallow it. I stood up from my chair and said, "Excuse me, I'll return shortly!" I proceeded to a dark corner of the tavern hall to spit out the unchewed piece. The place smelled damp with mildew and urine. A filthy-looking rubber plant stood in the corner. I spat out the meat.

Lynnyk ate a lot, hurriedly and greedily. He stuffed his mouth with large pieces, hastened to swallow, choked on his food. He leaned low over the plate. Having forgotten everything in the world, deadened to what was going on around him, he immersed himself in the meal. His red goatee, soaked in beer, was littered with crumbs. Without lifting his twisted fingers from the

---

[48] A thick and sour soup popular throughout Eastern Europe.

food on his finely ornamented plate, he blindly searched for a glass of vodka or a mug of beer on the table.

Clearly, he was famished and exhausted. Who knows how much time had passed since he last ate! Perhaps he had not left his home for several days, locked himself in the workshop, and set himself to work in a gloomy mood of hysterical desperation, in self-denial. This is how tramps eat in the seaport dens when they finally get their hands on something filling.

The periods of fasting were compensated by this voracity. He made up that night for what he did not eat yesterday and would not eat tomorrow. His goatee twitched. His fingers trembled, clinging to the bone handle of the fork; debilitated and overcome, he fidgeted in his chair.

I watched him with amazement and horror. I imagined the helplessness of his isolation, and a sense of despair awakened in me. I vividly perceived the loveless chaos of his disordered life.

We left. The twilight flowed by, just as motionless and quiet as before. The surrounding silence betrayed the fact that the night was still unraveling. Lynnyk, drunk on vodka, was staggering. We had managed only a few steps when he suddenly felt unwell. Pale and exhausted, head hanging down, he leaned against the wall of a building. He opened his mouth wide and breathed heavily.

A policeman standing at the corner of Morskaia Street approached us. Watching with reproach, he pointed out patronizingly that gentlemen should not behave this way. Then he began demanding that we go to the police station to sober up. I declared that we would do nothing of the sort. He insisted, alluding to the need for "order." I cursed at him. He reached for his whistle to blow it.

Irritated, I referred to Lynnyk as "His Excellency." In a commanding tone, addressing him informally, I ordered the officer to summon a carriage.

This made an impression on the policeman. It was a tone he was accustomed to, the tone in which all of his God-like "superiors" addressed him, and with which he spoke to all the "inferiors" to whom he was the absolute embodiment of power.

He called a coach. With the help of the policeman and the coachman, we loaded the unconscious Lynnyk inside. We set off. I supported Lynnyk, who kept sliding down from the seat. His legs in their worn-out boots stuck out helplessly, dangling over the edge of the cab.

Purely out of habit, the policeman straightened up and saluted. It was his first time encountering His Excellency: the man in the elegant top hat and boots resembling a tramp's clogs, who passed up *Medved* and would rather get drunk in a coachmen's tavern.

To conclude this description of Lynnyk, I should add that he dressed entirely randomly, as if on a whim. He paid no attention to his appearance at all. He might wear his old wide-brimmed hat, or a straw hat from his provincial uncle, or an English top hat of the finest brand. He might wear the most expensive, fashionable shoes bought on trips to Paris, Stockholm, or Tsargorod, or simple polished boots bought at the fair in Zlatopol or Konotop. It all depended solely on the occasion. He would pair the boots with a top hat, and the lacquered shoes with worn-out trousers. The circumstances of his tragic demise are widely known, and I do not need to dwell on them in detail here. They have been widely discussed in the press. They are always mentioned in his biographies, as well as in monographs dedicated to his work.

Like Nikolai Sapunov,[49] Lynnyk drowned in the Gulf of Finland. Was it an accident or intentional? This remains a mystery. Various assumptions have been made, with no definitive conclusion.

In the summer of 1911, he traveled from Petersburg to Kuokkala.[50] He visited Ilya Repin at his *Penates*, dined and drank with Leonid Andreiev. Then he had a falling out with Kornei Chukovskii.[51] After that, he was seen at the station, alone, sitting at a buffet table and drinking, looking focused and gloomy.

That evening, instead of returning to Petersburg, he went to the shoreline, took a fishing boat, and sailed into the expanse.

The black silhouette of the coffin-like boat looked distinct against the red-yellow, flat sea surface. Lynnyk

---

[49] Nikolai Sapunov (1880-1912): Russian painter and stage designer, follower of the school of Symbolism.

[50] Currently Repino, an area of Saint Petersburg. In the 19th and early 20th centuries, Kuokkala was part of the Grand Duchy of Finland, where many Russian artists, writers, and intellectuals had their summer houses.

[51] *Penates*: Ilia Repin's estate in Kuokkala. Leonid Andreiev (1871–1919): one of the most talented Russian playwrights and novelists of the Silver Age, whose works are evocative of deep pessimism and audacious treatment of sexuality. Andreiev's writing displayed the features of Expressionism and Symbolism. Kornei Chukovskii (1882–1969): Russian and Soviet popular children's writer.

rowed, rhythmically leaning forward and backward, raising and lowering the oars into the molten liquid gold.
The sun stood motionless on the horizon. The sky
shone with the same shade as the sea: a boundless, continuous flow of golden light, seen as if through a pale
haze; a lace curtain that softened all hues.

Lynnyk set the oars down. He rose. He straightened
up. He spread his arms. From the shore, he looked like a
faint silhouette of a black cross.

And then… One could only speculate. Perhaps the
boat tilted. Perhaps, standing up, he slipped on the wet
bottom of the boat and, having fallen into the water,
could not hold on.

No cry, no plea for rescue ever reached the shore. Or
perhaps it all happened too far away for anybody to hear
anything.

An elusive moment came and went. Destiny passed
by without a sound, swift and hurried. The black figure
of a man standing up in the boat, vanishing suddenly
into the red blaze of the sea. The dark, heavy boat
swayed on the surface. Ripples slowly spread across the
mirrored glass of the water. Ripple after ripple.

They never found Lynnyk's body. Perhaps an under-
water current carried it far into the depths of the Baltic
Sea.

XVII

The master perished, leaving only his creative legacy.
Lynnyk occupies a significant and distinctive position in
the history of Ukrainian art. His name is often men-

tioned alongside Narbut's.[52] There is an unquestionable logic to it; both of these masters, so dissimilar in their essence, overcame in themselves the populist traditions of a naive ethnographic landscape, rooted in sentimentality and tenderness toward the people and nature of Ukraine.

Sentimentality? Tenderness? What use did Lynnyk have for any of these notions?

He understood art along Ingres's formula, "To paint is to think!"[53]

Art had to become a doctrine in itself. Or, more precisely, it had to become a component of a doctrine.

Lynnyk's art was not emotional. It was anti-emotional. Shall we argue that it was rational?

He did not paint cherry orchards.

He did not paint a single sunset or a house surrounded with mallow flowers; no girls with youngsters standing near a stile, no groups of young women engaged in divination around the time of Epiphany; and neither did he paint pumpkins or tomatoes in the market.

Others painted mornings and evenings, sunny and rainy days, winter, spring, autumn, and summer; moonlight, Bohdan Khmelnytsky's entry into Kyiv,[54]

---

[52] Heorhiy Narbut (1886–1920): prominent Ukrainian graphic artist and painter, famous for his designs of the Ukrainian National Republic currency and stamps, as well as his creation of a unique typography of Ukrainian letters.

[53] Jean-Auguste-Dominique Ingres (1870–1867): French Neoclassical painter.

[54] A famous 1912 monumental painting by Mykola Ivasiuk (1865–1937), depicting the ceremonial entry of the founder of Hetman State, Bohdan Khmelnytsky, into Kyiv in 1649.

garden lilacs, bales of hay; a waning crescent hanging like an icicle in the sky above the outskirts of the village; heavy clouds dragging watery hems of rain across the land; paths trodden through the chaff; squares in Hlukhiv, churches in Chernihiv.

He did not paint flowers or dawns, winters or springs. His canvases did not exude the golden autumn, the bright-yellow hues of the trees, or the gentle warmth of the sun.

He did not seek to touch anyone's soul. He mocked art that moved others. He suffered, seethed with indignation, acted out.

Meeting Lynnyk at some art exhibition meant confronting a public scuffle, consciously orchestrated by him.

Once, I happened to arrive at an exhibition hosted by the Union of Landscape Painters, precisely at the moment when Lynnyk was wandering through the galleries with the appearance of a sick, desperate man. He was visibly overjoyed to see me—so long as one could characterize an outburst of vengeful fury as a type of joy.

"Look who's here," he exclaimed. "You too came to look at this heap of shit? I reckon you've never seen such ugliness…"

He pulled me towards the painting that disturbed him the most.

"Just look at it!" he implored me, gazing into my eyes, seemingly ready to grab me by the chest or kick me in the throat if I dared defend any aspect of the piece.

"Well, what would you say? Utter shit—the utmost, even! What did I tell you?!"

I do not remember in front of what painting we found ourselves. In all likelihood it was some entirely conventional landscape. Red poppies atop yellow clay cliffs. Golden fields of ripe wheat. Flower beds in the garden, autumn asters in front of the terrace. Something like that.

"Such worthless filth ought to be destroyed, burned, torn apart!" Lynnyk's voice boomed. "They should be hanged for this!"

"In due time," he lowered his voice conspiratorially, "artists of this low caliber will be done away with. They'll be tortured, put in cages, shot. Send them all to Siberia!"

He whispered with pleasure, filled with insatiable revenge against the art he loathed with every fiber of his soul.

Fortunately, he had neither a knife nor his walking stick on hand to pierce the canvas.

He was content with clearing his throat, spitting, and saying indignantly, "Prudes!"

The gray shadow of a woman guarding the peace in the galleries separated itself from the doorway and, gliding silently on the polished parquet, stood in front of us.

"Sir, spitting is forbidden here. There is a spittoon in the corner for that."

This agitated Lynnyk. He became enraged.

"Did you hear? Seeing such trash, one can't even spit?! Let's get out of here, let's go! We'll have breakfast somewhere! That is," he paused, looking at me with bitter regret, adding, "if you do not object!"

Object to *him*? It would have sounded like utter ridicule coming from Lynnyk, if not for the fact that behind all these antics, masked by the clamor and the mischief, hid the acute pain of a personal and creative loneliness that never revealed itself.

He winked at me slyly and gripped the wedge of his red beard. The walking stick was left with the doorman. This time, a restaurant napkin served as the flag above Lynnyk's battles and victories.

We sat together at a table at *Dominique*, where he initiated me into the secrets of the ritually pompous dish names read aloud from the menu.

After placing the order, he turned again to his favorite topic: art and its theoretical underpinnings. Today he delivered various diatribes against landscape painting. Against portraying objects or external images of the world.

"They imagine," Lynnyk waved his napkin-standard, "they imagine that they are creating art when they paint nature, the actuality of the natural world! I am telling you, that is not art."

And he carefully poured glasses of vodka for me and himself from the carafe. God, what had he done to me—an innocent and inexperienced adolescent whose family never consumed a drop of alcohol! Back then, I was far from being a connoisseur of complex gastronomy or spirits. Lynnyk was my Virgil, and I was his timid and bashful Dante.

Lynnyk preferred strong drinks, and under his confident guidance, I learned to distinguish the taste and quality of white- or red-capped vodka, rowan-berry tinctures, absinthe, schnapps, and whiskey. With Lynnyk as my mentor, I traveled simultaneously through all nine circles of Vodka-Hell and of Theory-Paradise to discover the highest truth of Art—my beloved Beatrice—in these conversations. I came to understand that art must transform itself from an art of objective reality into the starting point of an image-system of a newly organized, orderly, and fully constructed reality.

XVIII

The artistic creativity of Stepan Lynnyk and Yuriy Narbut represents a stage within the history of Ukrainian art when painting was transitioning from populism to anti-populism. However, the similarity between Lynnyk and his younger peer ends there; in all other ways, they were polar opposites.

Narbut's style, themes, and form were defined by the seventeenth century, the Bohdan Khmelnytsky era, the heyday of the Ukrainian Baroque. Lynnyk's creative attention was drawn to a completely different era, the ninth and tenth centuries, the empire of Sviatoslav and Volodymyr, the great waterway "from the Varangians to the Greeks," from Scandinavia to Byzantium. One was attracted to the state, the other to its nascence, its instability, a state in the process of becoming.

Narbut was a stylist. For him, the historical forms of the seventeenth-century Baroque embodied a distinct continuity of an established style. He conjoined, rearranged, and combined individual elements of this style, affirming its completeness. Lynnyk, though, did not create out of what was stylistically *given* but what could be stylistically *determined*. He based his art not on existing forms but on those that were lacking, on what would be and should be. He did not combine elements of the extant Baroque or any other style; what interested him in art was not what had already taken shape but what was taking shape; not what existed but what did not exist; society, country, people, and styles not when they had already formed, but at the moment when they were just forming. A state that was being born, a people in the process of creation, a style that was only just beginning to cohere.

Amorphousness, nascence, chaos! The chaos of his lifestyle, of his personality and art—that's who Lynnyk was. His artistic creativity was precisely that. Unlike Narbut, he did not seek predecessors to lean on; he sought to destroy them. The art of a post-apocalyptic world in the aftermath of an unforeseen catastrophe— that was the only genre of art recognized and asserted by Lynnyk.

Thinking in terms of epochs and their internal contradictions, contrasting them became a standard way of reasoning for all of us, people of the mid-twentieth century who had lived through the catastrophes of two world wars. We are accustomed to mentally separating the world and seeing epochs in opposition: the monarchy of the Hohenzollerns and the Weimar Republic; Modernity, Our Times, and the Middle Ages; bourgeoisie and proletariat; Bolshevism and capitalism; Nazism and democracy... We despise the years that do not propel the universe forward or backward by a millennium. We perceive any given epoch not as a challenge that unravels itself within the indifferent, always-identical unambiguity of its daily appearance and disappearance, but as a stage in creating a new world, in its irreconcilable opposition to everything that has existed up to that point.

Today, this is hardly news to anyone. At the beginning of the century, such views were formulated individually, through the work of solitary and isolated loners, confined to their studies or prison cells. Lynnyk was one of them. He intermixed with people of similar disposition—whether consciously or not is another question. He dreamed of creating the art of the coming era, and he would not be satisfied with anything less. He also rejected the art of Modernity, just as Renaissance artists would reject medieval art as Gothic—by which they meant barbaric. Lynnyk was assured of his destiny. He hoped that some new Vasari would inscribe his name in history as that of the first artist: a name that would come to signify a new Giotto, founder of the art of an era that was just dawning.

Lynnyk was ready to discuss the "art of the era" with anyone willing to listen. Those who were not willing would be lectured anyway. He proclaimed this idea with prophetic zeal, full of wrath and hatred, aroused and unrestrained.

Upon meeting someone and grabbing them by the sleeve, swinging his famed stick ripped from a village fence, Lynnyk proceeded to dispense his trademark vitriol:

"Artists of Modernity, starting with the Renaissance," he would say, "propagated the reality of the external, spatial world, perceiving it as a collection of random, disparate, episodic things: a person, a cow, the rooks have returned,[55] a lad in a black lamb's wool hat, an illustrated *Aeneid*... But we have no need," Lynnyk continued shouting, "no need for this hodgepodge of isolated images depicting separate things!"

His mouth, filled with decaying, yellowed teeth, was wide open. The red wedge of his beard trembled. A withered arm extended from under the fringes of a tattered sleeve.

These were beyond mere utterances. This was a manifesto. Lynnyk's oeuvre contained no paintings that depicted individual objects. He did not paint anyone or anything in particular. He was not interested in isolated things, separate events, individual beings.

He did not belong to the category of artists who painted their wives, lovers, portraits of acquaintances or patrons, themselves, impressions of nature. He strode past himself and nature. He lived his life without noticing his own existence, or that of nature. Flipping through the stacks of his art exhibition catalogs, any search for such works as *Self-Portrait of the Artist*, or *Portrait of Mrs. M.*, or *Crimean Landscape* was doomed to fail.

This was not the result of any self-imposed limitation but merely a different approach to the self and the world. He believed that there existed more essential things than

---

[55] The title of a popular 1871 painting by the Russian landscape artist Aleksei Savrasov (1830–1897).

"myself" and the "woman who loves me," the essence of his lust for her, the color of her eyes, the shade of her body as she lay on the couch, shining through the black silk of her pantyhose.

He did not equate the world with his feelings, the world with himself, his impression of the world with the world beyond himself. He did not seek to transform his impressions into a source of artistic understanding of the world, nor did he reduce the world to his impressions. This was a time of pervasive enthusiasm for Cezanne; apples on the table did not concern Lynnyk. He was no impressionist and cared little for either Manet or Monet.

Monet deconstructed the external world, and so did Lynnyk. But their motives, their purposes differed. Monet sought out the relative, Lynnyk the absolute. Monet preferred the fleetingness of subjective sensations received from the external, objective world; Lynnyk delved into the passionate study of its essence.

One painting by Monet depicts the Reims Cathedral. The reflection of sunlight on the cathedral walls was Monet's way of showing how, in the oscillations of the glowing mist, the cathedral loses its massive grandeur, how the stone becomes weightless. In Monet's painting, the Reims Cathedral seems to be built not of stone but of variously pale-colored masses of air.

For Monet and Manet in art, as for Flaubert and Maupassant in literature, reality possessed neither degree nor quality. They considered everything that existed equally worthy. Lynnyk approached the world from a completely different perspective. He parsed reality into its manifold planes. Contrary to the idea of a one-dimensional world, which came to characterize modernity in politics, economics, theater, philosophy, and art, he proclaimed the hierarchical structure of the world. He saw all that existed as layered, contrasting, and multi-dimensional. The idea of an art uniformly acceptable to all seemed to him an abhorrent mockery of art as it was meant to become.

XIX

What is progress? During Lynnyk's time, this question stirred lively discussion. Some believed it was all about a change in theme: no longer rural but urban. Not the sentimental idyll of an affinity for nature, but the social tragedy of an exploited proletariat. Not black soil but factories, plants. Not a cherry orchard by the house but the monotonous stone of barracks, black chimneys beyond an endless fence, murky air saturated with soot. No longer a maiden and lad in traditional attire near the stile, "my Halochka!",[56] but a boulevard at night, a tattered bush, a gas lamp with shattered glass in the lantern, a couple alone, a harmonist in boots, a vest and a linen shirt on display, the red glow of a cigarette stuck to dry lips, a drunken prostitute in a semicircle of trembling dirty-yellow light. Or: red flags of demonstrators, a black

---

[56] A quote from *Natalka-Poltavka*, a famous operetta (ca 1819; published 1838) by the founder of modern Ukrainian literature, Ivan Kotliarevskyi (1769–1838).

horse's corpse, a bloodstain on the gray stones of the pavement. White lime on colorless prison walls, barred rectangles in the windows.

No, this narrative naturalism did not captivate Lynnyk. To paint factories, chimneys, furnaces, iron, bricks, and reinforced concrete—was that to reproduce the sense that the clock had lurched forward by a millennium?

Moving forward? But why not backward? The concept of movement became an ideological category unto itself.

In those years when most were unwavering in their belief in the theory of evolution, in progress, in straightforward movement without interruptions, Lynnyk was fascinated by the images of great upheavals and decisive changes, the terrifying phantoms of catastrophe that would bring destruction to the old world.

In terms of affiliation, Stepan Lynnyk belonged to the *Mir iskusstva*. It always struck me as strange, however, to see the works by Stepan Lynnyk and Aleksandre Benois side by side.

One approaches Benois's painting. Silvery light shines calmly and evenly. Droplets fall gracefully onto the surface of the pool. The mirror-like gleam of the transparent fountain water reflects the immovable green tapestries of the garden and the white marble of female statues. Further back, along the perspective lines of distant alleys and the broad expanse of segmented lawns stretch rows of slender, meticulously trimmed trees. On the pale-golden sand of the footpaths, leaning on a cane, in a high wig and silk caftan, strides His Majesty Louis XIV, the Sun King.

Benois aestheticized the world that had passed, the world receding. That world was gallant, geometrized, stylized to resemble Versailles's own proportions, to prioritize palace and garden—such were the works of Benois. And next to them, right there on the wall, hung crude, carelessly painted, and monotonously brown works of Lynnyk, bleak and apocalyptic visions: a city-tower in the ocean of the universe; the Whore of Babylon condemned to destruction.

The city, enclosed by walls, ascended like a solitary island above the abyss. Red tongues of flame, rising from the dark, engulfed the mountain. They reached the walls, and the stones sparked, reflecting the hellfire. Below, in the abyss, a serpent wrapped around the mountain with the ring of its repulsive body. It raised its head, opened its jaws, ready to devour the city-tower. And above, angels were already blowing their trumpets, proclaiming the end of the world, and slowly rolling up the scroll of the sky.

Art critics—Tugendhold, Levinson, Volkonskii, and Grabar—considered Lynnyk a Symbolist.[57] Nonsense! He did not belong to that circle. The self-contained cliquishness and sectarianism of the Symbolists was foreign to him. He did not mince his words; he did not stutter.[58]

---

[57] Yakov Tugendhold (1882–1928): Russian and Soviet writer and literary critic. Andrei Levinson (1887–1933): Russian theater critic. Prince Sergei Volkonskii (1860–1937): Russian theater and literary critic. Igor Grabar (1871–1960): Russian painter and art historian.

[58] The word usage in Ukrainian—"сюсюкав і шепелявив"—might be a reference to the futurist poet Mykhail Semenko's characterization of

Lynnyk did not merely proclaim; he took action. He worked passionately and persistently. He left behind hundreds, even thousands of paintings, entire enfilades of canvas. He painted in series, one after another. He sought to develop the principles and methods of the painterly art on a practical level; with these he intended to replace the principles laid out as the artistic foundations by Renaissance masters and their successors at the onset of modernity. In those years, there was a renewed fascination with icons and frescoes. But Lynnyk did not follow the path of medieval art restoration. Far be it from him to declare icons and frescoes as the ideal forms of all artistic creation. He despised stylization.

"You have to be a total idiot," he said with typical harshness, "to copy icons."

He could not imagine the future as a return to the Middle Ages, nor the Middle Ages as the ancestral home of humanity; the art of the future could not be a mere copy of antiquity, as the present was not a reproduction of the past. Neither did there exist a proven cyclical motion to history. There could be no new Prince Yaroslav with his family, no newly-copied frescoes from the tower stairwells of Kyiv's Saint Sophia.

Among the art of the Middle Ages, what mattered to Lynnyk was not style or form, but the principle of the singular purpose of the artist and of art.

---

contemporaneous Ukrainian poetry in *Meeting at the Crossroad Station: a Conversation Between the Three / Zustrich na perekhresniy stantsii: rozmova triokh,* 1927 (translation by Roman Ivashkiv, in *Mykola (Nik) Brazhan's Early Experimental Poetry,* eds. Oksana Rosenblum et al., Boston 2020, pp. 248–49.

He sought a universally binding connection between everything, a hierarchical subordination of things in terms of their belonging to the absolute. His search was rigorous and devoted, fanatically persistent.

"The greatness of medieval art," Lynnyk proclaimed, "lies in valuing the absoluteness of the real—and the reality of the absolute."

Clarifying the principles on which art should be based, Lynnyk said,

"Our task is to affirm the relevance of each thing to the absolute, the subordination of each individual thing to the absolute. To create a system of artistic images, as solid and necessary as it was in the Middle Ages, where there would be nothing contingent, and each image would occupy its predetermined and defined place. Everything in this system of images has to emanate from one central point and to that source return."

XX

The negation of everything that art has endured over the past five hundred years defined the content and direction of Lynnyk's creativity. His paintings, his series of canvases represented individual fragments of negation, the result of his destructive raids on art.

This series of paintings represented a series of denials, rebellions against light, color, laws of perspective, orchards, black soil. He sought the primitive, the foundation, the real at its point of inception. He did not paint flowers, poppies, or orchards around the house. He painted not flowers but stones—rocks from Scandinavia brought by the glaciers to Ukraine; the barren moraine soil that predates black earth and in which nothing grows; a landscape that remained unchanged in all its archaic, primordial existence, since Paleolithic times.

In lieu of Goethe's formula "In the beginning was the deed," he proposed his own: "In the beginning was the stone." He reduced the world to the reality represented by the existence of stone.

But he did not stop there.

In his disdain for Renaissance art, he eradicated from it what was most important—light! Renaissance art centered the problem of light. Lynnyk's principal concern was darkness. For artists of the modern era, it was important to show how light revealed the form of an object and altered its color. For Lynnyk, something else mattered: to show how, in the absence of light, things would begin to lose their color and texture.

Thus began the struggle against light. It lasted many years. Lynnyk painted series after series, and with each successive one, gradually, the light diminished. It darkened, solidified, became motionless and solemn. In Lynnyk's paintings, one could not distinguish day from night or morning from evening, as if from time immemorial, there had never been any difference.

He did not paint mornings or evenings. Instead, he depicted vague fluctuations of darkness, clusters of twilit shadows. In the gloom, colors lost their boundaries, forms could not be articulated, existence became indistinct and contourless. An amorphous blue of early light prevailed over objects and phenomena.

Along the upper Dnipro, there was as yet no soil, no fields to be plowed. There was no black earth. There was yellow clay, blue stone, white sand. Harsh, pristine forest. Mossy trunks rose in silence. Fauna thrived in the hollows. Over the eternal swamps, the dreamy gray mists hung and shivered.

The bends of the river cut into the layers of forest, breaking their age-old darkness. People lived on isolated cliffs above the river banks. They burned the forest to grow their crops.

Behind black clouds of smoke, the sun disappeared—if it had ever been visible in this densely forested land. People, scorched by fire and using long poles, rolled burning piles of brushwood over the undergrowth. The blue ash glowed in the clearing between the charred stumps and tree trunks. Sowers in coarse, homespun fabrics tossed seeds into the ashes, handfuls of wheat and flax, covering the dispersed grain with chopped pine branches.

Lynnyk was drawn to the origins of states, cities, crafts, faiths. I recalled his painting *Hewing the City*. I observed every detail of it in my mind.

The strict law of the color blue was already on display in this painting. In the blueness of twilight, when one could no longer discern whether the sky had already cleared or the night still reigned, on a forest hillock, silent people in linen clothing and bast shoes hack away at oak trunks with axes. No free, unbound movement. No bright colors. In sullen silence, the enslaved work under the command of a man clad in black iron, standing in the distance and leaning on a Viking sword. The forest is being destroyed. An age-old tree falls with an ominous, piercing crash. Beyond the ravine, on an isolated hill, a city is being built. The city—a new historical category— insinuated itself into people's lives, but it would not bring joy to humanity. Life within its perimeter would not be radiant.

Lynnyk's paintings left a dismal, heavy impression. If art sought to liberate, his creativity oppressed.

Lynnyk left behind many sketches from his travels to the North and South. The fjords of Scandinavia and Tsargorod on the Bosphorus were the two poles, the two extremes of his sojourns.

In one of his paintings, he reproduced that northern longing for the South, the eternal female dream of the North centered on Tsargorod... Imagine primal, barren moraine. The harsh northern sea. Cold waves bearing white crests making themselves heard. On a desolate shore stands a lonely woman in a linen shirt, embroidered with red patterning. The wind stirs the clouds, brushes her face, flutters the shirt hems, splashes white foam from the waves on the rocks by her feet. A woman—Slavic Olga? Varangian Solveig?—dreams of lands far beyond the great seas: of the southern sapphire waters, the riches of Tsargorod, of an unknown faith and the kingdom's splendor.

XXI

Lynnyk approached his creative output with a meticulous selectivity. Out of the large number of paintings he created, only very few made it into exhibitions. He adhered to the steadfast rule of "exhibit less, paint more." Still, he highly valued his own canvases, sometimes to excess. In the first days after an opening, almost all of his paintings had a standard white sheet attached to the frame corner: "Sold!"

At the time, controversial art had secured a more favorable position for itself. Lynnyk elevated his art to the level of a theoretical issue. Art critics devoted considerable attention to him. He was written about extensively in journals and magazines, and a number of illustrated monographs on his work were published as well. It was a success. Despite all the controversy around his creativity, recognition followed. But from a creative perspective, something still failed to satisfy. Lynnyk had dedicated his entire life to his art, but that art could not satiate him.

The pieces intended to adorn the walls of private apartments—those of affluent individuals, professors, journalists, lawyers, bankers, and politicians who could afford to spend a few grand on their "own" Lynnyk— did not satisfy him. Enclosed, asocial art did not satisfy him.

He tried to transgress the boundaries of this isolated art, to overcome its subjectivity. He sought to contrast the subjective with the universal, the relative with the unconditional, the intelligent with the popular.

He attempted to move his art from private spaces, enclosed rooms, into open, public locations. He contraposed the idea of painting as an individual feat with architecture as an accomplishment of the many.

From sketches of set designs, from painting canvases meant to be hung above the bookshelves in the studies of the enlightened and wealthy, he turned to architecture and mosaic work.

The church that Lynnyk built in 1908 was more than just a refined tribute to his aesthetic fascination with Byzantium. Victor Hugo was mistaken in believing that "the book would kill the edifice," or that the enlightened particularism of a newly individualized society had definitively refuted the idea, nurtured by the Middle Ages, of a universal and absolute art.

As always, Lynnyk was fueled by his polemical streak. He constructed his stone church with a clearly defined contention: to contrast it with the brick structure of the Poltava *zemstvo*, designed by Vasyl Krychevsky.[59] Stepan Lynnyk introduced countless questions into the debates on Ukrainian artistic style: the Baroque or the Byzantine; the seventeenth century or the Princely era; the Cossack era or the reign of Sviatoslav; the Vorskla (that "*teeny-tiny river*")[60] or the great waterway "from the Varangians to the Greeks"; *khutorianstvo*[61] or the thoroughfare of world

---

[59] *Zemstvo*: an institution of local government that emerged in the Russian Empire as a result of the Emancipation reform of 1861. Vasyl Krychevskyi (1873–1952): a multi-talented and prolific Ukrainian architect, painter, graphic artist, and set designer; founder of the Ukrainian State Academy of Arts (1917). Poltava zemstvo, built in 1903-1908, is the first example of Ukrainian architectural Modern.

[60] A fragment of a Ukrainian folk song used by Ivan Kotliarevsky in *Natalka-Poltavka*.

[61] An idealization of the Ukrainian *khutir*, or farmstead, as a center of morality. The term *khutorianstvo* was introduced by the Ukrainian writer and ethnographer Panteleimon Kulish (1819–1897).

history; zemstvo or Sophia; liberal progress or explosion, rupture?

At times, it is worth revisiting Vasari. Reading his work, you begin to understand more clearly that no art spawns fully armed, with helmet and spear, from the head of Zeus; no "today" ever encompasses the entire epoch. It is challenging for contemporaries to separate direct paths from tangential ones, to distinguish the roads that lead to the future from those that lead nowhere.

Even now, as the fiftieth anniversary of Lynnyk's death approaches, it is difficult for us to guess just what parts of his chaotic and unfinished oeuvre contained the promise of the future, and what was merely slag tainting the bronze intended for the monuments to eternity![62]

XXII

All this time, the heat had grown unbearable!

I could not bear to sit on the stone bench any longer. The granite slabs were glowing with white flame. The scent of flowers felt too dense; the sweet aroma of fresh leaves from the trees and bushes was overwhelming. Everything around languished in the mugginess. Was it about to pour?

I rose from my seat and surveyed the sky. Far to the west, beyond the hill, I saw a dark blue cloud approach-

---

[62] Chronologically, that would have been around 1961. The novel was first published in 1942.

ing from the steppe behind the ridge. A drape of heavy velvet hung in the background.

The thundercloud moved slowly, in complete silence. In an instant, a sudden wind would rise, carrying away flowers, leaves, sand from the shore, and smoke from the steppe.

Perhaps it was time to head out to the meeting. I assumed it had already begun.

I checked my watch and shook my head. Good grief! It seemed I had lingered longer on this cliff than I intended. Undoubtedly, I had already missed Arsen Petrovych's presentation that was intended to inaugurate the Conference. What should I do? I suppose nothing could be changed now.

I gathered everything I had spread out on the bench and took my leave. On the steps in front of the church entrance, old grannies were seated—covered in black scarves, dry hands folded on their knees, forgotten by death. Motionless shadows frozen on the stones, silent creatures reminding people of the almsgiving mystery.

I looked at them, at their dark wrinkled faces, faded eyes, bony hands trembling as they reached out to me— a ritual gesture carrying an established symbolic meaning. Were they pitiful women-beggars? Elderly women? Supplicants, shamed by poverty and despair?

Our era of positivism scorned begging. It devalued the ideal of poverty. To be poor meant being a nobody. But these old women, reaching out to me with extended hands, reminding me of the need for mercy, belonged to a different era. They represented an age that deemed possessions as evil, viewed begging as a sacrificial feat and a lofty calling.

The women kept on repeating the ritualistic formula,

"Have mercy upon us, toss a coin!"

I stopped and gazed at those black silhouettes, as if seeing them for the first time, and a thought flashed through my mind. How did I not understand this before? Indeed, the point is not in the "coin" at all; the point is that there exists a certain category of people affiliated with a church—a community or an order, so to speak—who continuously implore,

"Have mercy!"

To maintain order in a city, we put a muscular, uniformed police officer, armed with a gun and a rubber baton, on every street corner. In the Middle Ages, for the same purpose, they would install the feeblest person—a cripple or an old man—in the same spot, whose duty was to remind every passerby of the need for moral perfection.

The policeman was taught to kill; the old man was taught to pray, sing, play musical instruments. The authorities made sure that there were as many beggars in the country as possible because this was the only known way to maintain order on the streets and market squares.

We might be surprised by such a conception of begging: the more beggars on the streets, the more morally perfect the country would be. Why are we not surprised by the opposite view that ties the prosperity of the country to the number of airplanes constructed, tons of steel transported by rail, barrels of oil extracted? Yes, our era puts smelted volumes of iron, produced engines, and generated kilowatts above all else!

A contemplative wanderer who made a profession out of meandering through ideologies and millennia—a "vagabond," even—this is how a good acquaintance, with a touch of sarcasm, chose to describe me.

"You are a drifter, a *brodiaha!*[63] he said to me upon learning that I had transitioned from studying ancient Armenian and Romanesque architecture to the seventeenth-century Cossack Baroque.

I must admit: he was right! I have always been tempted by intellectual vagabondism, ideological meanderings, philosophical musings. It was perhaps due to Lynnyk's influence that I could not resist such things.

There was a time when people sought to discover new lands. They traveled across the sea's expanse — Magellan, da Gama, Columbus. Geography was considered the fundamental doctrine; to be a cabin boy—the dream of every adolescent; and a map of the oceans, the sailor's Bible—the only thing worth reading.

But now, in lieu of unknown lands, we seek unknown truths. I feel a peculiar, insatiable thirst for immersing myself into the panoply of truths. I have always been baffled by the surprising conclusions we find when we follow a line of thought to its endpoint, ideas taken to their extremes. I valued doctrines that compelled humanity to transition from one opposition to another.

I stood there, surrounded by the elderly. I was enticed by the symbolism of tradition that prescribed re-

[63] Ukrainian: a vagabond.

nouncing one's property. I took out my wallet and started giving out money. I dropped coins, one by one, into the grannies' trembling palms. The old women asked for my name. I introduced myself,

"Rostyslav!"

I heard whispered prayers behind me as I climbed the stairs, like the rustling of dry autumn leaves.

On the very top, before stepping through the doorway, I paused to take another look—at the storm cloud advancing from the west; the rows of single-story buildings; the green carpet of trees; the black triangles of shawls, chiseled out against the white stone of the church steps. Somewhere, a bird was chirping, sparrows were tweeting. The tram hummed below the hill.

No one could have accused me of rushing to the meeting, nor of having the scantest desire to waste my free time on the tedious ceremony of an official meeting regarding a matter whose outcome, in all certainty, had already been predetermined.

XXIII

At the moment when I was about to enter the antechamber, I ran into a woman coming out of the church. I hastened to step aside to let her pass ahead, and lo and behold, I recognized her as my good friend whom I had met in Kharkiv a few days ago. What a complete surprise! I was just astonished. I had no idea that she also planned on coming here.

I was thrilled by this encounter; I could not contain my joy. I reached for her, showering her with a multitude of exclamations, dozens of questions, thousands of words.

"Valentyna Mykhailivna! Is it really you? How on earth did you find yourself here? When did you arrive? What are you doing here? Such a pleasant surprise! You cannot imagine how happy I am to see you. I am just drowning in boredom here; you are truly saving me. Where are you heading now? Might I accompany you?"

I upended an entire basket of questions, spilling out bundles of enthusiastic exclamations right in front of her. I wanted to hear all the news from her, all at once. I was triumphant. I felt victorious. Finally, there was something worthwhile for me to spend my time on.

I extended my hand, ready to feel the familiar, soft grip of her slender hand, which would make the scent of violets, her favorite perfume, linger and melt in my palm for a while. But at that moment, I started blushing excessively. I was embarrassed. I felt extremely perplexed.

Upon closer inspection, however, I was struck with the realization that the woman in front of me had nothing at all to do with my friend from Kharkiv.

She took a step back and replied,

"You are mistaken, sir! I don't know you!"

A shadow of dissatisfaction passed over her face. She waited for me to step aside and let her pass. I was, however, dumbfounded and stood listlessly, as if rooted to the spot.

Such idiocy! The illusion of the initial impression dissipated. In front of me stood a stranger, entirely unknown to me, hardly resembling Valentyna Mykhailivna. I was cursing myself. My fervent enthusiasm, the burst of excitement, a thousand greetings addressed to no-body. All I had managed today was to find myself constantly confused, lost, mistaken.

In utter confusion, I rushed to apologize.

"I am sorry! Please, do forgive me! I am truly sorry!"

She hurried down the stairs. One by one, the old women bowed to her from the waist, nun-like, extending their hands.

I stood there bewildered, my gaze cast downwards. Why had I imagined that I had known her? Is it because she resembled an acquaintance of mine? But that could not possibly be the case; they were completely different—their height, hairstyle, and stature.

As I scrutinized her more closely, I grasped this with a particular clarity.

The woman was walking along the path between the white-cedar bushes. She passed through the gate before looking back, perhaps out of habit, as she would normally do when leaving the church, or perhaps to see if I was still standing there. She noticed that I kept looking at her; blushing slightly, she quickened her pace, crossed the square, and disappeared into the shadows cast by houses up the street.

XXIV

A somber, silent cloud stretched upwards, enveloping the entire horizon. The birds flitted about. Skimming low to the ground, wings aflutter, anxious swallows darted past. The old women were getting ready to leave.

They crossed themselves for a long while, bowed towards the church several times, and then vanished into the unknown, their shadows impenetrable to the eye.

I contemplated what had happened: I had made a mistake. But every mistake has its meaning. The mistake came from the depths of the subconscious, but surely there must be some logic to the irrational.

I followed the woman with my eyes, trying to fathom the roots of the illusion to which I had just fallen victim.

Indeed, I should not be standing here; I should be attending the meeting, I have been dallying too long already. I was getting annoyed with myself. It was absurd: fixating on trivial nonsense when I should be at the meeting. But what could I do with myself? Hesitating between the obligation and the possibility of avoiding it, I finally acquiesced to the latter. I am never in a hurry to do what must be done. Why bother? Above all, I have always valued the capricious whims of desire that would suddenly awaken in me. One should always be true to oneself. Is that not the case?

I ought to admit that I am a person of fleeting moods. Instead of sitting listless at the meeting, it is so much more pleasant to immerse myself in thoughts on a matter of no importance or think about nothing. Or ponder why this unfamiliar woman, whom I had met just now at the entryway to the antechamber, seemed so stunningly familiar to me from the very first impression.

I entertained all possible scenarios. Perhaps I had met her once at a party organized by a mutual acquaintance: we had sat together at a table, I served her caviar on a plate, poured wine into her glass, entertained her with jokes, danced a two-step with her to the music of the phonograph. After that, I might have escorted her home and kissed her on the stairs, in the darkness, before parting ways. A meeting and a kiss that happened unintentionally, never to be repeated.

Or perhaps all of this played out quite differently. We were vacationing together at a sanatorium somewhere in the south, in Crimea or the Caucasus; my eyes glanced over her as we ate at the same canteen table; she was my beach companion; we stood together in the same queue to take the baths. On the way from the beach or while waiting for the bath, I entertained her with stories of various adventures, and she laughed without a care.

A brief flirtation for a few days or a few weeks, and then I had completely forgotten about her until today, when these images resurfaced in the depths of my memory, washing away the accumulated sediment of later impressions.

Or perhaps it was something else altogether. Among the ashes of forgotten experiences, a spark of sentimental recollection about a former student at the Institute rose inside me—a bouquet of lilacs placed on the lectern, before the lecture; a meticulously prepared presentation; a handwritten confession passed to me hastily in the vestibule?

Or perhaps it was a chance encounter somewhere in the foyer of a theater or cinema, at a concert, and her face unconsciously etched itself into the depths of my being, to reawaken from oblivion on this exact day, with renewed vigor, initially evoking by association the illusory thought of my acquaintance, only to dissolve and return to oblivion later on.

I agonized over these efforts, impatiently burrowing into the chaos of the past and perhaps orienting myself in an utterly wrong direction. All the while, this matter might not have concerned any real fact or vignette of life, but rather something else entirely—some complex concern, the context of shattered, multidimensional fragments that had congealed, fragments whose origins were profoundly distinct, holding nothing at all in common.

I continued my quest into the labyrinth of memory, hoping vainly to catch the end of Ariadne's thread that might lead me out of these depths. I surmised that the roots of the illusion should be sought in the realm of my professional experience. This concerned a portrait, a painting of some eminent master. In my mind, I sifted through thousands of paintings, meandering the halls of the Hermitage, the Pinakothek, the Louvre. I flipped through endless catalogs, illustrations, collections of drawings I presented in my lectures. All in vain!

In the most secluded and remote corners of my erudite memory, I hoped to stumble upon the slightest of analogies.

Those that came to mind were crossed out one by one.

I was weary of names, dates, art movements, paintings. I was exhausted by the kaleidoscopic interplay of female features. I was in possession of a decent, one could even say professionally rigorous memory, and I could ascertain:

"No, I have never met her in my life, and neither does any painting give me justification to claim that the memory of some artistic work had merged with the impression of encountering this woman."

I scorned myself: what was any of this to me? Why did it matter whether I knew where she had come from? I did not want to give in.

I was overwhelmed with excitement. One way or another, I would get there: *I will know.*

Skipping several steps at a time, I ran down the stairs. Walking briskly, I followed the same path she had just walked. She had not gotten so far that I was unable to catch up.

I could state with all certainty that I had never seen her in my life, and she did not resemble anyone I could have known from any portrait. Yet I was certain that somehow I knew who she was. Unfortunately, I was neither schizophrenic nor a poet; I was far too rational. I have never experienced a headache. I did not know what a cold felt like. Even when I had typhoid or influenza, I was never delirious. When I was tipsy, I did not lose my composure. I had to use an iron crowbar to break through the layer of ice separating my subconscious from my consciousness. I was accustomed to perceiving the subconscious without any dimming of light, not after sundown but in the full brightness of day, outlined by the clear contours of logical, rational categories.

I had to see this woman once more. I reached the street that ran along the hill. I noticed: the woman turned to the right. Yes, I saw her at a distance. I followed. I began to catch up.

She crossed the street and stepped over the tram rails laid below the hill. Now she was walking down the alley planted with young maple trees.

I could clearly see her slender figure against the backdrop of the hill covered with gray-green weeds; her red high-heeled boots; light-colored stockings; narrow linen skirt; white cardigan with lace sleeves; pale-yellow hair, gathered at the back in a heavy bun.

Everything about her was extraordinarily simple. Perhaps it was her refined, artistic simplicity that initially caught my attention.

I wanted to watch; instead, I should have listened. But listened for what? Perhaps I was on the wrong path all along. I should have sought not a visual but an auditory image, not a painterly but a musical one. I should have searched for a spot where the former transformed into the latter.

I gazed at the woman, at the silver nakedness of the bulging hillside, which stood before me like the oxidized metal of an old Sasanian bowl. I felt a bitter taste on my parched lips, like that of dusty wormwood from the steppe. Who could tell whence and why this melancholy came over me, enveloping my heart and inciting this tightness in my chest? The mournful mood that had no name, appearing uninvited, obscuring and extinguishing the joy of light?

Above the distant crest of the soaring hill, above the rooftops of buildings and the treetops that stretched out in a green strip above, a dark storm cloud was creeping, beginning to cover the sky.

Suddenly, from above, a prelude to the storm—a whirlwind broke loose and descended, tearing leaves from the trees, lifting dust from the gray pavement of the street and yellow sand from the alley.

The woman quickened her pace, ducking her head.

I know: the wind will carry the cloud over the city, banishing the rain.

There will be no storm!

XXV

And that was when the music emerged!

Measure by measure, the melody was being born. It originated in the anxiety that preceded the storm, in the whirlwind that arose from the distant expanses of the steppe, sweeping over the green fields of wheat.

The sounds vibrated clearer and clearer, more sonorous and resonant. A river of music flowed. I dove into it, dissolving myself. In an instant, in just a moment, I would recall the melody, embrace the sounds, remember them, identify that musical phrase that grows from the scattered sounds and individual measures within and around me, as yet only vague and unformed fragments.

I kept gazing at the golden glow of this woman's hair, at her heeled red shoes, at her slender and unsettled posture. Inside me, with a final labor of will, from the depths of memory, from the sensation of bitter wormwood, from the melancholy that arrived from some unknown place, a few measures emerged, very transparent and simple.

They resounded, pushing aside the dubious anxiety of vague, amorphous patches of memory. I reined in the skittish uncertainty that had plagued me. I recognized those measures. *There* it was. They fell into a certain, clear, and distinct musical phrase.

Once the scattered, individual measures formed a musical phrase, I had no doubt anymore: the roots of my current search, of my half-understood impressions lay right here, in this fragment of music.

I kept repeating the phrase over and over. Now I knew where it came from.

"It's a leitmotif from Szymanowski's Symphony No. 2! Yes, that's it! It's the leitmotif from that second "ecstatic" symphony, saturated with the flames of passion, which brought recognition and global fame to the young composer, immediately catapulting him into the fore-front of the greatest masters.[64] *Ta-ra, ra-ra, ra-ra!"*

I kept repeating variations of the leitmotif, one after another. The main theme, that very simple and transparent phrase, grew within me as I gazed at this woman, trying to understand why, upon that first encounter, it had seemed to me that I knew her.

The leitmotif expressed fervent, immediate feelings of love, ascending to the level of ecstasy and capable of scorching, rocking, captivating, but never satiating.

The musical sensation awakened in tandem with the visual, merging, intertwining, overlapping and ultimately mastering it. It was a melody that I was seeing, a visual

---

[64] Karol Szymanowski (1882–1937): Polish composer and pianist, a member of the modernist *Young Poland* movement. Even though Domontovych refers to Szymanowski's Symphony No. 2 here, it is the composer's Symphony No. 3, created in 1914–1916, that has been described as an "ecstatic night-time love song."

image that I heard. It was love, unfolding simultaneously in both the auditory and visual fields.

Ahead of me walked the woman whom I could hear. Yes, it was her. Her gait, her slender figure, the gold of her blond hair, the dark blue of her eyes—blue cornflowers scattered amidst the wheat—her quick, hurried steps. And her voice, which I heard in reply on the church porch:

"You are mistaken, sir! I don't know you." Her resonant, gentle, deep voice. I no longer held any doubts. I was completely sure, and nothing could undermine my certainty. This melody was her. It was her, this woman whom I had unexpectedly met here, who was the object of love expressed in this theme. Only she, and no one else, resounded through each variation of the leitmotif.

This discovery was thrilling. I wanted to beat the drums, blow the horns, leap and run. I had to share my discovery with someone, tell somebody everything that had happened.

Why not tell her first?

I am someone who is prone not only to changing moods but also impulsive action. If I set my mind to something, I will do it. I was catching up to her. I was coming up beside her. Up close, I could see her heavy hair gathered atop her head; her high cheekbones and smooth forehead; the light rose of her tanned cheeks; the narrow, finely-shaped nose; the deep blue of her eyes.

I had no doubts. I pictured it: he, tall and broad-shouldered, still a young man, once walked beside her, just as I was at the moment. Their steps were synchronized, and he was looking—eagerly, impatiently, with excitement—into the blue of her eyes. And then these transparent and simple measures emerged in him, speaking of larks in the sky, of dark blue cornflowers amidst ripening wheat, of a cloud rising on the horizon, a prelude to the whirlwind that would inevitably break loose and sweep over the fields, the steppe, him and her.

Having taken a step and leaning toward her, I said,

"Excuse me! I beg your pardon. I understand that this is completely inappropriate, almost rude of me. I hope I am not too forward in approaching and addressing you like this. I am a complete stranger to you, but please do not misunderstand my intentions. I simply wish to ask you something. Just one question. I want to see whether I am right. All of this came as unexpectedly to me as it did to you. Please, tell me, are you familiar with Symphony No. 2, the one they call 'ecstatic,' by Szymanowski?"

I watched as surprise, concern, and finally anger ignited the blue flame of her eyes. She looked at me, hesitating in her final judgment: Was I cocksure? Insane? Or just an idiot?

She was clearly disturbed and did not hide it. I noticed an instinctive gesture as she tightly clutched her purse to herself. A smart precaution in this deserted place! She looked around in hopes of calling someone. But in the empty alley under the hillside, there was no one, just the two of us. She was likely wondering: *would it have been better, without responding to this man at all, to seek immediate help by crossing the street?*

She raised her voice with indignation.

"What is it that you want from me, exactly? What is this? This is the second time you have approached me. I ask you to leave me alone."

I wanted to soften her anger, so I responded with naivete:

"Nothing at all, I swear! Just a simple yes or no! That's all!"

I tried to explain.

"When you were crossing the tram tracks, I glanced at you, and the leitmotif from Szymanowski's symphony came into my mind."

I had a feeling that what I had just said sounded even more absurd than what had come before. The woman blushed slightly, hesitating. She was not entirely certain as to how to handle the situation.

And at this decisive moment, unexpectedly to myself, I remembered the dedication printed on the piano score of the symphony.

"Larysa Pavlivna!"

A cloud covered the sky from the west to the north. A shadow hung over the city's outskirts. In the twilight, dim and inaudible bolts of lightning flashed one at a time, while the sun still shone in the southeast. Maple leaves drifted on gusts of wind. A whirlwind erupted, carrying with it the steppe smoke, the beach sand, acacia leaves and flowers in waves of aroma. It ruffled the woman's clothes, pulling strands of hair from under her comb. If she was saying something to me, I could not hear it.

She turned her back to the wind, bowed her head and shouted as she held her hair with her hand.

"This is completely unamusing—knowing who I am, approaching me, not introducing yourself but teasing me like a schoolboy!"

I objected vehemently.

"I assure you that I would never have permitted myself such poor pretense. I really don't know who you are."

The whirlwind passed and she raised her head. There was utter confusion in her eyes. She did not understand at all. Hesitantly, she tried to interject,

"But..."

Then she furrowed her brow.

"So, what is it that you want from me?"

"I wanted to find out..."

"Find out... what?"

"What I had asked you. Are you the woman to whom Szymanowski dedicated his Symphony No. 2?"

She flared up,

"Are you a journalist? Did somebody tell you?"

"Not at all! Neither the former nor the latter! Like I said, this situation is as unexpected and incomprehensible to me as it must seem to you."

Finally venturing a guess, she pondered aloud whether I had met the composer in person. She uttered his first name and patronymic.

"He told you about me? Did he send you?"

"Nothing of the sort! I am familiar with his works and I appreciate his creative genius. I am one of the sincerest admirers of his talent, but I have not yet had the pleasure of meeting him in person."

The wind tilted the treetops, sprinkling Larysa Pavlivna's stockings with sand and playing with her hair.

She turned sideways to the wind and tucked her head. Now she was looking at me askew.

"Where is it that you know me from?"

"From nowhere! I told you—I don't know you!"

She threw up her hands helplessly, like a child.

"But *how?*"

Bewildered herself, she then asked me with a sincere directness,

"You aren't from around here, are you?"

"No, I'm not. I arrived from Kharkiv only yesterday."

She was likely unsure why she had posed the question. But she was undoubtedly starting to enjoy our whimsical conversation. Slowly, she found herself drawn into the game.

We reached the intersection where the maple-lined alley, running along the hillside, met a cross-street, descending from above, nestled between two empty, weed-grown wastelands.

I asked the woman if she would not object to my accompanying her.

"Of course not, we aren't far!"

And she stretched her hand toward a group of tenement buildings on the hill.

We turned left and walked uphill; I shielded her from the gusting wind.

I took advantage of the opportunity to clarify what had happened. I myself did not understand everything that had transpired. Certainly, in my attempts to explain, I managed to confuse myself even further; clarity was out of reach, but I kept talking. Sliding inevitably into pontification, I set out to analyze the minute details.

"Allow me," I said, "at the risk of boring you, to start from the moment when you and I met unexpectedly in the antechamber of the Varangian Church. You were leaving and I was about to enter. That's when I had the sudden impression that I knew you well."

I sighed.

"'*I know*' is an expression we repeat automatically, and yet it preserves its manifold and often contradictory meanings. I knew you and, at the same time, I did not. But this was about *how* I knew you. Our consciousness doesn't always produce straightforward and truthful interpretations of what we perceive. You and I collided accidentally, and my first impression of you told me that I *had known* you. My consciousness, however, suggested the first offhanded answer, an arbitrary and superficial one, 'You know her because she's your good friend!' It was a mistake, an erroneous answer from my conscious mind. I ended up feeling embarrassed and asking for your forgiveness. The most beautiful denizen of the deep, tossed ashore, turns into a heap of disgusting slime."

I glanced at my companion. She was listening. I continued.

"So, there were two things: the impression of familiarity that came from nowhere, and its false interpretation. May I continue?"

"But of course!"

"Usually, we completely ignore such incidents that populate our lives. We take no notice of them. We overlook them as trifles, although oftentimes they deserve our careful attention. In this case we might risk coming across as tactless or intrusive."

I smiled at her. She smiled back. My ironic posture led her to be more forgiving.

"You left," I continued, "and I stayed. I made every effort to find an explanation for this impression of familiarity. Naturally, it was too amorphous to really grasp. It was vague and fleeting. Try catching and holding onto a glint of sunlight from the chandelier, reflected on the wall! I was chasing an illusion. I strained my mind. I demanded a clear answer from my memory. I handled myself like the strictest investigator. I was stubborn. And yet, all my efforts were in vain. I was on the wrong track."

"I assumed that the impression was visual, and I achieved nothing. Why hadn't I assumed that it was not a visual but an auditory—even a musical—impression of something familiar? I decided to alter the trajectory of my search. I followed you, totally exhausted. I blamed myself. I lamented. I was desperate. And at that moment, when you were crossing the tram tracks, when your silhouette stood out against the hill and my impression of you turned clear and solid—that's when I heard those transparent, simple, distinct musical phrases that make up the leitmotif in Szymanowski's symphony."

"I suppose," I turned to her, "you wouldn't see this as a complete coincidence or a mistake, would you? Here is what happened, in my opinion: a musical impression was born out of a visual one. I was looking at you, and the longer I did, the clearer and more powerful the symphony resonated within me; the musical phrases kept emerging. I had no doubt: it was you!"

She did not know how to react, either to me or to my story. Was I a charlatan, or did I simply possess an active imagination? Should she take what I had told her as a factual account or as something spur-of-the-moment? She tried to resist,

"Either you're taunting me," she said, "or you're just having a laugh!"

She demanded honesty.

I reassured her that everything had transpired exactly as I had told her and that my story had not been embellished by any sort of trick, jape, or flight of fancy.

"Why should we imagine," I said, "that the creative act cannot be replicated? Why should I not recognize your image in the composer's theme, just as he recognized his theme in you?"

She grew excited,

"That can't be possible!"

"But it's a fact! Why," I said bitterly, "why would you insist that the Green Bird was merely that? Why wouldn't you, like Gozzi, believe in talking statues and trust that only the Green Bird can bring happiness to mankind?"[65]

I bowed and kissed her delicate hand with its narrow, oval-shaped nails. I kept looking at her. Her heavy hair, gathered on top of her head, strawberry blonde with a golden tinge; her thin-lipped mouth; her neatly outlined nose; her slightly blushed face.

We stood on the hill. The vast skyline stretched out in front of us, the distant silver steppe, darkened by the

---

[65] *The Little Green Bird* (Italian: *L'augellino belverde*) is a 1765 commedia dell'arte play by Carlo Gozzi (1720–1806). In the play filled with magical transformations, statues become human, while the Green Bird turns into a prince, who believes that philosophy is the path to happiness.

heavy cloud hanging over it, and the Dnipro. Shrouding the sun, the cloud was approaching the river. The wind kept bending the poplars.

The young woman glanced at the clouds, at me, at the wind. And again: at the clouds, at me, at the wind. She was uncertain.

She said,

"It seems like a storm is coming."

I said,

"The wind will chase that cloud away!"

She hesitated.

Then, with trust and sincerity, she said,

"Let's stop by our place! No one is there. My husband is teaching. You can wait out the storm!"

We crossed the street. A noisy crowd of children was playing on the sidewalk by the tenement house. Two toddlers broke away from the group and rushed to the woman, squealing. They hugged her legs, pulling at her skirt with their tiny hands, greeting her with excitement.

I asked,

"Are they yours?"

Nonchalantly, she replied,

"Oh, no!"

We entered a white, spacious, empty foyer. We went up the wide marble stairs to the second floor. Silence, emptiness, tall white doors. A fly buzzed, beating itself against the window. On the door, there was a brass plaque with the inscription "Professor." The spelling of the word, in the old style, suggested that her husband must have been about ten or fifteen years older than her.

The spacious corridor resembled a parlor. Open doors revealed an enfilade of large, bright rooms with high ceilings.

I caught her gaze and said,

"I have no hat to remove!"

She invited,

"Please, come in."

XXVI

I stepped inside the room. An antique *panskyi kilim* of bright golden hues, with pink roses woven into it, stretched across the entire width of one wall.[66]

My young hostess, noticing that I had approached the carpet and was examining the threads from the reverse side, mentioned with a hint of pride,

"We have a date for this carpet! It's from 1728, and it comes from the carpet workshop of Danylo Apostol."[67]

Carpet weaving was by no means my specialty. I had never written anything about this area of Ukrainian baroque art.

I contented myself with a brief comment.

---

[66] Ukrainian carpets from the 17th–18th centuries, characterized by the eastern patterns and popular in the milieu of nobility.

[67] Danylo Apostol (1654–1734): *hetman* of Left-Bank Ukraine in 1727–1734. According to legend, this particular *kilim* from 1720–1730 was found in Apostol's crypt in the village of Velyki Sorochyntsi, in present-day Poltava oblast. In 1922, the tomb was robbed by the Special Liquidation Commission, which expropriated objects of historical and artistic value from the churches. Currently, the kilim is in the collection of the National Museum of the History of Ukraine in Kyiv.

"Based on the dimensions of this carpet, could we not reproduce the scale of those late-seventeenth and early eighteenth-century manors, just as Cuvier recreated the visage of a prehistoric animal from a single bone?"[68]

Having satisfied my vague, amateurish interest in this precious item, I turned on my heels and surveyed the room. Bright, glossy parquet. On the lid of a black grand piano near the sidewall languished a typical bust of pensive Beethoven. A table occupied the center of the room. The petals of a red tulip gleamed inside the tall green glass sitting on the white tablecloth.

Larysa apologized. Would I allow her to leave me for a moment to fix her disheveled hair?

"But of course, by all means!"

I was left alone in this large room with its windows open to the east. Beyond the abundant trees, one could discern the silvery strip of the distant river and the blue of the sky.

I took the opportunity to look at the photos hanging on the wall above the wide Turkish divan on the other side of the table. With my hands folded behind my back, I examined the pictures closely. Immediately, I said,

"Oh, yes! No, I made no mistake!"

I took off my glasses and gave them a closer look. Instantly, I recognized a young face, a large lock of hair hanging over the rectangle of a forehead, tender, plump lips, and a firm, determined chin, reminiscent of Wagner's—the face of the young composer, so familiar from

---

[68] Georges Cuvier (1769–1832): French zoologist and the founder of paleontology.

the magazines, concerts, and posters. And here they were together: him and her. The seashore, black lancets of cypress, cliffs that evoked a southern exoticism. I contemplated the radiant joy on her face in this small image, where she stood on the shore in her white linen dress—such boundless joy that it evoked envy in me. Why did I remain uninvolved in all this bountiful full-ness of life?

A series of her photos. Various angles. Interplay of light and shadow. Shades of gray and sepia. Experimen-tal studies by famed photographers; masterpieces of imagination; earnest attempts to refute strictly realistic methods.

A portrait of a portly, bearded man with a professo-rial air—probably her husband.

Numerous other photos of people I did not know. My eyes passed casually over these images which seemed to have nothing to communicate to me.

I sat down on a sofa. Through the doorway to the adjacent room, much larger than the one I was sitting in, I could see the blue-gray silk furniture in Louis XIV style and the massive, black boulder of a grand piano, whose bulky triangular shape filled almost half the spa-cious hall.

A solemn silence filled this apartment of many rooms. In the distance, children's voices could be heard. I had the opportunity to contemplate in peace. Two expensive musical instruments; stacks of sheet music lying on the stools; large decorative photos that had no place in an ordinary professor's residence; and her own association with the composer. All of these spelled out some sort of close connection between my new acquaintance and the world of music.

Could I draw any further conclusions? Let us ponder further. Her name, according to the dedication inscription on the piano score, was Larysa Pavlivna. What could this name tell me? Did it convey some meaning or nothing at all? Was she an opera singer? There was a well-known chamber vocalist by that name: Larysa Solska. Her concerts had enjoyed considerable success. Critics and audiences placed her on par with Zoya Lodii.[69] Should I assume it was her?

As she entered the room, I rose up to greet her. I said,

"If we continue with the game we started, unraveling further this knot of mysteries, then I would have to confirm that today I had the pleasure of meeting Larysa Solska. I hope you would not wish to disappoint me by saying that I was mistaken?"

She laughed and extended her hand for me to kiss:

"No, I won't do that, my dear Cagliostro! You are a magician, a trickster, a clairvoyant, a daydreamer! I bet you'll be pulling your Green Bird from a pocket or a sleeve any minute now!"

What a charming woman! Smiling back at her, I said,

"I must atone for my failure before you: I have never had the chance to attend your concerts. But our mutual friend, Dmytro Revutsky, has spoken highly and enthusiastically of you. I wonder how, in visiting him, I have never once met you."

---

[69] Zoya Lodii (1886–1957): Russian lyrical soprano.

My hostess asked me to sit down. She sat on a divan, while I occupied a round chair.

I sat by the piano and touched the lid with my hand. I opened the keyboard and placed my fingers on the keys. It happened automatically, without a second thought. One movement led to another.

I am not a musician by any means. I am only an amateur. My playing is not flawless. I am aware of this, but I have a musical memory, and I don't think anyone would accuse me of being poorly-versed in music or unable to appreciate it.

Touching the keys gave me an impulse. My fingers ran over the keys; arpeggios rang out in the room. Perhaps I did it just to hear the sound of the instrument. It was full and resonant: grains of fine, heavy wheat fell into the palms of my hands.

I asked,

"Do you mind?"

She responded with a succinct and polite "Not at all!"

I cannot say exactly why I allowed myself to reproduce the leitmotif, this short and resonant musical phrase that echoed in my memory that day. Perhaps I did so purely out of inertia. Or could I have been embarrassed by the presence of this woman, to whom this wonderful piece had been dedicated?

Of course, it was careless, even tactless on my part, but what could I do? I could not hold back anymore. This was beyond my control.

Music filled me. I no longer existed. There was only music, and I completely surrendered myself to it.

I was not interested in conducting psychological experiments. No coercion. No attempt to play on her nerves or mine.

Knowing that she, the one who had triggered these sounds, was here, right next to me, I had to recreate the music.

The silvery harmonies of the symphony's first measures spread throughout the room, evoking first love, the first stirrings of emotion, and then abruptly the stormy flood of passion, the uncontrollable frenzy of ecstatic ardor. Within the imagined confines of the room, the music emerged and unfolded. The music was overwhelming; the feeling was overwhelming. The tension of passion turned into abstraction. The real was annihilated. The physically impossible became the metaphysically possible.

I immersed myself in the sound. I dissolved into the harmonies. The world turned into music. There was music and there was a musical, auditory abstraction of the world. The world and this woman were discerned and embodied in the music.

And now she was sitting by the table, where the flower threw a fiery glow on the white expanse of the tablecloth. She was listening. Her hands lay on the table. Her fingertips touched the glass with the tulip. Her face had grown pale. She seemed absent altogether.

At that moment, the wind burst into the room. It whirled through the dwelling, shaking the walls of the house. Throughout the building, windows clattered, doors slammed shut, window panes shuddered. The tinkling of shattered glass was audible from somewhere.

The cries of frightened children and women's screams rang out,

"Shut the windows! Shut the windows!"

The room was rapidly darkening.

"There will be no storm! The wind will scatter the clouds!" I said.

"I'll be right back!" she shouted and ran to close the windows.

XXVII

She returned. I said to her,

"This music is dangerous. If I were married, I would forbid my wife to listen to this piece!"

Larysa burst into laughter,

"Just play!"

Her voice sounded curt and impatient. It was simultaneously a command and a plea. She was begging for mercy. Who knew whether she was actually in control of herself?

I kept on playing. I played the tensest, most ecstatic part of the symphony, the one that gave the entire piece its unofficial title. A passionate fervor was ignited. The flower's petals were opening. The flames turned white.

She stood by the piano, her face very close to mine. Her face was now pale as chalk; it resembled a mask, and her painted lips trembled, dry from anticipation.

She completely surrendered to the emotional flow of the music. She listened, and in doing so, she listened to herself, for the music was her and there was no music outside of her. She *was* the music. Through her, I recognized it; through it, I recognized her.

Her closed eyelids trembled like night butterflies. Her cheeks turned pink. Her lips parted. I kissed her. She did not push me away. Did she realize it was I?

The wind scattered the clouds. Light filled the rooms again. The day sparkled with the sun's radiance; the azure of the sky grew denser still.

"We need to open the windows!" she said and, pulling my head close, she kissed me. Then she stood up and walked away.

I considered the taste of her kiss: bitter, like wormwood. Was it just my imagination, or was there an insatiable desire in that kiss, like the music, with neither end nor beginning?

She opened the windows and the balcony doors, and the room became flooded with sunlight. In the blue haze of sunbeams, dust particles floated and whirled around.

I adjusted my tie in front of the mirror that hung over the piano. The mirror reflected my face, the hunched neck of the plaster Beethoven, and the red blob of the tulip in the depth of glass against the white tablecloth.

I simply stood there. Before me was the piano—a white path of keys interrupted by black railings. The path led nowhere; or rather, it led to some hypothetical reality, created by art, that would give more credibility to our everyday existence.

Larysa entered the room in a new outfit. She wore an evening concert gown with a long train. Catching my alarmed gaze—whence this change in attire? —she replied,

"I'm going to sing."

And added,

"For you!"

Then she explained her outfit.

"Think of it like a uniform! Everyone behaves differently depending on what they're wearing. I have this inclination; I prefer to sing only in my concert attire. Singers, like children, are allowed to be eccentric."

She suggested moving to the adjacent room, where the grand piano was.

"The resonance is better here," she explained.

She stood by the grand piano, pressing her palms on the keyboard lid. The white gold of her hair contrasted sharply with her black attire. I was the sole member of the audience at this peculiar performance, notwithstanding the odd sparrow chirping and fluttering on the balcony, occasionally taking a wary peek into the room.

Her voice was strong and well-placed: the soft voice of a chamber singer, brimming with intimate lyricism. It was a restrained voice of the highest purity.

One song followed another in a casual, effortless sequence. Her style was very simple, but behind the simplicity of her singing one sensed an austere and demanding discipline. Everything superfluous was discarded. She infused her songs with feeling without ever veering into sentimentality. It was a musical exemplar of the Empire style.[70]

---

[70] A phase of Neoclassical art that developed in France in the early 19th century, placing emphasis on long and graceful lines, femininity and elegance.

A ring at the doorbell interrupted her singing.

"My husband!" Larysa called out.

She examined me from head to toe. It was evident that she would prefer to avoid deliberate family complications. She made sure I looked alright and then, supporting the train with her hand, hurried into the hallway, straightening the crumpled and scattered pillows on the couch along the way.

A clumsy, fifty-something man with a graying beard and swollen bags under small red eyes entered the room. He was corpulent but agile, animated. His beard, the bags, his belly, the black satin jacket buttoned halfway— all of these gave him the appearance of a typical pre-revolutionary professor.

I stood up and waited.

Larysa, following him, introduced us.

"My husband!"

Laughing, she added,

"In a married woman's life, *husband* is a purely formal category. He is a legal fiction, a necessary evil. Without him, a married woman could not be considered married!"

"Larysa, you say such dreadful things!" The man rebuked his wife playfully.

"What can I do? she said. "I am only stating the facts."

She continued the introduction ritual.

"This is my good acquaintance," she pointed to me.

Then she paused. She could not say neither my first nor my last name. She only knew that I was not local and that I had arrived from Kharkiv the day before.

"From Kharkiv!" she added to complete the sentence and fill the awkward pause.

Standing behind her husband, with a playful expression in her eyes, she looked at me. She needed support.

I hurried to her rescue. I introduced myself, naming my occupation, my title, stating the reason for my visit. I even said that we had met at the Varangian Church on the occasion of the conference, adding,

"I am a sincere and long-standing admirer of Larysa Pavlivna's musical talent."

I bowed in her direction, and the man and I shook hands.

In my situation, what else could I do with the limited resources at hand? I was creating a myth out of nothing! But I was fortunate: it appeared the professor was familiar not only with my name but also with my academic writings.

"Are you him?" he asked, and mentioned my name.

I smiled and replied playfully, matching his tone.

"Yes. I am him."

"Well, then I know who you are! Although I am, in fact, a geologist by profession, I have always sought out indigenous architectural landmarks during my research expeditions throughout Ukraine, the Caucasus, the Altai, and the Pamirs. You yourself might find a few things of interest in my photograph collection. Have you," he continued, "for instance, ever been to Afghanistan?"

I hastened to answer,

"Unfortunately, I have not managed to make it there yet."

"Well, I have indeed!" he exclaimed. "You'll see!" He brought out a folder of photographs from his office, as well as several of my own works.

"I have," he said, "your *Catalog of Baroque Monuments in Ukraine: Seventeenth and Eighteenth Centuries*, but unfortunately, I am missing what interests me the most: the French publication of your report on the journey to Armenia. I have been hoping to compare your photos with mine and find your comments on the monuments I had seen with my own eyes. I only have clippings from newspapers about your presentation."

I assured him that upon my return to Kharkiv, I would promptly send him a copy of my book.

"This edition is out of print, but I will certainly arrange for a copy for you," I said.

"I would be most grateful! I do appreciate art," he went on, glancing at me with his narrow red eyes; there was something Kalmyk about his tanned face, "and I have quite an art collection; if we were to include my wife, a singer, to it, then my collection could be considered very valuable and tastefully curated. This," he noted, "is my compliment to myself!"

We laughed at his joke and continued talking for a while longer, until I glanced at the clock.

I was dumbfounded.

"Can it be that it's already past four?" I asked.

"Yes, indeed," the professor confirmed.

I jumped from my seat. I approached the hostess and kissed her hand,

"I have lost track of time completely," I said. "Today I have no sense of time at all. This morning, I woke up at the crack of dawn. I came to the meeting too early and that's why I ended up running late. And then I lingered here all this time."

But Larysa did not want to let me go.

"You'll stay for lunch and after that, we will still have the evening at our disposal. Are you otherwise occupied tonight?" she asked me.

I replied that I had no plans this evening and was entirely at her service, but that I really could not stay for lunch.

The host energetically supported his wife's offer but I firmly refused.

Larysa relented.

"Well, all right then," she said, "let it be as you wish this time. Off you go to your important matters, but whether you desire it or not, you'll spend your evening with me!"

"Happy to oblige!"

"Then it's agreed!" Larysa concluded with a smile. "I'll come to pick you up. We'll spend the evening together. Unfortunately, my husband is too busy and won't be able to accompany me. He sends his apologies. It will be just me. Where are you staying?"

I gave her the name of the hotel and the room number.

The host meekly accepted the stipulation his wife shared on his behalf. I did not know if he was accustomed to hearing such statements from her, but I could not register any reaction while observing his face. Nothing about the situation appeared to bother him.

I ought to admit that I am not particularly fond of arranging meetings in the presence of a husband. But

Larysa preferred to be direct and open. At least, more or less open, as women tend to be, especially when they are beautiful.

The host escorted me graciously to the stairs and offered a firm handshake. Standing on the landing and leaning over the railing, he kept calling out as I descended, urging me to visit once more at the earliest opportunity.

"We'll always be happy to welcome you here!"

He seemed accustomed to being exquisitely polite with Larysa's friends. He exuded friendliness.

I thanked him, expressing the hope that this would not be our last meeting, that we would have the opportunity to see each other again.

In the lobby, opening the door and stepping onto the street, I felt myself blushing. I considered his kind invitation.

Yes, there exists that type of courtesy which always carries a trace of ambiguity. There is kindness that makes one ill at ease.

I suppose I have never lacked in reticence.

XXVIII

I lit a cigarette. Before reaching the tram stop, I decided to turn onto Poltavska Street.

I recognized familiar places. Nothing had changed over the years. It was the same steppe town. No new buildings. No new sidewalks. A pile of trash on the corner, unfenced wasteland, weeds around the building where the Mariyinska Women's Gymnasium used to be, and now housed the Vocational School.

Only, some of the sidewalk bricks had chipped; the acacias along the avenue had aged; the bronze pedestal of Catherine had disappeared from the cluttered square between the Museum and the Mining Institute; and on the Institute building, under the cornice, a new, large inscription appeared in gold letters: "In the Name of Comrade Artiom."[71]

I stood there, waiting for the tram. I smoked. The chubby goats that had been gobbling young plants in Soborna Square that morning had disappeared somewhere. The shadow from an unfinished red brick tenement house stretched eastward. A tram descended the hill. It was mine. I stepped onboard.

The tanned legs of the conductor flitted once again along the footboard around the car. Colorful paper ribbons slithered from her leather bag. Trees, laden with blossoms, rose upwards. We rode down—or rather plummeted, at breakneck speed, into an abyss, as if the brakes had failed.

In the hotel lobby, Ivan Vasylyovych Hulia rose from the bench and rushed towards me. The encounter felt like an explosion, a calamity. He gripped my hand for a long time, gazed into my eyes, and embraced me. His fingers fumbled about my back, as if he wished to convince himself firsthand of the veracity of my existence.

---

[71] The *nom de guerre* of Russian Bolshevik revolutionary Fiodor Sergeiev (1883–1921).

Hulia was thrilled to know that I still existed, that I had not perished or disappeared for good, that he still had the opportunity to see me alive. He was so incredibly concerned that something might have happened to me. He entertained a thousand scenarios,

"Arsen Petrovych, I, the representative of *Zavoblono*,[72] none of us could manage without you, dear Rostyslav Mykhailovych, we have been wondering what had happened to you: perhaps you fell ill and fainted, exhausted from the journey? Perhaps you were out of it. Or, God forbid, something worse had happened. You are so meticulous and punctual; forgive my familiarity, Rostyslav Mykhailovych, I would even say—you are a pinnacle of pedantic punctuality, and somehow... you were not present! This could not be. I proposed to Arsen Petrovych that we postpone the meeting; what sort of Council would it be without you? Arsen Petrovych was on the phone, I went twice to the hotel, I visited the Museum, everywhere, and—nothing! Nowhere to be found. I despaired, Rostyslav Mykhailovych, but what could I do? Of course, you could have gone swimming. Do you imagine I hadn't checked any of the beaches along the Dnipro? Of course I did, especially with this storm in mind..."

Instantly, without adjusting his tone, filled with the same enthusiastic fervor, Ivan Vasylyovych Hulia began recounting the morning meeting.

"What a pity, Rostyslav Mykhailovych, that you were not present in person. You missed a great deal! Arsen

---

[72] Russian: Заведующий областным отделом народного образования, or the Head of the Regional Department of Public Education.

Petrovych's report was wonderful. It was flawless. He clarified everything: the history of the Varangian Church, its artistic significance, the figure of Lynnyk, his position and significance within Ukrainian and world art—he thoroughly explained and contextualized everything. The Zavoblono representative himself thanked Arsen Petrovych for his report. I have the impression that the Varangian Church shall indeed be handed over to us and turned into a museum reserve."

He caught his breath, gasping for air, and squeezed my hand warmly.

He informed me that, according to the conference program, there would be no meetings tonight. The next session would take place tomorrow, not at ten in the morning but at eleven, and—he paused for emphasis—on the premises of the Art Museum. Then followed a humble request that I attend the meeting without fail.

I thanked him for the information and promised to be there. However, this conference and its associated matters concerned me far less than it might have seemed to eager Hulia at first glance. What is Hecuba to me, or I to Hecuba?[73]

Hulia and I dined together right there in the hotel restaurant.

[73] A paraphrase from Shakespear's *Hamlet*, Act 2, Scene 2.

XXIX

In the evening, with greenish twilight still shimmering through the open windows of my room, she knocked on the door three times.

Larysa entered the room looking elegant, dashing, lively.

But now she struck me as entirely different, nothing like before. In the morning, during our first meeting, she, her attire, handbag, and hairstyle—everything about her was unpretentious and modest. There was nothing overt in her mannerisms, no trace of deceit. She wore no adornments that would encroach upon her beauty or could seem even slightly excessive. There was an extraordinary restraint and definitive clarity in everything about her. The rhythm of her movements, the white fabric of her blouse, a simple linen skirt, and red high-heeled shoes. The weight of her fair hair, casually tied in a knot; the blueness of her eyes: dark cornflowers scattered in a wheat field.

Against the monotone background, this splash of color stood out more vividly. Beauty emerged from a few hues, from the rhythmic simplicity of a few lines. The white expanse of the tablecloth, restricted by the imaginary rectangle of its edges, and on it, the dense red paint of tulip petals.

Even the second time, dressed in black concert attire with a train, she maintained an overall restraint characteristic of chamber style. Her appearance took on more solemnity without losing any of its inherent simplicity. The long black dress accentuated the outlined strict contours of this simplicity. Nothing but the contrast of black and white. The blonde corona of heavy hair contrasting with the black background of the dress. Her slender, upright posture clearly outlined. It was that solemn simplicity of the Empire style, affirming the perfection of beauty through negation.

An elongated white Empire vase stood on the black cover of the grand piano. The style was adhered to with precision.

But now, in the way she appeared before me, she was completely different.

I have always struggled to comprehend the reason for the rupture that suddenly occurs in the leitmotif of Szymanowski's symphony. Such a transparent and simple musical phrase suddenly falls apart, rends itself, loses its transparency, with sounds jumping around nervously. In the music of the young composer, there appears an arrhythmia, a cacophonous tension, echoes of jazz music from restaurants and cafés. Szymanowski introduced instruments from a jazz orchestra into the composition of the symphonic orchestra, a move which provoked harsh criticism from supporters of a strict symphonic style. None of this comported with my impressions of Larysa, whose visual image today revealed the resonance of his music.

Now I saw her in a completely different light. No simplicity. No cornflowers. No vast wheat field enveloped in the breath of a spring storm!

A completely changed contour of shoulders, a distinct head posture. A new manner of walking, mirroring the rhythm of a syncopated foxtrot. Makeup, which was lacking in the morning and was now skillfully, expertly applied to her face. The standardized type of a made-up face, specifically designed for frequenting cafés, cinemas, restaurants. The eyebrows were blackened into straight lines, the eyelids saturated with blue; long, straight lashes shot out like arrows. Each individual eyelash was the product of meticulous work.

The shoes were chosen to match the dress. They caught the eye with their deliberate boldness. The sharp scent of unusual perfumes. A virtuoso hairstyle, expertly coiffed.

In her hand, she held a brightly-colored, extravagant parasol; her handbag was embroidered with gold—a small masterpiece crafted for women, designed to carry trifles.

I was impressed, even amazed. I hesitated a little, not entirely sure if there had been some mistake, and a stranger had accidentally entered my room.

She registered my surprise.

"Do you not recognize me?" she said, laughing.

But I recognized her voice, her laughter, the blue light of her eyes. She traced a colorful circle in the air with her parasol, placed the handbag on the table and, splitting her gaze between me and the mirror, aware of the deliberate alteration in her appearance, asked,

"So which version of me do you prefer?"

"You as you are!" I answered.

A hoarse voice, stifled with desire, uttered a single word,

"*You!*"

…We left the hotel.

Wanderers, vagabonds of emotion, urban nomads, we surrendered ourselves to the aimlessness of nocturnal explorations.

We moved from garden to garden. We transitioned from darkness to light; from light we plunged back into darkness. We discovered unknown countries, continents, lands. With our own selves, we started creating the universe anew.

I asked,

"Would you agree, Larysa, that the biblical story of Adam and Eve applies only to you and me, as today we are the first and only people in the world, and those for whom this whole world has been created?"

The night turned into a myth. Everything around us transformed into a whimsical phantasmagoria of feelings.

Waves of flower scent gushed forth. The fragrance was so dense and dim that it seemed it could be sensed by touch and rubbed between the fingertips.

Time flowed. We grew tired of our wanderings. We were hungry. I suggested getting dinner.

"Let's have some food and wine!"

She didn't object. She agreed to all the proposals: to dine, to drink, not to go to a restaurant, but rather, to the kebab-house that I learned of yesterday evening and dared to confidently recommend today.

A sideways glance from under the hat. Pressing against me, she said, softly,

"Darling!"

XXX

We took the battered stone steps down. Everything that happened yesterday repeated itself today.

As yesterday, we passed by the landscapes and genre scenes painted along the stairwell—the naive echoes of Persian miniatures, the evidence of the painter's helplessness. As yesterday, the well-dressed host greeted us at the doorstep. His shiny, bald head in a deep bow gleamed before our eyes; one hand he extended towards us, with the other placed over his heart.

The host recognized me, joyously expressing his delight at seeing and hosting me once more today.

In response, I shook his warm hand and affectionately patted his broad back with my palm.

We rejoiced in our meeting in that manner reserved only for people whose paths have crossed by accident, knowing that they will diverge, never to meet again.

Pointing his short finger at my companion, the host proudly told me,

"Here is our local *bulbul*, our nightingale!" And then, turning to Larysa, he scolded her for having neglected to visit for such a long time. He listened for the nightingales that flock to the city in spring, singing in the gardens. But he did not hear her voice among them, and he sadly asked himself more than once,

"Where is our bulbul singing? Perhaps she flew to some distant land, to the cold, dark, and icy north, to entertain the people there with her singing? To enthrall those who are deprived of the joy of listening to nightingales in their own gardens in spring."

Larysa clearly enjoyed this lengthy and colorful compliment, which sounded like a translation from Hafez.

We sat at a table the host found for us in a cozy corner.

Knowing the established custom, I casually brushed aside the menu with standard dishes. By today, I had accumulated enough experience as to how to behave here, conforming to the bazaar-like yet familial tone that the host had cultivated, as if all this were taking place not in an industrialized Ukrainian city, but in some small town outside of Yerevan.

"We're hungry!" I announced. "We want to eat, and we want something exceptionally good, something perfect and unique that isn't listed on any menu or carte!"

My words clearly excited the host.

"I understand... If such a distinguished guest as yourself," he pointed his finger at me, "and such a beautiful and young woman as yourself," he pointed at Larysa, "have come to me, I must treat both of you to something special!"

He was perplexed. He pondered. He bowed politely, lowering his oily eyes.

Typical for an occasion like this, the chef was summoned to our table. The three of us commenced the discussion, and gradually, as the passion intensified, the atmosphere turned electric. I quickly withdrew from the game. For my own safety, I avoided participating in this kitchen debate, especially since from the very beginning neither of them paid any attention to me nor cared to consider the thoughts which I attempted to interject.

The dispute between host and chef started with a selection of dishes and continued with their sequencing.

Each of them defended his own position.

They switched to Armenian. I understood enough of the language to realize that their difference of opinion had escalated into complete opposition. The dispute turned into a quarrel. They were no longer discussing. They were threatening each other. Their eyes burned with hatred and anger. It seemed that any moment they would lunge at each other and grab at each other's collars.

Those present became concerned. They pushed their chairs back and stood up. As a precaution, I moved the tablecloth, knives, and forks off to the side. Who knew how all this would end?

Trying to make myself heard over the clamor, I leaned over the table and called out to Larysa,

"Have you ever seen anything like this? Can any sum of money buy this?"

All of a sudden, everything subsided. The commotion died down. The chef and the host had reached an agreement.

The chef, looking preoccupied, quickly shuffled off to the kitchen, while the host, wiping his sweaty forehead with a napkin and beaming with tenderness, informed us politely about what was being cooked for us in the kitchen and what wine he intended to treat us with today.

"A wine for nightingales," he said, "cannot be ordinary. It cannot be like any other. It must be as sweet as honey and as fragrant as a rose."

He assured us that he had a wine precisely like this in his cellar. Only he had it, and it was just so: thick, sweet, and dark, like a southern night.

He wanted to assure us that not even the foremost wine connoisseurs had the opportunity to drink something similar. After all, not everyone was a friend of his.

As he spoke, he proudly tapped himself on the chest with his short finger. He was at the center of the universe.

It seemed that for him, the whole world and everything in it were divided into two categories: people who had the opportunity to be acquainted with him and savor his kind hospitality, and people who did not. All the world's imperfections and all of life's deficiencies stemmed from the latter.

"To savor even a drop of such wine is to preserve the memory of its taste for a lifetime!" he said.

"Wine," he continued, "is like a woman! There is *a* woman and *the* woman, as there is *a* wine and *the* wine. There is wine that you can drink every day but never enjoy. There is a woman whom you could have known your whole life—so what? But then there is a woman whom, once you've met her, you can never, ever forget, even if it was just a glance she accidentally threw at you, or a smile she bestowed upon you in passing."

He paused, as if lost in memory.

He could have elaborated on the matter, but there were times when words were unnecessary. And today, when such a beautiful, attractive woman was visiting him, along with the wisest and most learned of all men, who even when it came to women managed to choose the best for himself, it would have been a crime on his part if he did not treat them to the finest of all wines he had in his possession.

He called for one of his assistants, instructing him to fetch a candle and accompany him to the cellar.

He left.

I ought to admit: we had the opportunity to be persuaded that these were not just empty words uttered only to improve the lacking quality of the cheap wine and compensate for its hefty price. The wine we drank that evening was in fact thick, sweet, dark, and warm, like a fragrant spring night filled with the singing of a nightingale.

It was a precious liquid. Each drop of it had to be cherished, like a family heirloom passed down from generation to generation. The wine was worthy of comparison to the woman who drank it. All the joys and comforts of life were condensed in the pleasure we experienced as we savored that wine.

It was getting late. The tables in the kebab-house had gradually emptied. The guests dispersed, but Larysa and I, having finished dinner, were still sitting. A pink mist enveloped the world. We didn't want to go anywhere, we had no desire to move, engulfed in a sweet feeling of blissful numbness.

We drank strong, black Turkish coffee and invited the host to join our company. Immersed in a tipsy sway, we listened to his extensive reflections on wine, people, food, the meaning of life, and the purpose of mankind within universal existence. Naturally, he examined the universe from the perspective of a kebab-house owner.

He said,

"Among my friends who come here, one meets people of different tastes. There are people who don't care what wine they drink. They want to feel happy, they want their heads to spin. I love such friends. I respect them, and they respect me. They have a drink, and so do I. They are cheerful, and I am cheerful too. Holding my friend's arm, I help him to step outside, summon a coachman and wish him a happy journey and a good night."

"At the same time, I also have friends," the host continued, "who tell me something along these lines, 'My friend, I love wine, but not just any wine—a good one! I want to savor it, to enjoy its uplifting quality.'"

The host became animated. The rhythm of his speech changed. He turned to me, placing his chair opposite mine,

"Tell me, please," he addressed me, "how can I, having heard such words, call for Arshak and ask, 'Arshak, take the money from the drawer and go across the street to the tserabkop[74] store or to the other side of the *Prospekt* to some mom-and-pop corner shop and get me a couple of bottles of Kardanakhi or Kakheti wine!'"[75]

The host shook his head.

"No," he said, "I haven't stopped believing in God yet, and I haven't become an infidel. Yes, I call Arshak, but I don't tell him to go to the tserabkop for Kar-

[74] First mentioned in chapter IV.
[75] Prospekt: the main street of Dnipro (formerly known as Katerynenskyi Prospekt; now called Prospekt Dmytra Yavornytskoho). Around 1834, an alley with trees was added to the Prospekt, turning it into a boulevard.

danakhi; instead, I tell him, 'Go, Arshak, across the Prospekt to the city station and buy yourself a ticket to Yerevan on the Baku-Shepetivka express train. And when you arrive in Yerevan, hire a cart, go to the Sunday market and visit my friend's village, and get me the wine he pressed with his own hands, the one he has kept in his cellar since the year when his eldest son was born!' That's what I tell Arshak. And when a friend like you comes to me, I whisper in his ear, 'Listen, my friend, I have exactly the wine your heart desires!'"

Having finished his cup of coffee, to conclude our conversation, he said thoughtfully, mindfully, and instructively,

"One ought to respect people and enjoy satisfying their desires."

He rose from his seat and with a sigh from the utmost depths of his soul, he added,

"I believe that one should eat and drink only for the joy and comfort that food and drink bring!"

It was getting late. It was time to go. We had finished all our drinks, all our food. The dark coffee pot, handmade in the region of Van, had cooled.[76] By one corner of the table, a pile of salt-covered almonds darkened on a tray. The tablecloth was stained with wine. The crumpled napkins were carelessly tossed aside.

Feeling weighed down and lost in thought, we pushed back our chairs. We thanked the host for his sincere, kind hospitality and bid farewell, exchanging a dozen mutual praises and refined compliments.

---

[76] A province in the Eastern Anatolian region of Turkey.

He escorted us to the exit at street level, paused for a moment on the doorstep, yawned with his mouth wide open, turned off the light, and disappeared into the darkness of the cellar.

The remaining lights on the street faded.

XXXI

The night generously embraced us. With unabashed simplicity, it welcomed us into its fragrant, lush bosom.

Larysa refused to take the tram or a cab. She preferred to walk home.

"De-fi-nitely—not by tram! De-fi-nitely—on foot! I am telling you, Rostyslav—on foot!"

I took her hand and we kept walking, pressing tightly against each other; a solitary pair against the faded expanses of the night.

Around us—darkness, emptiness, stars. Sleep enveloped the city. Empty streets. Silent buildings. Nightingales sang in the gardens left untouched by the brick boxes of the tenement houses.

The nightingale's night enveloped us.[77] We walked up along Prospekt boulevard, intoxicated by wine, love, and carelessness. The scent of blooming trees seemed excessive.

She laughed with that mischievous, profound laughter from the chest that is known only to certain women,

---

[77] In Ukrainian folk tradition, the "nightingale night" falls on May 15th and marks the period of time when the singing of nightingales intensifies during the mating season.

and only when they are intoxicated by wine and love. This laughter stirred, excited, provoked, and renewed desire.

I could no longer control myself. I crossed all boundaries in the frenzy of the drunken night. There was no madness I couldn't commit. There was no measure to the excitement I wouldn't cross.

I begged Larysa to turn back. Not to go home.

"Larysa, let's go to my place!"

I kissed her hands, lips, legs. I was insane and thirsty for passion. And she, this petite woman, as mad as I, shook her head, saying "No, no, no!" Grabbing the back of a boulevard bench, she resisted—unyielding!—and then, slipping out of my hands, ran uphill in tiny steps.

Uncontrollable rage possessed me. I was filled with despair. I cried out,

"I'm going to kill you!"

She stopped, looking at me with the wide open, frantic eyes of someone suffering unbearable pain, and said with languor,

"Then kill me!"

She kissed my hand. She screamed at me,

"Go ahead, kill me!"

There was no measure to the excitement I couldn't cross. She did not know that measure either!

I walked away from her with my head down. She caught up with me, hugged me by the neck, kissed my eyes, and led the exhausted me by the hand.

Then suddenly, as if by an impulse, she pressed herself against me and whispered,

"Darling!"

We lost track of beginnings and endings. We walked into infinity, where there was nothing but an insatiable void of unfulfilled desire. We experienced all the temptations of the nightingale night, all of its charms. We became acquainted with all the dangers of the nightingale's song.

We were poisoned by the night melody, those warm, heavy scents, the starry darkness, the emptiness of space, the loneliness saturated with longing.

I couldn't say how long we walked, whether it was for a brief moment or an eternity. But when we reached the top of the hill, the greenish dawn already stood at the doorstep of the coming day.

The early morning wind blew. Young poplars rustled their leaves. The night receded, revealing horizons, things, the whole world; actions acquired substance.

I begged her again and again, kissing the palms of her hands.

She touched my hair with her hand and whispered,

"Enough, enough! Sleep, sleep, sleep!"

On the doorstep of her house, she uttered, one last time,

"I'll call you!"

XXXII

I sat in at the plenary session of the Council. Patiently and obediently, I performed my tedious duty. No, I was not fond of meetings.

On the table in front of me, a mountain of paper cockerels grew, alongside a pile of cigarette ash and stubs—an amassed rubbish heap of office debris, the discarded remains of my boredom.

One by one, representatives of different institutions took the floor. Individuals of various administrative ranks, clinging to accepted clichés and standard phrases. Representatives of the Regional Executive Committee, the District Council, Communal Services, the Union of Militant Atheists, the Pioneer unit of an exemplary Labor School, trade unions from various factories, the Institute of People's Education.

What did this squat girl, red-cheeked and dark-haired, in her flamboyant red Pioneer neckerchief, have to do with art, with the creativity of Lynnyk, with architectural and museum affairs? She began her speech with the statement,

"As a Pioneer counselor…"

I turned to my neighbor: Would he not agree that prior to her speech, it would have been appropriate for Pioneers to come to the stage and line up in two rows on either side of the lectern, blowing their trumpets?

"Moreover," I added, "I am curious to know who among those present will be awarded the honorary Pioneer neckerchief, and in general, what does any of it have to do with Lynnyk?"

He raised his eyebrows, eying me attentively, as if considering how he should respond. Then he smiled— apparently, my gold-rimmed glasses impressed him— and said,

"What a cynic you are, Professor!"

And added, after a brief pause,

"…And a dangerous person!"

V. Domontovych

I didn't quite understand what he meant by that. And, after all, I did not know who he was. Did it really matter?

I was bored to death. Not even my own wit was helping anymore. I kept yawning, not even pretending to hide it.

When the girl finished speaking and received her applause, she returned to her seat. I moved to an empty chair next to her.

"Congratulations," I said, "you spoke wonderfully. You have the true spirit of a Pioneer leader! Do you love poetry?"

For a while, she pondered what to say in such a situation, and then replied, "Yes, I love poetry!"

I shook her hand. "It's very nice to come across such a cultured young woman. Who is your favorite among Ukrainian poets?"

She felt confident in her reply. She had no doubts. She said, "Shevchenko!"

"Oh, yes, but surely there is someone else?"

"Of course!"

"For example?"

"Well, for example, Kotovskii."[78]

I didn't immediately grasp who she was referring to and how Kotovskii, that brave gangster, made it into our conversation, but I let it go and continued to question the girl.

"And who else?"

---

[78] Grigorii Kotovskii (1881–1925): a gangster and bank-robber who became one of the major Red Army generals.

"Who else? Lomonosov. He's a Russian poet, though. We studied him in school."

We walked through the thickets of untouched forests. With heavy axes, trails had been cut through the woods. Clearly, neither her nor I would stride along those trails. At any rate, she must have been a good pupil in school. Even at that moment, she still recalled material from her studies. After some reflection, I realized that she was referring to "the greatest poet of modern times, Maiakovskii," confusing him with Kotovskii due to the similarity in their names.

I thanked her. Feeling somewhat moved, I returned to my seat.

I sat there. I yawned.

That's exactly how Mykola Shtul, who represented the local Association of Revolutionary Artists at this Council, depicted me.[79]

The drawing was a success, and I begged the artist to give it to me, so that I could show it to Larysa.

She couldn't stop laughing and said, "A striking resemblance. That's exactly how you look!"

She stowed the drawing away as a keepsake, putting me in an awkward position before the artist, to whom I had sworn to return the sketch.

The speeches continued. I kept yawning. The ashpile grew. My boredom grew. I felt that I couldn't take it much longer.

---

[79] Association of Revolutionary Art in Ukraine (ARMU; active 1925–1932): an artistic organization in Ukraine that included the so-called *boychukisty* (the followers of the visual artist Mykhailo Boychuk, 1982–1937). Artistically, *Boychukism* strove to create new forms of Ukrainian national art through combining monumentalism and modernism.

And then I escaped. I fled shamefully, paying no attention to anyone, even though Arsen Petrovych rose from his presidential chair; someone in the audience shouted "Stop him!" I bumped into a chair, collided with someone, pushed another aside. Even the speaker paused for a brief moment. All around me, people were yelling,

"Rostyslav Mykhailovych, where are you going?! Rostyslav My…"

Unfortunately, I lacked the talent of vanishing unnoticed.

The enthusiastic Hulia managed to catch me in the museum vestibule at the last minute, just as I was stepping out onto the terrace. He tried to hold me back, persuading me to return. He grabbed me by the sleeve, but I broke free, muttering something indistinct, incomprehensible even to myself, and disappeared.

I walked down the green twilight of an unknown street. I took deep breaths of fresh air. I saved myself! What bliss, not to have to sit through any tedious meeting.

We tend to strive toward the attainment of specific types of gratification; we then forget the simple happiness that comes with the avoidance of nuisance.

XXXIII

Over the phone, Larysa and I agreed to meet for lunch sometime that afternoon in the Potemkin Garden.[80] She asked if I knew where it was.

I was indignant. Who doesn't know the Potemkin Garden, that neglected and idyllic place, overgrown with acacia bushes, scorched by summer heat?

But I couldn't find it. I didn't find it in the place where it used to be.

Nothing remained here of the former Garden except for the bare hillside above the river. People cut down the trees during the first lawless and destitute years of the revolution. Governments changed several times a week back then. Jurisdictions appeared and disappeared like cards on a green table cloth during a game of poker, when, feverish from sleepless nights, a person has lost everything, with only their life remaining for their final wager.

With an ax tucked into the belt of a coat—back then everyone, men and women alike, wore belted coats— exhausted people, straining themselves, would drag behind them the felled trunk of an acacia on sledges. In a hut warmed by a tin stove, on a sizzling-red skillet, they would fry pancakes made of cornmeal. Machine oil replaced animal fat. The teeth of the exhausted, starving people came loose. Their gums bled.

The former Potemkin Garden was an idyllic feature of the provincial center. Ravines spanned along the hilly

---

[80] The oldest park in Dnipro, it was known as Potemkin Garden from the 1790s up until 1925.

slopes, made sodden by summer thunderstorms. A layer of dust covered the paths trampled among the weeds. Under the tattered acacia bushes with broken branches, the chickens of the Palace staff dozed off. The wind fluttered the freshly-washed blue linens, heavy with moisture, hanging on lines between the trees. Spots where one could have imagined a lawn or a flower bed were populated instead by tiny roundleaf geranium flowers and large, lush grayish-green burdocks. Nature had been left to its own devices. No decorative designs. No attempts to alter or tame anything.

It was all gone. The Potemkin Garden had ceased to exist. The new garden had a completely different appearance. Young trees were subordinated to the regimen of paths sprinkled with sand. Special warning signs rendered the lawns and flower beds inaccessible for children, dogs, and drunks. A set arrangement of curbs enclosed their spaces. A unified standard of flowers adorned circular and star-shaped flower beds.

Flowers ceased to be mere flowers. They were now subjected to protocols. They had been registered, recorded in the ledgers of the Green Plantings Trust, verified in the accounts receivable and payable; the documents had been filed. The folders sat on the shelves of the offices of the institutions.

In the beds, the flowers looked as if they had been painted on plywood. The cap of Ilyich[81] and the biblical beard of Marx, laid out of broken bricks, burnt coal, and limestone, were repeated with deadly monotony. From

[81] Vladimir Lenin.

the entrance to the garden to the bank of the river, I counted five caps and eight beards. The size of these decorative motifs revealed a desire for grandeur, while the choice of material underlined the need for strict frugality. The material varied—for instance, a brick cap against a white background, or vice versa, a red-brick background under a white cap.

Along the banks of the Dnipro, amidst plywood, sand, coke, chalk, shattered bricks, decrepit trees, and cataloged flowers, arose the Park of Culture and Recreation, a product of meticulous accounting, corporate directives, and bureaucratic formalism.

Only the Dnipro and the sky remained unchanged: majestic and limitless.

In place of pieces of blue calico, sparingly sliced by the crevices of the city's stone streets into narrow strips, here, in the vastness of space, stretched the pure, eternal sky. Imperceptibly, in liturgical tranquility, little clouds drifted across the sky, one after another in a slow chain.

Personally speaking, I am a city dweller. I do not know the names of trees, plants, or birds. It's not my specialty. Knowledge of these names is the purview of botanists, dendrologists, and mycologists. I do not care for nature as it is. It gets on my nerves. I endure nature only after it has already been adapted for human benefit. The landscape should unfold from the terrace of a restaurant. Nature should be served at a café table: good coffee and pastries; the colorful fabrics of vast horizons all around. Asphalt sidewalks in a pristine forest. Paid admission and handrails to lean on while peering into the abyss. Nature should be comfortable.

Unfortunately, in the garden I could not find a single café or even a snack bar with a couple of tin chairs and tables under a tree, where one might order a single shot of vodka and a standard portion of Krakow sausage.

I had to settle for a wooden platform overlooking a cliff, a long terrace intended for dancing and concerts.

XXXIV

I sat facing the river, allowing the sunbeams to fall directly upon me.

The spring sun. The scent of damp earth. The wind blowing in from the river. An ordinary day. Emptiness. Solitude.

My generation no longer feared the sun. We didn't wear hats and didn't seek out shade in the heat. On a sunny day, we didn't cross over to the shady side of the street, where the cool drift from the stone buildings smothered the hot pavement.

Our parents avoided the sun; we, on the contrary, sought it out. Perceptions of good and evil, of utility and harm, of desirable and undesirable changed arbitrarily.

The view was stunning. But what a pity that there was no way of indulging in a cup of coffee, or at least a shot of vodka, around here. The city stretched out to the left, beyond the gorges cutting across the shore. The granite cliffs immediately brought to mind fjords, Scandinavia, and Lynnyk. My gaze ran along the riverbank, reaching the horizon.

The bridge—a wrought iron box thrown between the two banks and comprising several arches—hung in the expanse like an intentionally positioned metal ruler that would opportunely permit an amateur to test their perception of distance.

Squinting through the blue veil of air, I gazed at the distant golden glow of the opposite shore. Before me, in all its majesty, sprawled the azure of the Dnipro. Out with the worrisome meetings, chaotic hustle and bustle of disorderly weekdays! Observing the sky, the river, listening to the silence, I felt a sense of liberation, tranquility, and clear, undisturbed joy.

I completely immersed myself in contemplation of the deep radiance reflected in the Dnipro's magnificent clarity. Everything beyond the azure slowly evaporated. Within me and around me, there remained nothing but the impression of color, perceived in its complete simplicity. Like a precious liquid, the colorful light absorbed me, creating a sensation of abstract, self-contained color. This color, and only this color, remained isolated from everything that it was not.

Slowly, this sensation of color faded, the hue paled, and the self-contained feeling dispersed. I woke up from my half-conscious state of oblivion.

Today she came to the garden looking like a simple girl—her fair hair tied up with a red scarf, wearing an outfit that consisted of no more than three pieces. If it weren't for her high-heeled shoes, an integral component of her persona, she would have undoubtedly come in ordinary ballet flats—white with blue trim.

"I slept wonderfully!" she announced. "I feel like a newborn baby or a sixteen-year-old! Regardless of what you say, my friend, love is always so invigorating for a woman!"

Love!? Was she talking about love? I bit my lip quite hard. I've always been a skeptic. Was she speaking of genuine feelings, or was she just teasing me? I looked at her, at her narrow, tanned, pinkish face, at the blueness of her eyes. If only I knew!

As she talked about love, a bitter jealousy awakened within me.

Every game had its rules. The game of love was not an exception, just like the game of lawn tennis. The ball was served, and I had to hit it back. I responded in light jest.

"Oh, yes! Love surely invigorates a woman. But not love alone. Your formula isn't quite complete. I would say: love and clothing."

She raised her thick lashes, devoid of any extravagance today. She didn't yet know how she should react to what had been said. I continued anyway.

"Every encounter we have brings out a side of you that I hadn't noticed before."

She matched my tone, albeit a bit dryly.

"You're right, I have quite a selection of dresses! Like any woman, I love to dress for my own show the most! What exactly are you suggesting for today?"

"It seems to me," I said, "that we don't have a lot of choices: a boat or sand on the beach. Which would you prefer?"

"If you can row, let's go with the boat."

"Alright," I said, "boat it is!"

In the garden, none of the old trees had survived. Only down below, near the bank by the boat rental, tall willows leaned over the river. They reflected in the mirror of tinted water, with its greenish shimmer, stretched along the shore.

Crossing a swaying footbridge, we reached the boats. We had plenty to choose from. An old man who accompanied us, barefoot and sporting a copper cross on his hairy chest, asked me for a cigarette.

We chose a narrow white boat. Leaving the inlet, we set off downstream, and I removed the oars from the water. We were alone. The current silently carried us along. The soft azure enveloped us.

Larysa requested a cigarette.

We smoked. On the horizon, among the greenery, the stony aureole of Lynnyk's Varangian Church gleamed. I told Larysa about Lynnyk, the student years he had spent in Saint Petersburg, about the Neva. I compared the Neva and the Dnipro. The azure of the Neva and the azure of the Dnipro.

"Up there," I said, "the azure is dusky and elusive, like a haze. On the White Nights, it sleeps motionlessly over that northern river confined in stone. How can I convey to you the glimmer of this soundless light? It melts imperceptibly into the shadows of the columns of the Winter Palace.[82] And in this whimsical azure, under a night sky lit by nebulous, almost imaginary light, I see the staggering figure of a man whose temples already show a touch of gray. Swaying, the drunken man stands on the stone slabs of the bridge delineated by the precise compass of a geometer. The theatrical figure of a person

---

[82] An official residence of the royal dynasty of Romanov in Saint Petersburg between 1732–1917.

lost in his fantasies, a factitious Hermann who, despairing of loneliness, is dreaming someone else's dreams about the love of a woman who does not love him."[83]

I looked into Larysa's eyes. She looked at me. She didn't say anything. She didn't ask me anything regarding Hermann and Liza, Hermann's obsessive dreams, the lack of recognition, and I didn't ask her about the love of a woman who did not love me!

Around us hung the floating azure, shimmering in the translucent sunbeams. The sky and the white clouds reflected off the water, leaving neither sky nor river, nothing—only hazy fluctuations of blue.

After a pause, an excruciatingly long silence, Larysa stated quite unexpectedly,

"But you are mistaken: Hermann wasn't in love with Liza. Liza was in love with Hermann!"

She crushed her unfinished cigarette and threw it overboard, and the current carried away the crumpled stub, marked with traces of red lipstick.

XXXV

We were lying in the sand of a distant shore. No trace of human life. No goats. We were alone, as if in a fantastical desert.

We conversed, recalling shared impressions from the previous day and evening. We began with memories of the hospitable host from the Caucasian kebab house.

---

[83] A reference to Alexander Pushkin's 1834 story *The Queen of Spades* (*Pikovaiia dama*) and its two main protagonists, Hermann and Liza.

"He was charming!" Larysa exclaimed. "I fell in love with him!"

The statement seemed to convey either too much or too little. A feeling of jealousy awakened within me. She was on her back, gazing at the sky, her shoe hanging on the tips of her toes as she crossed one foot over the other. Her profile was framed by the golden backdrop of sand. The tanned pink of her cheeks stirred and moved me.

"Is there," I pondered, "greater happiness than making another person happy? Is there anything more pleasant than evoking joy in another person, without any ambiguity or disingenuity? This probably sentimental truth dawned on me only after our yesterday's visit to the kebab house."

"I'd like to know," Larysa inquired, "aren't you even a tiny bit sentimental?"

I said nothing in response, continuing to develop my thoughts on the archaic traditions of trade, elevated to a refined Epicureanism, where buying and selling had not yet separated from gift-giving and offerings; where the buyer had not yet ceased to be a guest and a friend.

Larysa joined in my observations, making a slight correction.

"You spoke of trade elevated to the level of Epicureanism, but wouldn't it be better to say to the level of Epicurean aesthetics?"

I didn't object, and Larysa continued,

"We made one significant mistake yesterday: we didn't ask our host about his relatives. He has a strong hand and short fingers. He gives the impression of a

177

simple peasant from the Yerevan area, but who knows? Perhaps his brother is a bishop in Armenia, or his uncle is a bank executive in London. He could be a world-renowned conductor, or a theater director like Vakhtangov, the producer of Gozzi's *Princess Turandot*.[84] Just as subtle and fantastic! A poet. A philosopher."

She put her head on my knees, looking up at me, and after a brief pause, remarked didactically,

"To sell wine, one must be a poet as well. I'm repeating what our host said yesterday, 'There is wine and *the wine*! And there's *the* woman! Wine, like a woman! There's wine that, having sampled only a drop, would be remembered forever. The same goes for women! It seems to me that you are one such woman.'"

My hand delved into the thicket of her hair. While exploring, my fingers retained images of once-felt sensations, shades of half-forgotten memories, waves of delight that seemed forever lost or yet to be discovered.

Women have different types of hair. Sometimes it's strong, firm, and resilient; its touch feels like resistance and coercion. Sometimes the hair seems to melt between the fingers, disappearing in the sensation of touch like a light foam. Soft linen, like the one that is used for dolls' clothing. Larysa's hair was fine and heavy, having preserved its life untouched by electric current or deadened by chemicals.

My fingers felt each individual strand distinctly. I sifted through them like stalks of ripe wheat.

The conversation turned to the initial details of our acquaintance. This subject never loses its weight and

---

[84] A 1762 *commedia dell'arte* play by Carlo Gozzi (1720–1806).

interest for those in love. It allows for the renewal of feelings just beginning to take root in a common pool of memories.

Somehow, Larysa introduced a shade of premonition into the conversation. This was felt in her manner of asking questions. She was skeptical today. There is never a conciliatory gentleness in female skepticism; on the contrary, one always detects an element of hostility.

Our acquaintance began in a manner too extraordinary to be simply accepted. On that day, Larysa was filled with doubt. She couldn't believe what she had agreed to the day before.

To perceive a stranger as the sound of a musical phrase! Am I out of my depth here, stating this as a fact? What sober, realistic person needs such fantasies? Larysa didn't want to be deceived and then mocked. She was defending herself. She was on the offensive. She wasn't Liza, I wasn't Hermann. She had no need for fairy tales.

She resorted to laughter. With it, she masked the deliberate provocativeness of her questions. After all, she had no desire to fight with me. So she kept laughing, fully aware of the sound's seductive power. She was stubborn. She demanded explanations. She began from afar,

"Can you know a person from the first impression they give?"

I confirmed,

"I believe you can!"

My answer, a simple assertion, didn't satisfy her. She refined the formula of the question,

"Seeing someone for the first time, never having seen them before and knowing nothing about that person, absolutely nothing?"

"Well, yes," I said. "Seeing someone for the first time, never having seen them before, knowing nothing about them except for that very first impression."

"Nothing at all?"

"Nothing at all."

The proof appeared to be insufficient for her.

"That's impossible."

She was disappointed. She interrupted the conversation, taking her head off my knees, and stretched out on the sand, feigning indifference. With her palms folded under her head, she gazed silently at the white clouds drifting past, like sails of unfamiliar ships headed toward an unknown land.

Silence, like the sharpened blade of a sword, divided us. The cold of steel separated us. I was bewildered. She was clearly frustrated with me and didn't hide her annoyance.

I recognized the immediacy of the danger that threatened me: in her questions and objections, unexpectedly precise and demonstratively emphatic, as well as in my inability to handle confusion or find any satisfactory argument to even slightly reinforce my position. The delicate thread of our recent, so unexpectedly initiated acquaintance could be severed equally unexpectedly. At any moment, she could rise from the sand, cast a casual, indifferent look in my direction, and yawn: "I am growing bored! or "It's getting late!" or "Looks like it's going to rain!" And it could all be over.

I understood this too well. Today was the day of reckoning. Today she was going to review everything that had happened the day before. Today she was going to question me and herself. She was doing what every woman would do—trying either to find justification for herself or to blame me.

Up until that moment, this beautiful, naked woman had been laying there, stretched out on the sand. Now she sat up, with her feet tucked under her legs. She said nothing. Melancholically, she sifted sand from one hand to the other. A thin stream trickled between her narrow fingers, landing around the soles of her feet, forming a slowly growing mound.

Should I not immediately acknowledge my guilt and present to her, as a gift, the sincerity of my repentance, a humble redemption for all my existing and non-existing sins? Surrender to her, accept all the blame, and seek salvation in her mercy? Put on the mask of a great shaggy dog, good-natured and incapable of anything but jumping and barking loudly, being completely and unreservedly devoted to its mistress?

I was aware of the fact that at this moment, the fate of my love was being decided: to be or not to be, and if the former, then how?

To lie by her feet, faithfully, like a dog; to surrender my freedom, myself, my thoughts, and my feelings to her, for good. I gazed at her. Hesitantly, I touched her hand.

"Perhaps," I said, "you are right!"

I made every effort for her not to sense my uncertainty.

181

She stood up, as if signaling that the conversation had taken a hopeless turn and there was nothing for me to hope for any longer. I wouldn't save myself this way. She looked at me with reproach. Gazing at the reflections of light on the lenses of my glasses, she asked mischievously,

"Is that all you can say? I expected more from you!"

I made a vague gesture with my hand. What could I do? What excuses could a drowning man offer?

I had to say something else. No matter what. She cut me off.

"I suspect that you are about to allude to intuition. It won't help you."

She warned me,

"Note that I do not tolerate clichés, especially awkward ones."

I hastened to assure her that I had no such intention whatsoever.

"On my honor!"

I knew one thing: the more unpredictable the paths I traversed to seek salvation, the better. After all, did it matter where the sailing clouds were headed?

In the final moment, I found rescue in referencing Boswell and Boswellism.[85] Larysa brightened up,

"And who is that?"

"An eighteenth-century English literary critic. It was he who had observed that a missing button on a poet's coat said far more about his creativity than reading all of his poems."

---

[85] James Boswell (1740–1795): Scottish biographer and journalist known for the detailed observations of his subjects.

"At least that's witty!" she admitted. Leaning towards me, she touched my cheek with her fingertips.

It wasn't much but I would take it. I understood that I had been granted some forgiveness; some measure of salvation had been confirmed. I kissed the palm of her hand.

"This is more than wit," I said. "It's an entire paradigm."

The observant critic chose an ironic form to express his opinion. He referred to a trivial detail: a missing button. It was a response to what was bothering Larysa right at that moment: the possibility of knowing a person, who they really were, from a fleeting impression. A useful ability that could greatly simplify human life.

"You can't deny," I said to Larysa, "that our acquaintance is entirely *à la* Boswell."

She sat down, clasping her hands around her knees. With her dreamy eyes, she kept looking into the blue distance, where a golden stripe separated the azure of the sky from the azure of the river.

She liked that our meeting happened in Boswellian fashion. She was picky, this woman, and like most women, she expected just one thing from love—for it to be extraordinary.

Even though satisfied, she continued.

"Yes, that's right! However, admit that all of it was accidental. When you encountered me, you happened to mention a fragment from a piece of music you knew. You connected the dots, and by chance, ended up solving the puzzle, even though it was just a missing button, a trifle, nonsense; something that was and wasn't, simultaneously."

She craved the imperative. She was tired of the non-binding nature of our feelings.

I protested vigorously; I challenged her. I disagreed with the contention that our meeting had been merely a random convergence of fleeting and incidental details.

"You and the composer's creation form a whole. You are embodied in the piece because the piece recreates you! Why won't you admit that I, too, am capable of a creative act? That from my impressions of you, I was also able to recreate everything that had found expression in the music—that you, the music, and my impressions of you are internally connected links of a single aesthetic process, just like..."

I leaned over her,

"...my love for you!"

XXXVI

Should I have mentioned that on that day I was not present at the meeting of the Committee of which I was a member, and which had been convened to develop a resolution?

Catching me was a hopeless endeavor. With participants of the meeting, the museum management, and everyone else who needed me or wished to see me, I maintained communication only in writing, exclusively through notes left in the hotel foyer with the concierge. I was elusive. Even to Ivan Vasylyovych Hulia.

As soon as I would appear at the hotel's doorstep, the concierge on duty, rising from his round chair and leaning over the bureau counter, would hand me dozens of notes, letters, briefs, and telegrams, reporting,

"They were asking for you..."

"They came to see you..."

"They waited for you..."

"They asked to tell you that..."

"They drove by to pick you up..."

"They called for you..."

"They requested your presence urgently, as soon as you..."

Urgently? I smiled. Why on earth? I was absent. I was not there for anyone.

At any rate, having retrieved the stack of letters from the concierge, I assumed a focused look. I looked at him through the lenses of my golden spectacles. I scrutinized him attentively and emphatically. Standing before me, he seemed like a student who came to sit an exam, having only the vaguest idea of the difference between the German and the so-called Jesuit Baroque styles.

I maintained the appearance of a person overloaded with affairs. I asked for forgiveness from everyone I accidentally ran into. I conveyed the fact that amidst the multitude of other tasks weighing on me, I simply had no time for this one.

I shrugged, pointing to the folder I held in my hands, pulling out a handful of papers,

"Have a look: a pile of papers, a thousand matters—each one urgent—awaiting resolution. I must attend to all of them. But when, where, how? You must understand that I am incapable of doing it all."

Such was my excuse. The impossibility of doing everything was the best pretext for doing nothing at all.

A government official in his office is represented by the briefcase he places on his table upon arrival. I, on the other hand, was represented by a key on a large brass ring in the narrow slit of the concierge's chiffonier.

Visitors who sought me, having received one of the two standard responses from the concierge—"He has not yet arrived!" or "He has already left!"—understood all too well that I, forced to split myself between too many places, could not possibly be in any specific place at any given time. I was summoned to the *Vykonkom*, to the *Oblono*, to the Museum, to the *Oblarkhiv*, to the *Istpart*, to the Monument Protection Commission.[86]

This was what the notion of a responsible worker now entailed: the complete impossibility of catching him anywhere.

I replied on the fly,

"I'm sorry, but I cannot. I must hurry. A colleague has summoned me... I have a meeting..."

Without reading them, on the go, I signed the minutes of the Resolution Committee meeting and the draft resolution produced by the Committee.

I was not present at the final session of the Conference, just as I was not there at the first.

From the three notes left for me by Hulia, I learned that the Conference's work was complete, that I should

[86] Executive Committee; Regional Department of Public Education; Regional Archive; Commission for the Study of the History of the October Revolution and the Communist Party.

go to the Museum's accounting office to receive my travel and consultation allowances, that the Regional Executive Committee had approved the Conference's resolution to transform the Varangian Church into a reserve, and that Arsen Petrovych Vytvytskyi has been looking for me all this time, while he, Hulia, would like to see me.

Hulia concluded his note with the question,

"For which date shall I book your train ticket?"

I shrugged. What did I know anyway?

I tore open the envelope with the letter from Arsen Petrovych. He had invited me to visit him the following day at exactly five o'clock for dinner.

All other letters and notes were left unread.

XXXVII

Arsen Petrovych Vytvytskyi, the director of the Art Museum, was a very kind and pleasant man. I met him in 1927 or 1928 in Kharkiv at the Committee for the Preservation of Antiquities, which he had attended on Museum business.

Already at our first meeting, he struck me as a very decent and, at the same time, a very restrained person. More than restrained—cautious. Watchful even. His restraint bordered on an almost fearful vigilance. At least, that was my impression.

It seemed to me that behind his softness there was a kind of alertness, or perhaps even tension. Not in the gentleness itself, sincere and open, but in something hidden behind it, akin to a distant, muted echo of some long-gone catastrophe. A wound, now healed but always there.

Later I learned that this was in fact the case. Already at our first meeting, I took it as a hint. With my finger-tips, I touched the haze that enveloped his actions, words, and gestures. Everything he did or said seemed to be saturated with a sense of immobility, some unspoken preoccupation. There was a muted, veiled, perhaps even melodic tenderness, an evening silence in this haze. His words were subdued, but his gestures resounded. His movements reverberated.

He enchanted me with his delicate manner. There was nothing conspicuous about him. I was pleased with this acquaintance. It revealed to me the charm of friendship, which had no place for reservation or prejudice.

He wore an oversized gray jacket. He was tall, slender, agile, lively, yet extremely correct. He never allowed for anything jarring or fussy in his behavior.

He was imposing. Light-gray attire; silver hair slicked back; a slightly graying beard, slightly longer than usual—all of these saturated his appearance with a priestly solemnity. He exuded an impressive, elevated presence. He hadn't grown heavier with age, hadn't fattened up. He retained his youthful aptness and lightness. He seemed to be floating.

I knew that he wrote poetry. Two or three collections of his poetry had been published. It seemed he had access to the wellspring of being and nourished himself on the shoots that had grown from it. He possessed an uncommon ability to perceive life in its premonitions: in myth, poetry, music. Eternity revealed itself to him in its embryonic state. He recognized the universe in the rhythms of poetry, the colors of music, the images of myth. If I dared to say that he had something of the poet-musician in him, according to the classic formula proposed by Verlaine—"Music first and foremost!"[87]— then I would have to make a correction: he was something of a philosopher who was simultaneously a poet and a musician. I knew that what I had said was inaccurate. Having called him a poet, I was forced to retract my words. He *was* a poet but it meant only one thing: he was nobody, nothing. A person who had a calling but no recognition. From the beginning of the nineteenth century and up until the revolution of 1917, he had served in local self-governing bodies in Chernihiv, Poltava, Podillya. Zemstvos were a common refuge for the vast majority of Ukrainian writers of that time who lacked the financial means to pursue a university education, or for those who could not move to Saint Petersburg to take up positions in the Ministries of Finance or Agriculture.

Working as a statistician in a zemstvo[88] was neither heaven nor hell. It was a way to exist. In those years, everyone was certain that the most important thing in the world was to carry on: to marry; to have or not to have children; to eat lunch every day; to button up the collar and cuffs of one's shirt; to make monthly bank

---

[87] A quote from Paul Verlaine's poem *Ars Poetica* (transl. by Normal Shapiro).
[88] See note 59 on p.110.

payments for building one's house; to go to the *English Garden*[89] on Saturday evenings and drink a bottle of beer; to drop a calling card with the governor and chairman of the zemstvo administration on New Year's Eve. Meanwhile, Vytvytskyi was able to create. He was not engaged with physically strenuous labor; instead, he encountered a moral dilemma: the impossibility of revealing, expressing, or just being himself.

He confessed to me, bitterly,

"Never in my life have I been *myself*!"

Being himself meant this: observing how the grass grew; how the trees dressed in the green smoke of fresh leaves; how the telegraph wire sang in the field; how lilacs bloomed in spring. Since childhood, he had loved old gardens, the cold wind, the night clouds, the bitter taste of lonesome melancholy. The sorrows of the heart. The air filled with the scent of old books and the light smoke of candles. The steppe's blue expanse. The dry smell of grass in an abandoned cemetery.

His calling was to dream, to fast, to pray, to become a saint. But in his times, such matters were not given any importance—they were disregarded. A man who was called to become Francis of Assisi was forced to wear socks mended by his wife, to work at an office compiling consolidated statistical tables: heads of livestock, hectares sown with spring crops, cartfuls of manure taken out to the fields; agricultural inventories, population movements, the rates of various diseases, typhoid,

---

[89] A chain of so-called *English clubs*, gentlemen's clubs in the Russian empire. The one in Katerynoslav opened in 1838.

cholera, influenza. He probably knew the percentages of each grain crop, but had only a very approximate idea of what bitter vetch was, or how to tell barley from oats. He was a city man.

In his time off, he wrote poetry. His first collection had been published in 1906. Back then, people marched with red flags, sang *La Marseillaise* and the *Warszawianka*. They led choirs in the newly established *Prosvita* clubs. They protested against the punitive squads.[90]

The October Manifesto; the State Duma elections; revolutionary enthusiasm; red-clad editions of *Donskaia rech*; socialism, sectarians, and political issues in their dozens; the agrarian question; university lectures in Ukrainian; Mukden and Tsushima; Portsmouth; terror, bombings, revolver shots, and barricades; bailiffs beaten in the streets by gymnasium students; Ingush, Cossacks, and gallows; Lenin's slogan *All Power to the Soviets* and the liberals' motto *Let the executive power be subordinate to the legislative power*—none of these found reflection in his poetry collection.[91] It was as if none of this had ever ex-

---

[90] Warszawianka: a Polish patriotic song written in support of the Polish November Uprising of 1830–1831 led by the army of Congress Poland against the Russian rule. Prosvita (from Ukrainian: enlightenment): a Ukrainian educational organization active in the 1860s-1940s, primarily in Galicia. Punitive squads: here, referring to the reaction of the Russian autocracy to the massive uprising, including riots and terrorist assassinations, during the Russian Revolution of 1905–1907.

[91] October Manifesto: a document issued by tsar Nicholas II in October 1905 that marked the end of unlimited autocracy in Russia and ushered in an era of constitutional monarchy. State Duma: an elected legislative body that constituted the imperial Russian legislature from 1906 until its dissolution at the time of the March 1917 Revolution.

isted, and it was a sufficient reason to condemn the poet as anti-social.

Breaking away from the traditions and phraseology of civic poetry and its leading slogan—*I am not a poet, I am a citizen!*—enclosing himself in an ivory tower, he cultivated pure poetry. Poetry for its own sake. He was a modernist, perhaps the most consistent of them all; the most uncompromising anti-populist.

His name appeared alongside Oles and Voronyi. In the background, but always in the same context, it appeared along with Filyanskyi, Kapelhorodskyi, and Tarnohradskyi.[92]

He wanted to be himself at least in his poetry. Exoticism was his way of fighting; aestheticism, his path to liberation. He tried to elevate the fragile and fleeting

---

Donskaia rech: a socio-political and literary newspaper that had been published in Rostov-on-Don in 1887–1905. The Agrarian Question: an 1899 book by the Czech-German philosopher and marxist Karl Kautsky (1854–1938). Lectures in Ukrainian: in the aftermath of the Revolution of 1905, the previous restrictions on education and publications in Ukrainian were lifted. Mukden and Tsushima: the names of two battles of the Russo-Japanese war (1904–1905) between the forces of imperial Russia and Japan. Treaty of Portsmouth: the peace agreement that ended the Russo-Japanese war. Ingush, Cossacks: during the Revolution of 1905–1907, some of the Ingush and Don Cossack detachments supported the uprising and were subsequently jailed or executed.

[92] Oleksander Oles (1878–1944): Ukrainian poet, whose collection of 1909 reflected the disappointment with the failed national liberation after the Revolution of 1905. Mykola Voronyi (1871–1938): Ukrainian modernist poet and theater director. Mykola Filyanskyi (1873–1938): Ukrainian lyrical poet. Pylyp Kapelhorodskyi (1878–1942): Ukrainian writer and journalist. Valeryan Tarnohradskyi (1880–1945): Ukrainian lyrical poet. Except for Oleksander Oles, all the poets mentioned in this footnote were the victims of Stalinist purges.

conventionality of modern poetry. It was also a protest and a rebellion, albeit of a peculiar kind, the meaning of which he could hardly comprehend. He had been published in Yevshan's *Nova khata*; later, his poems began to appear, though infrequently, in the *Literaturno-naukovyi visnyk*.[93]

Several failed idioms, contradictory linguistic innovations, inappropriate phrases that occurred in his early poetry; the individualistic aestheticism inherent in his poetry, as in the oeuvres of other modernists—all these features gave a certain critic, one who stood guard over public opinion and populism, the opportunity to publish a sharp article against Vytvytskyi.

A long review, written on the occasion of the poet's first collection, appeared in one of the *Kievskaia starina* books under the title *The Omen of Our Time*.[94] Populism armed itself against modernism. The pamphlet's tone was temperamental and harsh. This critic did not refrain from brutality. Directing his biting attacks against the verse itself, portrayed as a dangerous threat to the people, he did not hesitate to make scathing remarks bordering on personal insult. He condemned, vilified, accused.

Naive realism and philistinism guided the aforementioned critic throughout his own life. Before and after

---

[93] *Nova khata* (New Home): a magazine for women published in Lviv in 1925–1939. *Literaturno-naukovyi visnyk* (Literary-Scientific Herald): the first All-Ukrainian literary and socio-political journal, issued by the Shevchenko Scientific Society, in Lviv and Kyiv, in 1898–1932.

[94] Kievskaia starina (Kyivan Antiquities): a leading historical and literary journal of Ukrainian Studies, first published in Russian (1882–1906) and then in Ukrainian (1907).

the revolution of 1905, he assumed the role of a representative of the nation and took responsibility for the fate of many other people.

In his review, the critic accused Arsen Petrovych, along with his entire group of modernists, of insufficient knowledge of the Ukrainian language. He began by outlining the sins committed against the written language, with crimes against the spirit of the people's vernacular, and this formed the basis for his diatribe. To this he also added accusations of moral decay, ideological inconsistency, attempts on and crimes against both word and spirit, against the conscience of the Ukrainian people. None of this was particularly profound or subtle, but in any case, it was consistent.

The article led with an epigraph from Taras Shevchenko: "And as a guard, protecting, I shall set my word around them."[95] The critic considered himself a guardian, posted at the entrance to the temple of the people and their language.

This critic remained faithful to his promise to elaborate on his statements.

He regarded the people as a linguistic unity. He equated the people with the language. He proceeded from the assertion, "The people *are* their language!" Thus, he laid the foundation for the ideological doctrine that he had preached, determining its content and scope, and the program and method of its political action. Language became the basis of the dogma; compiling a dic-

---

[95] Taras Shevchenko, *Paraphrase from Psalm XI*, transl. by Vera Rich. (Kyiv, *Mystetstvo*, 2014), 302.

tionary of the living language, writing articles for magazines, publishing primers, grammars, and popular booklets for the people became the guiding principle of all social activity. This led to amateurism in the field of linguistic studies and deprived social action of its main criterion—the awareness of scale. He couldn't care less. He preferred to be both a scholarly and a political leader, lacking the background and knowledge for the former, and the character for the latter.

To be a political figure is to be a visionary, to have something of a prophet in oneself. He, however, was only an empiricist. He was not sufficiently broad-minded. He perceived the attempt of the modernists to emphasize the Ukrainian literary language, to set aesthetic values at the forefront, as a dangerous deviation for Ukrainian culture; an assault on public decency in general and human morality in particular.

In the aforementioned article in *Kievskaia starina*, he observed: "We put emphasis not on the self-assertion of literature, but on the self-assertion of a million-strong nation in which literature—in case it wants to be *Ukrainian* literature—must play a supporting role as a means to such an assertion." In his opinion, modernists who did not want to write like Borys Hrinchenko placed themselves outside Ukrainian literature.[96]

The modernization of poetry? Poetry that breaks away from populism? An errant path, harmful tenden-

---

[96] Borys Hrinchenko (1863–1910): prominent Ukrainian public figure, writer, journalist, ethnographer, and linguist. His literary writings in a realist style focused on peasant life and social questions.

cies. A non-cep-tion, the corpse of creativity, the stench of decay, carrion for dogs.

Our critic defended the internal self-sufficiency of the calling, the autarky of writing, *khutorianstvo*-isolationism,[97] the village in its removed self-sufficiency. He saw the purpose of the intelligentsia in educational activities for the benefit of the people. He showed reluctance towards literature that depicted matters not of its own people, but of someone else's. He fiercely attacked Vytvytskyi who, according to the critic's wording in the same article, "sought themes beyond his people, in someone else's distant past, rehashed other people's songs, cradled other people's children!"

A game of préférence, a hat of black lamb's wool, a jacket worn over an embroidered shirt, a cherry orchard by the house, a lonely street on the outskirts of the city, a buzzing silence! Like all political figures of the first quarter of the twentieth century, the critic could not roll his *R*'s properly and sounded somewhat dim-witted.

The review in *Kievskaia starina* crushed Vytvytskyi. He didn't try to determine the extent to which the accusations against him were substantiated. He made no attempt to refute or justify himself. He was accused, and that was enough. He would rather degrade himself than others. He began to seek his own guilt when anyone else would have experienced merely a bruised ego.

The review descended on him as an utter catastrophe. Already reserved, he became even more reticent. Already indecisive, he became even more cautious and tentative.

This did not mean that he had changed his attitude towards poetry or compromised his views in the slightest. He continued to write just as he had before. He didn't deviate from his path. He was not capable of compromise. Too sensitive and impressionable, he could not shake off the feeling of fearful bewilderment.

As a poet, he completely isolated himself. He separated himself from his environment, from place and time. He transformed his poetry into an abstraction of aesthetics.

Every time he had to submit a poem to a journal, he hesitated. Perhaps it would be better to let it sit? Self-doubt made him sick.

He lacked the necessary dosage of persistence to advance his literary career, which other poets, more resourceful though far less talented, successfully managed.

They would tell him, "You have to elbow your way through to make it!" He didn't care for crowds or elbowing his way through. He avoided overcrowded tram cars. Of course, he walked home from the zemstvo after work.

Cynicism was not inherent in his nature. Perhaps that was why he wrote poetry, why he became a poet. Because of this, he never tried to stand out in his craft.

He was not dim-witted; nor was he outspoken.

Too soft and polite, he refrained from bothering anyone over matters that concerned him personally, especially in matters as strictly private and intimate as his poems.

V. Domontovych

If the editorial board of a journal wrote to him asking that he send some work, following up with a second and a third request, then he would send a few poems. If they didn't reach out or remind him, he would leave them sitting in the drawer of his writing desk.

The man himself showed no outward initiative. It wasn't unusual for his poems not to appear in any periodical publications, even though he had worked eagerly and persistently on them. He was unable to bring himself before an editorial board, taking along a notebook and demanding, "Print this! I am a poet!"

He published far less than he wrote, and he wrote far more than he managed to bring to completion.

XXXVIII

After the revolution of 1917, either due to personal modesty or because he lived in such a provincial place, he remained on the sidelines of developments in the literary sphere, just like many other representatives of the older generation. Oles emigrated; Chuprynka was executed; Filyanskyi and Kapelhorodskyi fell silent. Samiylenko, upon his return from emigration, lay dying from tuberculosis in Boyarka, near Kyiv. Mykola Voronyi, in vain, was trying to retain his place in the current literary process.[98]

---

[98] Hrytsko Chuprynka (1879–1921): Ukrainian modernist poet, who led an anti-Bolshevik rebellion in 1919 and was subsequently executed by the Cheka. Volodymyr Samiylenko (1864–1925): Ukrainian poet, dramatist, and translator.

While others were pushed aside, Arsen Petrovych stepped back of his own accord. He never appeared anywhere, never announced anything about himself, never made any attempts to remind the public of his existence. It was not even fully known that he, one of the founders of modernist Ukrainian poetry, perhaps even the most talented of all contemporary poets, was still alive, living in a southern steppe town and working as a museum director. He was forgotten, as if he had long since died or had never existed at all. Several of his poems, which appeared in *Chervonyi shlyakh* and in the local *Zorya*, edited by V. Chaplya, went completely unnoticed.[99] They received no response. They seemed either too exotic or simply outdated.

The new revolutionary era ignored this introverted poet. He didn't take offense. His earlier, amateur fascination with art became a profession; his autodidactic tendencies became a craft. Immediately after the revolution, at the first opportunity, he left the zemstvo. While his other colleagues plunged into the whirlpool of party-revolutionary struggle or transitioned into the cooperative movement, he chose museum work, becoming completely absorbed in it, finding satisfaction in his calling.

"I'm no longer involved," he said. "I no longer deal with numbers, statistics, tables, percentages. My God, what happiness! Finally, I feel free. Is that not enough? I

---

[99] *Chervonyi shlyakh* (Red Pathway): a leading Ukrainian literary journal published in Kharkiv in 1923–1936. *Zorya* (Star): an illustrated journal that focused on literature, culture, and politics and was published in Dnipropetrovsk in 1925–1934.

deal with paintings, porcelain, antique glass, furniture, rare and exquisite things, and I enjoy it. The feeling of comfort brings peace, and that is what is most important."

To speak of peace and harmony in the early years of the revolution could only be done out of *épatage*. But the fact remained: the local art gallery owed its preservation and further flourishing solely to his perseverance and unwavering energy. From abandoned houses in the city, he collected artifacts. He traveled to villages, scouring peasant houses for scattered property removed from manors and estates. He saved what could still be saved.

He did all of that in those turbulent, murky years, the dreadful years of devastation, when all ties were severed, and everything that had thus far been absolute, became contingent. Life was ruled by chance. The fate of a person, let alone the fate of human creations, was of least importance on the scales of social existence. Somewhere there existed an unknown, imaginary line separating what had been, what had ceased to be, from what was about to be born but had not yet emerged. People lived beyond the present, in the decreed future.

In the great and formerly prosperous city, there was nothing to eat, not a crumb of bread! People swelled from hunger and silently submitted to death. When a man who happened to gorge himself on *varenyky* developed an intestinal obstruction, he said, crossing himself right before death, "Thank God; at least I am dying with my belly full!"

In these uncertain, desperate times, Arsen Petrovych—emaciated, hungry like everyone else, staggering from fatigue and exhaustion, taking occasional rest stops to catch his breath—struggled to pull a cart loaded with paintings, furniture, books, and manuscripts. He brought things to the Museum from private collections: miscellanies, heaps of rubbish, and abandoned property—anything that he stumbled upon and could later have value as an exhibition object or simply end up in the trash.

Machine gun fire rattled in the street. Arsen Petrovych would abandon the cart and crouching down, run to a gateway to hide. After the gunfire subsided, he would pick up the cart shafts again and continue dragging it along.

Like others, he became accustomed to the war as a backdrop against everyday life. The city turned into the frontline. He did his job at the Museum—just as he wrote his poems—out of inspiration: he was heeding his inner calling.

In this steppe city, exposed to all the winds of the world, the authorities changed with dazzling regularity. They alternated out of an almost natural necessity, like the ebb and flow of the tides. In the short term allotted to each authority, its representatives acted hastily and inexorably, with the cruel desperation of conquistadors, the invaders of a newly discovered, as-yet unknown continent.

No one could tell how long a given regime would hold out in the city. With every transfer of power, Arsen Petrovych would abandon his house and his wife, his own property, everything he had, and move into the Museum. The Museum was more important than anything else. He was accountable for the Museum. Accountable to whom? To no one, only to himself.

For days, sometimes weeks, he would be trapped in one of the Museum's unheated premises. He guarded those disorderly rooms, filled with objects haphazardly accumulated.

And when the threatening figure of a cursing soldier would clatter at the Museum entrance, festooned with grenades and weapons, half-mad from executions, alcohol, exhaustion, typhoid, from the absoluteness of the power he embodied, Arsen Petrovych knew how to behave with dignity and maintain composure.

They would stand facing each other. One sporting a battered, scorched, and bullet-riddled gray coat and red or green *gallifet*[100] made of velvet curtains ripped from a brothel or a restaurant. The other—a poet, a museum director, a civilian in a black coat with a karakul collar, cinched tightly with a belt. They would stare at each other. Under such circumstances, an instant could change everything. In one moment, a person's fate would be decided: to be or not to be.

What Arsen Petrovych felt in such moments was not fear. It was something else—some physiological sensation of emptiness, a feeling of nausea—as happens when a ship at sea, lifted upwards, suddenly plunges into the abyss.

Arsen Petrovych was not inclined to succumb to fear or confusion when threatened. Ultimately, among the junk that filled the hall, there was nothing that could be of any use to a person with a gun. Most often, disputes

---

[100] Soviet military trousers reminiscent of riding breeches.

arose over some teacup, some vessel from which one could drink. Arsen Petrovych made concessions. He offered his own enamel jug that he had brought from home in order to preserve a Sèvres cup for the Museum. Of course, at that time, an enamel jug was from every angle far more valuable than the most expensive Meissen or Sèvres porcelain.[101]

So these two men went their own ways, feeling the deepest fondness for one another. They had become friends. And the soldier, pulling a loaf of bread from his pocket, broke it in half to share with the person he had threatened to kill before.

Each new authority that appeared in the city denounced the preceding one as destructive and barbaric. They accused it of perpetuating hunger, violence, executions, terror, contempt for the people, and tyranny.

The prison was emptied in the name of humanity and justice, and to clear much-needed space for the newcomers.

And in the name of the same highest and holiest ideals of humanity, in the last hours before departing, when the enemy's cannons were already pounding the city from Amur or Chokolivka, while machine guns were muttering somewhere in Mandrykivka, those in charge set about destroying everything: people, food supplies, cultural treasures, bridges, power plants, water pumps, cellars with ammunition, and factory machines tools.[102]

---

[101] Meissen and Sèvres: important centers of German and French 18th-century porcelain-making.

[102] Amur: a suburb of Dnipro on the left bank of the river. Chokolivka: possibly Chechelivka, one of the old working-class neighborhoods in

Nothing would fall into the hands of the enemy, advancing from beyond the Dnipro or from the steppe, bringing ruin, damnation, and death.

If a new regime established itself in the city for a while, Arsen Petrovych's situation did not improve; in fact, it worsened considerably. They began to scrutinize him. They began to investigate. They demanded that he submit an inventory and attach the necessary documents. He was accused of collaborating with the previous authorities, that while others resisted, were executed or jailed, he had held a responsible position, gained trust and recognition, enjoyed all sorts of benefits, received a ludicrously high salary, received the rations of the especially privileged.

Clearly, the situation was hopeless. How could he prove that, in his capacity as the Museum director under the previous authority, he had committed no crime against the current one? On the contrary, had he not exerted all his efforts to preserve the Museum collections and protect the artistic treasures from destruction?

As gently and calmly as possible, he laid out the inventories of museum property before a disheveled fellow in a cap pulled askew, wielding a revolver, the handle of which protruded from the torn pocket of his pants. But the lists, swept angrily from the table, could go to hell. What did the lists matter when it was proven that he had collaborated with the enemies of culture, order, and humanity? He deserved to be shot, crushed

---

Dnipro, on the right bank. Mandrykivka: a historical Cossack settlement in Dnipro, on the right bank.

like a flea. The first time, however, they let him go, muttering grimly to some imagined interlocutor,

"The comrades upstairs will sort it out!"

Some pale and indistinct figure would appear at the Museum, a person who was trusted more than Vytvytskyi. An official order with a stamp and a large seal of appointment would be slipped onto the lacquered surface of the table. Arsen Petrovych would rise from his director's armchair to sit sideways on a stool when visitors came. But after a few visits, the phantom figure would disappear from the museum horizons without a trace, while Arsen Petrovych, still in doubt, would be back in his armchair. The most important thing was that during the years of the civil war, that is, between 1917 and 1923—when the city changed hands twenty-two times—he was neither shot nor hanged, nor did he succumb to starvation or typhus.

As for the Museum, it had grown over the course of a decade, enriched with artifacts, and had been relocated to a larger premises. Arsen Petrovych had gained authority. He commanded respect. His opinion mattered. There was an illusion of stability or certainty.

But there was no certainty. The ground was shaky. It slipped underneath his feet. Arsen Petrovych was keenly aware of this. They demanded a thorough restructuring of the exhibition. They commanded him to present criticism and self-criticism, to recast his own essence, to unmask others—those who hid or refused to recast themselves, those who evaded self-criticism.

Arsen Petrovych began to worry.

Agitated, he confessed to me, "I know that my exhibition is somehow out of line, but what can I do?"

He shrugged his shoulders helplessly.

What could he do? What did they want from him? No one could explain it clearly to him. He had to figure it out for himself.

But that was beyond his abilities. He felt like a person lost in the woods. Taking advantage of my arrival, he asked me to inspect the Museum's exhibition and advise him on how to restructure and rebuild it.

We perused the exhibition halls of the Museum. Upon completing our inspection, Arsen Petrovych asked me,

"Well, what do you think?"

He looked into my eyes, as if trying to read his fate.

What was I supposed to tell him? That he was no museum professional, no art historian? That he was an amateur, a provincial who held nothing in common with modernity, an individual from a different generation? That he knew art history no better than he did dialectical materialism? That the years of work as a statistician left an imprint on him which could not be corrected? Why tell him any of this?

Out of caution, I refrained from answering him directly. Touching the bronze candelabra that sat on his lacquered office table, featuring the three ancient graces, I looked through the tall window at the green treetops and said,

"You do have some impressive pieces here. The foremost museums of the world would envy you: van Dyck, Cranach, Tilman Riemenschneider, and finally, a truly exceptional rarity for us, El Greco!"

He rejoiced immensely.

"Really?"

It was he who had collected everything that was here. He had sought them out, rescued them from destruction, acquired them for the Museum.

"Is this not enough? Hmm?"

Was this not enough to redeem him? To justify himself? Was it insufficient for his struggle against the current epoch, for his ongoing race against time to endure, after decades had passed, just as he had kept standing, kept holding his ground during the years of the Civil War?

He spoke somewhat louder than usual. He repeated his question several times, as if he couldn't hear properly. He grew agitated. Tears welled up in his eyes. The magnifying glass in his hand trembled, or perhaps it was just my imagination.

I added nothing more. Why bother? Let things follow their course. Why try analyzing things when neither their trajectory nor their inner transformations could be predicted?

As for the Museum exhibition, I had to admit that from any perspective—professional or amateur—it was abysmal. At the very least, it was incompetent. In the exhibition halls, hopeless junk appeared alongside masterpieces. Generally, these were collections of random things that had found their way into the Museum by chance. There was no system or principle applied to the arrangement of paintings; nothing was put at the foundation of the exhibition except the Director's own preferences. It was a cabinet of curiosities; nothing more.

V. Domontovych

"They accuse me of *recheznavstvo*.[103] But how could I build a museum exhibition without objects? I don't understand!"

Dear God! In his case, being accused of recheznavstvo was a compliment. The objects were there, but the knowledge was missing.

His left eye teared up as an old man's might. Arsen Petrovych pulled out a wide, white handkerchief from his pocket and wiped his damp cheek.

In other museums, to insulate themselves from accusations of recheznavstvo, workers would take down paintings from the walls, remove objects from the showcases, and instead hang posters, slogans, magazine clippings, portraits of leaders, and enlarged photographs. The exhibition would begin with a popular print featuring a genealogical tree of human origin according to Darwin's theory of evolution. A model of a gorilla-like Neanderthal usually served as an introduction.

I made no effort to convince Arsen Petrovych that sometimes a poster, a quote, a slogan, a magazine clipping, a clumsy depiction of a shepherd with a lamb on his shoulders that had been scratched with a nail into the walls of latter-day catacombs could be more meaningful than the marble of a statue carved by the skilled chisel of Praxiteles.

I said:

---

[103] From Ukrainian: categorization of things. The term has a negative connotation of focusing on separate objects and their characteristics, origin, and provenance, instead of reinterpreting them in the Marxist-Leninist context. In the 1930s, *recheznavstvo* was a common accusation against archaeological and museum workers.

"From the images in the catacombs to Raphael's Sistine Madonna, fifteen centuries have passed. Can you traverse all this time in fifteen years?"

But it appeared that Arsen Petrovych didn't understand what I meant by that.

We were back to the enamel jug, not to the elegant refinement of Van Dyck, or the exoticism of El Greco, or Tilman Riemenschneider with his depictions of saints. Things were dubious and uncertain.

I glanced at my watch.

"I'm terribly sorry, but I'm in a hurry!"

I quickly shook Arsen Petrovych's hand. Before my eyes flashed his white handkerchief, the silver of his temples, the gray of his beard, the stoop of his shoulders, the darkness of the bronze candelabra, the red shine of the varnish on the polished surface of the table.

I rushed downstairs. In my heart, I felt a pang of sorrow for the man and an awareness of my own helplessness.

Leaning over the marble balustrade, Arsen Petrovych called out to me from above.

"Don't forget—we're expecting you at five today!"

My hand touched the fluffy softness of the velvet on the railing. I nodded.

"Right, indeed! Five it is!"

I ran along the sunny side of the street. There was a faint cloud of sorrow in my heart. I crossed the street. The pebbles on the boulevard made a gritting sound under my feet. My gaze swept past the rows of green benches. With my eyes I searched for Larysa's hat. My heart was beating tensely.

XXXIX

One can afford to be lax when it comes to the timing of a lecture. One can even be fashionably late to a meeting. Under no circumstances, however, can one be imprecise when it comes to a reception or a celebratory dinner.

This time, I was there right on the hour. To verify my timing, I deliberately glanced at my watch, turning off the avenue onto the side street. It was seven minutes to five. I walked leisurely along the cozy alley, which ran past houses nestled amidst trees and flowerbeds, searching for the third house on the left from the corner, as was precisely indicated in the note handed to me by Arsen Petrovych.

Yes, here it was—a squat house with several windows, with an acacia tree unfurling its green foliage and white clusters of blossoms over the beet-colored tin roof.

I stopped by the gate and slowly opened the wicket, anxiously expecting a wild horde of enraged, barking dogs to set upon me any moment. But all was quiet. A brick path led me along the solid wall of the house and into the courtyard. In the corner of the tenement house, as was customary, a large black barrel stood under the rain gutter. Whether to wash one's hair or launder the linens, there is nothing better than rainwater.

The heat was subsiding. The colors grew deeper. The tall greenish-gray weeds covering the courtyard reminded me of childhood. Trampled paths, intertwining and intersecting, led from the house to the utility buildings, the icehouse, the cellar, and a barn.

They opened a passage to my memories. I recognized this unfamiliar courtyard as a revisited recollection of my own past. The barn, assembled from weathered, almost charred planks, confronted me from the opposite side of the courtyard—not only in space but also in time. The gates of the barn sagged and could no longer close; to prevent them from falling, the owners had propped them up with a stake. The world had changed its face. Cosmic storms swept over the globe, revolutions transpired, fronts ebbed and flowed, millions perished, but the stake that once supported the barn gates, torn from their rusted hinges, remained unchanged.

Behind the black barn, I saw a small orchard. Neat rows of whitewashed apple trees, green bushes of currants, rich beds of black topsoil, the glazed frames of greenhouses, yellow rectangles of reed and straw mats scattered nearby. Arsen Petrovych was a good housekeeper and a diligent gardener. The sun ignited the weedy courtyard with a green flame. In its jungles, yellow chirping chicks roamed; one could hear the worried clucking of the busy hen. A light breeze carried the scent of flowers and, along with it, the comforting thought that the day had ended. In its place, evening's gentle quiet, translucent dusk, and tranquility were on their way to take over the world.

I returned. Within my field of vision, I registered a blue-pink flowerbed, dark cherry tree shoots along the fence, the gray planks of a table with its legs hammered into the ground. On the table—with his long tail held downward, deft and slender, aware of its dignified grav-

211

ity and indifferent to everything—stood a greenish-blue peacock.

This is how feelings, impressions, thoughts, and memories accumulate. Consciousness has not yet grasped their inner urgency. They emerge—patchy, noisy, and disorganized, guided by my own motions, appearing and disappearing with them.

I stood before the façade of the house. My eye casually glanced over the porch, overgrown with wild grapes; the wide steps; the doorstep scraper nailed to the baseboard to clean off the oily mud brought from the garden before entering the house.

The white-bearded host appeared on the porch steps.

"Rostyslav Mykhailovych, how delightful to see you!"

We shook hands warmly and sincerely. That's how he has remained in my memory up until today, as I write these lines ten years later. Alive, cheery, gentle. It's hard for me to imagine him otherwise: broken, sad, weary, as he became after being let go from his position as Director.

"Marusya!" he called out affectionately, his voice resounding, to his wife. "Come outside, Rostyslav Mykhailovych is here."

She came out—chubby, full-faced, rosy, no longer young but still beautiful, wearing an apron, with her sleeves rolled up. Arsen Petrovych looked at her affectionately, with tender pride. He clearly took pride in his wife, in the way she remained so good-looking at her age, in addition to being such a good homemaker.

I bowed my head and kissed her plump hand.

We dined at a long table set on the porch. The peacock, spreading the feathers of its fantastic tail, traipsed across the courtyard in front of the porch with an air of importance. Hens bustled under the porch—red-black, yellow-red, pigeon-gray, and white. We threw them bread crumbs. Pecking at each other, the birds fussed about, loud and disorderly as if at a market.

Decorative glasses, dark green and bear-shaped, and squat, ribbed jars gave the table a rustic look. Large, puffy pies were piled high inside a white willow basket sitting on a stool by the table. These were authentic pies, baked in a stove—not an oven—on wide tin sheets. Likewise, borscht was cooked in the oven, in a large cast-iron pot. The borscht was made with lamb, sautéed and simmered, as should be the case with any good Ukrainian borscht.

We toasted to my health, the health of our hosts, everyone who was present, and each one individually. Raising my glass, I expressed regret that important scholarly research and other official duties beyond the Council, as well as the desire not to waste even a drop of time, precious like wine, had hindered me from devoting sufficient time to the Council's work and from being present at all the meetings.

Ivan Vasyliovych Hulia reached out to me across the table, holding his glass,

"Rostyslav Mykhailovych, how could we... But you! If it weren't for you..."

The noise at the table disturbed the agitated hens on the other side of the porch, testifying to the unanimity of the guests in supporting Hulia's words of welcome. Along with him, everyone sincerely shared their sympathy for me, knowing I was overly burdened with work and disheartened by the strain of official duties placed upon me.

We toasted, we greeted one another, and, still standing, finished our glasses of pungent cherry brandy with a touch of sour pits.

Enthusiastically, Hulia began singing *Mnohaya lita.*[104] Like everything that Hulia did, it was moving, chaotic, and somewhat absurd.

After lunch, seemingly endless in its extravagant grandeur, and at the hosts' invitation, all of us moved to the central section. On the walls of the cozy rooms, I noticed an interesting, small, but tastefully selected collection of paintings by Ukrainian artists. Next to a beautiful river landscape in lilac hues, painted in tempera by Vasylkivskyi, which was done in bold decorative manner, hung a painting by Vasyl Krychevskyi.[105] In the alcove between the two windows open to the street, where the acacia generously extended its blossoming clusters, hung a luscious landscape by Burachek; a study by Repin for *The Zaporozhian Cossacks*; and baroque etchings by Narbut.[106]

"What about Lynnyk?" I asked. "Why is it that you have none of his paintings here?"

---

[104] From Ukrainian: "many years." A traditional Ukrainian celebratory song originating in the Byzantine Rite.

[105] Serhiy Vasylkivskyi (1854–1917): Ukrainian painter and art scholar who worked in the styles of Realism and Impressionism.

[106] Mykola Burachek (1871–1942): Ukrainian impressionist painter and art scholar.

"Lynnyk?!" the host responded almost reverently. "I have a collection of his sketches, drawings, and photographs of his paintings, which, I'm certain, you won't find anywhere else."

And on a table covered with a crocheted tablecloth, he laid out several large folders and bulky albums bound in heavy leather.

Indeed, it was something quite exceptional, entirely extraordinary. With eager curiosity, I delved into the collection, discovering some surprises. Especially impressive were Lynnyk's sketches and drawings from 1907 and 1908 when, during the construction of the Varangian Church, he often visited and stayed in Katerynoslav for long stretches of time.

We have ample cause to talk about the Katerynoslav period in the work of my beloved great master, the world-renowned Lynnyk. In these years, the chaotic spontaneity of his early works, somewhat unbalanced and too impulsive, gave way to monumental finality. His work incorporated elements of Byzantinism, the universality of Sophia-Wisdom, classicism endowed with stern pathos and, at the same time, mystically penetrating.[107] While Lynnyk's early creations were marked by the Varangian spirit of Sviatoslav—conqueror, horseman, ruiner of kingdoms—a different Varangian theme dominated his interests in his Katerynoslav period. Volo-

---

[107] Sophia-Wisdom: a concept that was developed among the circles of Kyivan theologians and philosophers in the 13th–17th centuries. Drawing on the idea of neoplatonism and hesychasm, the concept of Sophia provided a middle ground between the Byzantine East and Catholic West, between the emotional and the rational approaches to Christianity.

dymyr—founder of cities, builder, basileus—and his trajectory stood at the center of Lynnyk's attention in those years.

Arsen Petrovych, too imposing for this modest room, stood beside me.

"Critics have been entirely right to note the influence of the frescoes of Vrubel in the Kyrylivska Church on Lynnyk's frescoes and mosaics in the Varangian Church," I said.[108] "But it is worth noting that Lynnyk eliminated the morbid reverie, the pallid tone that Vrubel's works displayed. While Vrubel was inspired by Dostoevskii, Lynnyk paid homage to Konstantin Leontiev."[109]

I thanked the host for sharing his treasures with me, and added,

"If jealousy could contain even the slightest hint of nobility, I envy you for being the owner of such a beautiful, I would even say, unique collection."

Arsen Petrovych was clearly pleased with what I had said. He removed Lynnyk's drawings to make space for an album with samples of peasant embroidery. Those were followed, in their turn, by the drawings of folk murals.

After a pause, a red-wood casket appeared on the table. What mysteries did it hold? I expected all sorts of surprises. We had by this point drunk enough to approach the greatest marvel with edified and calm reasoning and

---

[108] Mikhail Vrubel (1856–1910): Russian Symbolist painter and designer who spent a number of years in Kyiv, where he supervised the restoration and creation of frescos for the Kyrylivska Church.

[109] Konstantin Leontiev (1831–1891): conservative philosopher and monarchist who advocated for Russia's closer ties with the East.

to accept the most ordinary object with enthusiasm, as if it were a magical phantom *à la* E.T.A. Hoffmann.

The metal lock opened with a mysterious ringing. I saw Arsen Petrovych's fingers tremble as he reverently retrieved from the casket a package tied with silk cord. He handed us the yellowed sheets of letters by Mykhailo Kotsyubynskyi—precious relics of a friendship that had remained unknown to the writer's biographers. Arsen Petrovych was overwhelmed with sorrow and regret. His heightened emotions prompted him to bring forth words full of tenderness and sadness.

He showed us letters from Lesya Ukrainka. Arsen's and Lesya's paths crossed in a bizarre, tensely interwoven way. Perhaps these letters concealed the psychological resolution to Lesya's inner drama and could have helped to reveal the creative sources of her little tragedies, those dramatic masterpieces.

As for the correspondence with magazine editors, it would have certainly attracted the envious attention of literary scholars who have made a profitable profession out of publishing correspondences of famous, lesser-known, and completely unknown authors.

We drank coffee. The conversation shifted to a subject that was of interest to everyone—the construction of *Dniprelstan*,[110] which was nearing completion. The

---

[110] *Dniprelstan* or the Dnipro Hydroelectric Station: other names used for the Dnipro dam are mentioned in Chapter III. It was built between 1927-1932 on the right bank of the Dnipro, near the city of Zaporizhya. The goal of this project was to inundate the Dnipro rapids, historically significant locations on the river that had long been connected with the history of Ukrainian Cossacks.

question was examined from all possible angles. Most of all, we talked about the rapids that would be flooded, and how in a short while they would become auxiliary facts of history. Ethnographers were curious about the fate of maritime pilots from Lotsmanska Kamianka[111] and worried that the profession of a pilot will become of no use. Many found the idea of sailing down the Dnipro from Kyiv to Kherson quite attractive. Others passionately discussed the cutting-edge transformations that technology would bring about. In the course of a few years, these changes would substantially alter the face that these lands had inherited from ancient times.

There were enthusiasts, and there were skeptics, who imagined colossal, excessive technological transformations, catastrophic in character. The conversation veered off from present times to the past, from fear of the future to reminiscing on the changes and fractures that Ukraine had experienced in the previous millennia.

We talked about the eras that had vanished; the peoples who once inhabited these steppes. We agreed that we knew ourselves too little in the present, let alone our past.

In our midst we had archeologists, both locals and visitors, who had come to take part in the excavations organized by the Dniprelstan archeological expedition. We attempted to find refuge in archeological discoveries.

The archeological findings led us on a path through the millennia. The Paleolithic site in the Rebrova gulch outside of town,[112] the Neolithic burial ground near

---

[111] A 17th-century Cossack settlement in present-day Dnipro.
[112] An archeological site near Kislovodsk, Russia.

Ihren on the Samara River,[113] stone burial cists from the Bronze Age,[114] excavated Scythian burrows near the rapids—all of these discoveries predetermined the stages of our imaginary travels.[115]

Finally, we touched on the burial grounds from the first through the fourth centuries CE, excavated by Pavlo Kozar[116] in Voloske, a village in Dnipropetrovsk oblast. Back then, was he aware of the importance of his excavations?

Our conversation centered on the monuments of antiquity. We passionately exalted the significance of this grand and majestic stage in Ukrainian history. In the first two centuries of the Common Era, a beautiful high culture covered vast territories of ancient Ukraine, from the Black Sea to the Desna, and from the Desna and the headwaters of the Vistula far to the east, all the way to the Donets and the Don.

Back then, a bearded Scythian with disheveled hair, completely drenched in horse sweat, his locks fixed on his forehead with a narrow strap, dressed in long trousers made of animal skin and wearing *carbatina*, would wander the steppes with his herds.[117] He survived on mare's milk, sweet and intoxicating *kumis,* and, having

---

[113] A neighborhood in present-day Dnipro; formerly a separate town.

[114] Cist, or stone chest: a stone burial box used to contain the remains of the dead.

[115] A group of nomadic Indo-Iranian tribes that controlled the steppe of Southern Ukraine in the 7th–3rd centuries BCE.

[116] Pavlo Kozar (1898–1944): Ukrainian archeologist and historian who took part in the Dniprelstan archeological expedition (1927–1930).

[117] Carbatina: a kind of a leather shoe popular among the rural inhabitants of ancient Greece and Rome.

kindled a fire for the night, cooked meat and millet porridge in large metal cauldrons. For the first time in his life, he shaved his beard and cut his red hair.

He changed his way of life. The militant Scythian cast off his barbaric attire of the herder-horseman and dressed appropriately and decently, as it fit someone who belonged to the civilized ancient Mediterranean. He was no longer clothed with animal skins, as a rider would be, pulling them over his naked body without a shirt, matching his clothes to his profession of herdsman. Instead, he wore linen and wool, woven in a hut by the hands of hardworking women. Instead of leather pants, he wore a white linen cloak that he fastened on his shoulder with a bronze or gold fibula.

Leather gave way to linen. Instead of killing an animal for its skin, he would shear it instead.

A razor with a wide, rounded blade became a common accessory for daily grooming. A sophisticated woman who wore tiny canisters of precious fragrances (delivered from the best perfume shops of Rhodes or Alexandria) in her earlobes would demand that her husband shave at least twice a day.

Our formerly belligerent nomadic cattleman, plunderer, and horseman had disappeared. He gave way to a settled agrarian life in a densely populated country, where the cities in the south were surrounded by stone walls, and the villages were scattered at a distance of several kilometers between one another.

The flocks of sheep minded by the shepherd, who stood leaning on his crook, grazed in the field. The rooster flew up to the fence, singing, stretching out his throat, and the chicken, having laid eggs, cackled in the yard. Heaps of fragrant grain filled the granaries; stocky cone-shaped barns protected the chaff from the autumn rains.

The September wind was blowing in from the sea. In the port tavern of Pontic Olbia,[118] holding a glass of Falernian wine in his hand, sat a red-haired indigenous dweller. He was clean-shaven and wore a white cloak fastened with a fibula. Rapt with attention, he listened to the tale of a tanned, skinny sailor, his head tied with red cloth. The story focused on the current year's grain harvest in Africa. The local dweller was alarmed by the rumors of fluctuations in exchange prices on the grain markets of Cartagena, Alexandria, and Antioch.

Having carelessly tossed a couple of silver coins on the tavern table, the local dweller made his way to the city to visit the ship and bank offices of the grain exporters. He stood in front of the city gate. The blue-white sea stretched into infinity. The white sails of the *triremes*[119] sparkled against the blue of the sea. The ships were carrying the grain harvested in Ukrainian fields to Asia Minor, to Greece and Rome.

In the villages, the women were no longer engaged in making pottery by hand, providing for their own needs and the needs of their families. Pottery no longer involved making mediocre imitations of the imported tableware. Sitting on a bench, an experienced craftsman,

---

[118] An archeological site of an ancient Greek city located on the shores of the river Buh in southern Ukraine.

[119] A type of galley used by the ancient civilizations of the Mediterranean.

now a professional, produced perfect pottery of exquisite shapes and colors on a wheel. He now competed instead of making copies.

We enthusiastically applauded the refinement of artistic taste, the perfect restraint that guided the master in his work. He had no interest in gaudy embellishments. He avoided color palettes that might have come across as too loud. These were the attempts of a skilled artisan to curb his creative fervor in pursuit of perfection, balance, and a sense of measure.

In his search for a color palette, the skillful potter had the courage to renunciate intensely bright colors. He sought to reduce color, achieving the necessary effect with the help of hues and shades, instilling a fascination with matte colorlessness among the laymen. He managed to prove that the glow of diffuse gray light could be no less intense than any pure color, be it green, blue, or red.

He valued monotony and tried to preserve it. He created a vast expanse of empty space. He exposed the surface to display the perfection of the material. He let the flow and interchange of hues to live as a play of shadows on the jar's curvature, in the profile of its rim. Shades of color emerged from the changes within the contour and shape of the vessel, as if they were shadows or reflections of the surface's primary color.

We experienced genuine delight in recalling the colors of clay pottery from ancient Ukraine—light-gray, greenish, blueish, ash gray, and reddish with all its transitional hues, from pale brown to coffee and black.

In a similar fashion, a foundryman leaning over the workbench inside his hut, near the window tightly wrapped by a stretched bull bladder, was making fibulae, bending and carving bronze, iron, or gold wire. Through his meticulous work, the craftsman arrived at an austere and simple, precise and balanced style.

The spirit of the ancient golden ratio hovered over the golden fields of Ukraine. We would venture to suggest that among those poets who represented the Silver Age of Latin in Europe, from the circle of the contemporaries of Ausonius, as well as his rivals and friends, were not only the poets born in Galia but also those who had been nursed in the steppes of Sarmatia.[120]

Who were all these exporters of grain, artisans, poets, builders, and owners of tenement houses, living in villas and praying in temples adorned with columns? Were they the Hellenized Scythians mentioned by Herodotus? Their offspring? Vlachs? Veneti?[121]

---

[120] Silver Age of Latin: one of the stages in the periodization of the history of Latin literature (18–133 CE). It was proposed by Wilhelm Sigismund Teuffel, a German classicist, in 1870. Decimius Magnus Ausonius (ca 310-ca 395): a Roman poet and teacher of rhetoric. Sarmatia: a large confederation of ancient Eastern Iranian nomadic peoples of classical antiquity who dominated the Pontic steppe from about the 3rd century BCE - 4th century CE.

[121] Vlachs: an indigenous population of Romania and Moldova, claiming descent from the inhabitants of the Roman province of Dacia. Veneti: an Indo-European people that inhabited the region of central Europe east of the Vistula River. First described by the ancient Romans in the 1st century CE, the Veneti are postulated by some to be the ancestors of the Slavs.

XL

Out of fragments and trifles, out of nothing, combining facts, assumptions, and snippets, inflating isolated details to create a momentous image, we kept searching for the path that connected the past with the future. We determined the horizons and limitations of the highly evolved cultures that had come into existence on Ukrainian lands and, after having persisted for six or eight centuries, suddenly disappeared in the span of only a few years.

As we continued our discussions—on the laws of emergence and decline, on the rhythm of disappearance—images of demise came to our agitated imagination.

Anxiety and fear flared up inside every one of us, and certainty dissipated. Our hearts contracted and sank to the bottom in despair.

Without a sound, night entered our mellow and warm house.

The night exhaled the sweet aroma of flowers into the open windows.

Black Mother-abyss, dark and warm, was pregnant with incredulity; its wide bosom was filled with birth and demise.

I approached the window and, leaning over the sill, took a look outside. I dove into the darkness, insatiably inhaling the fresh air of this fragrant night.

I looked at the flickering stars, at the space that connected all beginnings and endings, everything that was, is, and would be. I remembered the night when, engulfed by delirious desires, Larysa and I wandered around drunk on the hallucinations of the nocturnal abyss.

Arsen Petrovych approached. He lightly embraced me, leaned out of the window by my side, and asked, "Are you watching?"

His question betrayed feelings of meekness, a faint sadness, and a docile acceptance of fate's whims. I felt the sadness that saturated his being. I was filled with compassion and yet, what could I possibly do?

The word *destruction* affected Ivan Vasylovych Hulia like a spur in a horse's side. He interpreted these images of demise as a personal reproach. He represented the Protection of Sites of Cultural Heritage, Antiquities, and Art Committee (*KOPKSiM*). As a representative of the Committee, he carried full responsibility for any disappearance or destruction. Nothing was to disappear. Nothing was to be destroyed.

He surveyed us all with a sense of concentrated gloom.

"I have always believed that the inactivity of the Committee representatives was the greatest evil. I have never failed to remind you of that. I used to warn you all the time. This is exactly what I spoke about in my speech during the Second All-Ukrainian Congress of Kopksim."

Hulia perceived the issue of destruction with the sensitivity of a professional, with the lofty awkwardness of an expert. For him, the history of humanity equaled the history of Kopksim's activities. Everything that had happened in the past depended on the activities of the Protection of the Cultural Heritage Committee. The chain of committees could be sufficiently or insufficiently developed, the representatives could have sufficient or insufficient powers; this would cause corresponding changes in the history of humanity, the preservation or decline of human cultures.

Representatives of the Committee have existed from time immemorial. The world might not have come into existence, but they did. Errors in the activities of the Committee have caused the decline of cultures. Here is what Hulia imagined the essence of the historical process to be, and he aimed his anger at the violators of the Bylaws. The Committee's Bylaws constituted the greatest achievement of humanity, its highest accomplishment, a version of the Bible, a kind of Kant's *Critique of Pure Reason*, albeit more perfect, more impeccable.

Hulia put his hands into his pockets and, overtaken by his thoughts, wandered around the room. Sounding on edge, he repeated the same words and fragments. He had just a handful in his arsenal.

"We have to adopt measures…Turn to those in power…Appeal to public opinion…Widen the circles of authorized representatives."

He paused. He folded his fingers, one by one.

"During the Second Congress of Kopksim, I pointed out (a) the inadequate activities of the local representatives of the Committee, (b) the inactivity of those representatives, (c) the fact that they are not reaching the necessary level, (d) they do not measure up to their purpose, (e) for the most part, they consist of low-skilled people, and (f) they are either indifferent or careless with regard to the cause that has been entrusted to them. In sum, I noted that all these factors might lead to a disaster."

I looked at a strand of black hair that, as if a tongue of fire, ascended gloomily from the top of Ivan Vasylovych Hulia's heavy, prominent forehead. I looked at his folded arms, his hanging head, and it seemed I understood him. It seemed to me that I understood his professionally abstract thinking, the obscure nature of his conceptions, his expert thought patterns. He perceived all things, ideas, and phenomena in terms of functions within the organization for which he worked. To him, the entire world and everything in it could be classified as sites of heritage, antiquities, and art. They were to be registered and protected, and they would be distinguished only on the basis of the extent of their importance, be it on the level of the republic, the Soviet Union, or the world in its entirety.

Hulia's ideal would be to transform the universe into a colossal museum, where every object would be registered, defined, described; all on an index card with an individual code, drawing, or photo attached to it, with the date of acquisition, provenance, and value.

The world needed to be cataloged. His, Hulia's, ideal world would be climate-controlled, the objects within preserved with formaldehyde according to the season. Moths, worms, humidity, mold, and temperature fluctuations, the direst enemies of humanity and culture, would be overthrown for good, liquidated. The decisions of the Protection of Heritage Sites Committee would be final and not open to appeal.

I remember well the extent of the annoyance, stubbornness, and burning enthusiasm that Hulia displayed in Kharkiv when, as a representative of the Committee, he demanded a typist for his staff on top of the already existing position of a clerk. Based on his words and arguments, humanity's fate depended on the outcome of this issue. Would the staff and budget distribution be increased in order to purchase a bookcase, folders, a mimeograph, ink, chairs, a fan, as well as a doormat? The Committee's accountant was as afraid of Hulia's arrival as he would be of a natural disaster. The accountant would scurry home and fail to show up at work. Even Petro Ivanovych Stryzhyus, a fish-like personality with constantly clammy palms, the secretary of the Committee, would lose his balance at times like this. He sat, all flushed and baffled, blinking or fussing about.

Hulia sounded the alarm bells. He stubbornly advocated the necessity of purchasing a doormat. He conducted a systematic siege of the Committee Head's office. He caused commotion in the *Narkomos*, the People's Commissariat of Education, terrorizing the entire office of the Chief Science Commissioner.

Only endowing the Protection of Heritage Sites with full powers could guarantee the continued preservation of human culture. Humanity would have access to the full corpus of published and deciphered papyri. We would have not just the fragments but the entire collection of works by Heraclitus. Humanity would not have suffered because of the absence of the perfect manuscript of *The Tale of Ihor's Campaign*,[122] and *La Gioconda* by Leonardo da Vinci would not have been stolen from the

[122] From Old East Slavic: *Slovo o polku Ihorevi*: an epic 12th-century poem by an anonymous author, an important literary work of Kyivan Rus'.

Louvre in Paris. All works and letters by Hanna Barvi-nok would have been published.[123] Old huts in Ukraine would have been described, photographed, and meas-ured. It would have been forbidden to plow up Scythian *kurhans* in the steppes.[124] A separate Museum would have been created, where experts would study the *kamyana baba* statues collected there.[125]

Hulia invited us to fill our glasses with plum brandy, strong as pure alcohol and sweet as candied honey, and drink to all those who understood the providential im-portance of protecting heritage sites. The words that would seem to be sheer blabbering coming out of someone else's mouth sounded moving and sincere coming from Hulia.

His passionate toast was accepted enthusiastically. People shook his hand. To be precise, it was Hulia who was shaking hands with everybody. He was greeted, thanked for his expression of the genuine sentiment shared by all present.

The atmosphere in the room began to liven up.

---

[123] Pen name of Oleksandra Bilozerska-Kulish, 1828–1911: Ukrainian writer whose works focused on ethnographic and social aspects of Ukrainian village life.

[124] Mounds of earth and stones raised over a grave which were in use on the Pontic-Caspian steppes during the 3rd millennium BCE.

[125] Ukrainian: *kamyana baba;* pl. *kamyani baby*: anthropomorphic female stone statues of Scythian and Sarmatian origin found in the Ukrainian steppes and dated 7th–4th centuries BCE.

XLI

Arsen Petrovych sat in a soft armchair, upholstered in gray and pink fabric. The chair was low, and the sharp angle of his bent legs came up to his chest, while the yellowed knuckles of his hand disappeared into the gray of his beard.

"You want to know what destruction is? We're all filled with fear of a catastrophe. We keep talking about upheavals and crises."

He paused briefly, raising his glass and examining the thick, transparent liquid that glowed in the light of the electric bulb like a ruby. He looked at us and continued,

"I can see your hesitation. You don't know whether to give preference to hatred or mercy. Hatred exhausts you, and you would rather seek salvation in mercy. I share your feelings, but I'm not sure whether you want mercy only for yourself or for everyone else. Is your mercy alive, or did it arise solely from the awareness of your irresolute nature?"

He spoke gently, yet his words sounded like a reproach to all of us. He said,

"Hatred is a concept of historical order, but mercy can be seen that way as well."

He listened to our silence.

"I think you are full of doubt. Can mercy be seen as betrayal, you wonder?"

He set the half-empty glass of brandy on the table and stood up.

He was too tall for this low room. He approached the bookcase and extracted a book bound in silk from a cardboard box atop the shelf.

On Shaky Ground

"This is *Fata Morgana* by Kotsiubynskyi," Arsen Pet-rovych declared solemnly, showing us the autographed book featuring a friendly dedication on the title page. It was as if he was espousing the Gospel from a pulpit.

"You might recall this passage," said the host, returning to his seat in the grayish-pink upholstered armchair, "in which Khoma Gudz and Andriy had arrived at the landlord's distillery, which was under construction. With your permission, I'll read a short excerpt."

His voice was calm and deliberate.

Andriy could already see a row of sleighs with logs and beams, bast baskets filled with red bricks [...] He ran from one sleigh to another, feeling the wood with his hand, knocking on the bricks [...] But Khoma's eyes shone with a green malicious light. 'Feeling like in seventh heaven? You'll be hunched-backed before you earn anything. Watch out! Some have bellies hanging over their belts, and they'll sap all the strength from your body, damn it all...I hope they burn and the wind scatters their ashes together with the human wrongdoings!' 'Wait, Khoma!' But Gudz couldn't be stopped now—the proverbial train had already left the station. 'I would take all of it and—wham, wham—I'd bust up the whole place, I'd flatten it to the ground so that there would be nothing left of it, now and forever!'[126]

Arsen Petrovych repeated,

"I'd bust it up... flatten it to the ground..."

He wanted to keep talking, but the hostess opened the door to the dining room, interrupting him. With a bow, she invited us to move to the adjacent room,

---

[126] Translation adapted from: Mykhailo Kotsyubynskyi, *Fata Morgana and Other Stories* (Kyiv: Dnipro Publishers, 1980). Transl. by Arthur Barnhard.

where a steaming samovar stood on the table near the gleaming glass of the goblets.

A snow-white tablecloth glistened. The monumental grandeur of the hostess, sitting by the samovar and pouring golden tea into glasses, accentuated the idyllic seclusion of this isolated world. The steam sang. The nickel of the sugar bowl glittered. Marusya's puffy cheeks and elbows spread around a pinkish glow.

Arsen Petrovych continued,

"Just as Gudz's grandfathers had burned Bernardine monasteries and noble castles to the ground in the seventeenth century, so too in 1917 did Gudzenko raze farms, tear down buildings, destroy cities, send trains off course, drag rails off their tracks and into swamps. They wanted to flatten everything—tenement houses, cities, bridges, railways—to the ground, so that there would be only soil, and on that soil—a hut, and nothing else except for the earth that could be plowed and sown."

Arsen Petrovych caught his breath. Only in that moment did I notice how weary he looked, the glimpse of fatigue in his eyes, how the glass trembled in his hand. Just like that morning at the Museum, only then it had been a magnifying glass.

"At the beginning of the revolution, I traveled extensively through villages, collecting what had survived. I remember how, sometime in the spring, I came to a village hoping to save a few canvases by Borovykivskyi and Levytskyi from an estate of the Likhachevs.[127] With great

---

[127] Volodymyr Borovykovskyi (1757–1825): Ukrainian iconographer and portraitist, a graduate of the Saint Petersburg Academy of Arts. Dmytro

difficulty, at risk to my own life, I reached the village. Imagine my despair when I found out that there was nothing left of the farm, the estate, the collections, the antique furniture sets."

He pushed the glass aside and clasped his beard with his hand.

"It was night time. I lay on a bench, listening to the typhus delirium of my sick hosts. In the entire village, there wasn't a single typhus-free house. Somewhere on the street, shots rang out. Someone ran through the vegetable patches in the darkness, shouting frantically, 'Help!' The alarmed dogs barked. The dark horizon was ablaze. Something was burning. My head hurt. I felt exhausted. I was tired of pointless wanderings, the road, the impact of ruin. I felt dejected. I wondered if I was beginning to come down with typhus myself."

He reached out for a jar of jam, raising it up as if it were a chalice. There was something liturgical in the gesture.

"I no longer wanted anything. I didn't aspire to anything. I just wanted to understand what it was: vengeance? Centuries-old, Shevchenko-inspired rage of the common people against the noblemen? A blind, spontaneous instinct of destruction? The demons of deafness?"

He didn't notice the jar in his hand tilting, thick globs of red liquid falling onto the tablecloth. The hostess

---

Levytskyi (1835–1922): a prominent Ukrainian portraitist of the classical era who developed a school of portrait painting in the Russian Empire. Likhachevs: a noble Russian family who owned a number of estates in the Yaroslavl and Tver oblasts of Russia.

looked at him with silent reproach; he caught her gaze and, concerned and blushing, placed the jar on a plate and started scooping the jam from the tablecloth with a knife.

Meanwhile, he continued,

"I lay in the hut, next to those sick with typhus. At night, in the deranged darkness, I lamented these people, the village mentality that denied everything that lay outside its scope of the known. To confine one's life to the boundaries of a village, refusing to accept anything beyond the fence, the pastures, the cemetery? The consciousness of the people seemed to me majestic in its confined greatness. I accused the people of being closed-minded."

The samovar hissed, its thin gray stream of steam escaping from the narrow hole in the lid. I stirred sugar into my glass with a spoon, and the glass clinked. With some hesitation, I surveyed the long row of colorful jam hues—yellow-green quince, translucent pink rose, the red darkness of cherry.

"Have you tried apple?" the lady of the house reminded me. But I opted to settle for gooseberry.

"Arsen, pass the currant jam to Rostyslav Mykhailovych!"

Arsen Petrovych obeyed his wife's command, handed me the jar of gooseberry jam, and continued.

"Back then, I was younger. Only with years one becomes conscious of one's prospects. It's like climbing: once you make it to the top, everything lies at your feet. My hair has become gray; I've become more restrained. I understood what I once couldn't understand. I am asking you: what are the people? What does it mean for the people to exist? What is history, or rather, what do we conventionally call history? The people endure. The people remain outside of history. They prefer to stay away. They either do not react to historical events at all, or they react to them other than how we would like them to, or demand of them, in the name of fulfilling those tasks we call historical. I am asking you: is the anti-historicity of the people an expression of their inadequacy or, on the contrary, is it evidence of the completeness of their wisdom?"

Arsen Petrovych gazed at us with his gentle and calm eyes. His presence evoked in me a sensation of priestly solemnity, a triumphant magnificence, that liturgical quality which permeated the poems he wrote.

To sum up, he observed,

"Let's take any given uncle who still plows, if not his field, then certainly his vegetable patch with the same plow that Volodymyr Monomakh had mentioned at the Dolobske Council.[128] He locks the barn with the same latch as in the twelfth century; he sharpens the same scythe with the whetstone that his ancestors used eight hundred years ago. Would it really be that unusual for our uncle to interpret the events in his village differently than we might?"

Arsen Petrovych was getting warm. He eagerly drank his tea and, extending the empty cup to his wife, asked for more.

---

[128] Volodymyr Monomakh (1053–1125): Grand Prince of Kyiv who sought to strengthen the unity of Kyivan Rus during his reign. Dolobske Council: a council of Kyivan Rus princes that took place in 1103 near Dolobske Lake (current-day Trukhaniv Island in Kyiv).

I ought to admit that Arsen Petrovych's populism did not captivate us. It seemed somewhat outdated. His conceits left us with the impression of an archaic stylization.

Not everyone grasped the essence of Arsen Petrovych's thoughts, or they didn't perceive them quite as he expressed them. Disputes arose. Everyone wanted to defend their point of view, and if after some time a certain consensus emerged, it boiled down to a demand addressed to Arsen Petrovych:

"We need evidence! Let's clarify once more!"

Arsen Petrovych placed his hands on the table, intertwining his fingers and slightly leaning his body forward over the table. I had had too much to drink; a murky fog enveloped my brain. In this posture of his, Arsen Petrovych suddenly seemed very large and unexpectedly bulky, as if with his broad figure he had managed to fill the entire space of the table. Everyone sitting around suddenly became very small, floating, melting, and swaying in uncertainty, while a voice resounded from some distant abyss.

I forced myself to listen.

"The Village sought to assert itself, to destroy everything that was not itself, was beyond it or stood against it! Alongside Bohdan, the villagers burned down the castles of Vyshnevetskyi in Left-Bank Lubny and Pryluky. With Gonta and Zaliznyak, they razed Polish houses in Right-Bank Human and Korsun.[129] With Gudz in 1905,

---

[129] Vyshnevetskyi (in Polish: *Wiśniowiecki*): a Ruthenian noble dynasty of Lithuanian, possibly Scandinavian origin, which became polonized in

they destroyed the nobility's distilleries, throwing pianos from the house windows, while with Gudzenko in 1917, they again burned and flattened manors, estates, railways, and townships. A steam locomotive lay overturned, pushed into a ditch, near the place where an estate had existed, and where now there was nothing but a mound of rubble and broken bricks."

He painted apocalyptic pictures of destruction he had witnessed, the scope of which he extended into the past and projected into the future. He conjured visions of catastrophe, while I floated from the abyss into some unknown void.

He widened the possibilities.

I was floating in an expanse. Everything was unstable.

XLII

I shouldn't have had so much to drink. I rose from the chair, set it aside and, with heavy steps, went out onto the terrace.

---

the 15th century. Lubny: one of the oldest cities in Ukraine (present-day Poltava oblast), destroyed by the Mongols in 1239 and rebuilt by the Vyshnevetskyi dynasty in the 15th–16th centuries. Pryluky: one of the oldest Ukrainian cities (present-day Chernihiv oblast) that belonged to the Vyshnevetskyi dynasty in the 16th century. Ivan Gonta (?–1768) and Maksym Zaliznyak (1740–?): leaders of the Koliyivshchyna rebellion, a 1768 uprising in which scores of Polish nobles, Jews, and Uniates were massacred. Human (Uman) and Korsun: old cities in present-day Cherkasy oblast of Ukraine, which were under Polish rule in the 15th-18th centuries and became sites of the notorious Haidamaka rebellions in the 17th–18th centuries.

Nighttime. The nightingales' song in the garden. The scent of flowerbeds in front of the terrace. The black darkness of the night sprinkled with stardust.

Everything was flowing: the darkness, the stars, the aromas of trees and flowers. Larysa. I was flowing too, dissolving in the stream of the unrealized and the unfinished. And onward I drifted. The blind, deaf expanses of the night space engulfed me. Through my "self" flowed the river of motionless darkness.

And then, from the depths of the night, I felt an indistinct sense of someone standing next to me. Someone had traveled an unknown distance and now stood beside me. I wasn't sure of anything, but it seemed to me that the silent and motionless figure belonged to Arsen Petrovych.

We were silent. I squeezed his hand. My hand was feverishly hot. I was drunk!

As we stood there, the fragments of the evening's memories flooded me—a chaotic mixture of sounds, colors, thoughts, feelings, words. It started to seem as if everything that had happened this evening was a phantom, that there was in fact nothing: the hieratic calm of the host, as he spoke, was feigned; he no longer believed in what he had said; the thoughts he had nurtured within himself for decades had become insubstantial; all the chains had been broken. Rolling across the terrace, they clattered loudly. Bowling pins fell.

"Pins? Do you like bowling?"

Pins? Me? Do I like bowling with pins? No, I don't. It seemed to me that I had already answered that I did not. Although it was possible that I had said nothing.

We fell silent. The river of silent darkness flowed through me. I lost myself again, lost all ends and beginnings. But I had to keep the conversation going, and I said,

"Paintings should be nailed to the walls with a hammer!"

Silence was filled with uncertainty. Uncertainty was to be avoided! Perhaps while saying this, I woke up, because then I distinctly heard the following,

"Indeed, you are right: paintings should be nailed to the walls. Actually, they should be hung on the nails hammered into the wall."

I agreed. I didn't object. I was thrilled by the idea of nails being hammered into the wall and paintings being hung on them.

"You have such wonderful things at the Museum," I said to Arsen Petrovych. "They should definitely be hung on nails!"

"But they accuse me of *recheznavstvo*!" he responded. "Tell me, is this a serious accusation, this recheznavstvo? Am I finished? Is this the end?"

I took notice of the tragedy that this person was experiencing, standing motionless next to me in the dark of night. And then, suddenly, I sobered up. I felt that this question, coming out of his mouth, sounded like a personal reproach. He was harboring hope that I could help him, that I could save him if I only wanted to.

"You are mistaken, Arsen Petrovych, if you think I could do something. Trust me, I don't know what materialism is. Moreover, truth be told, I am not generally interested in matters that don't concern me personally."

I knew that my answer sounded harsh, my words ruthless; they came across like a verdict, but what was the point of maintaining illusions?

"Well, well!" the host said, becoming pensive.

An internal struggle was raging inside him. He was filled with a sense of danger, and there was a burden on his heart that he couldn't shake. At this moment, he envied dockworkers on the pier, or old men sitting with outstretched hands by the gates at the entrance to the cemetery.

For the dockworker in his canvas robe, it was easier to carry sacks of grain on his back down the steep steps, from the shore into the black belly of the barge, than for him, the director of the Museum, to bear the dreadful anxiety in his heart. But he remembered his duties as host and kindly offered,

"Perhaps you would like another cup of tea, Rostyslav Mykhaylovych?"

"If you have Narzan or Selters, I would prefer them over tea," I replied.

We came back to the house. Bottles with green labels appeared on the table. I was thirsty, and now I savored the frothy coolness of Narzan. The nimble silver bubbles settled against the glass.

Arsen Petrovych eagerly drank tea, but the liquid tasted bitter now, and the sweetness seemed like medicine to him.

He couldn't control himself. Behind his usual restraint, it wasn't difficult to grasp the deep internal imbalance. I glanced at him. He shoved his hands into the pockets of his vest and his trousers, then felt the pockets of his jacket, as if he had lost something, searching for something but couldn't find it.

"Do you need something?" his wife asked.

"Me?"

He made an effort to smile, but his smile came out bewildered and awkward. Without taking his eyes off me, he stared intently for a while, as if trying to remember something. His gaze was fixed and mute. He was looking but he could not see.

"What's the matter with you?" his wife asked again.

"With me?"

He woke up from his slumber.

"No, nothing! I had wanted to ask Rostyslav Mykhaylovych something, but I already did that. So, nothing!"

Then he turned to his wife.

"You asked me what I needed? I wanted to ask you to pour me a cup of tea."

"It's right in front of you!"

"Ah! Thank you, I missed that!" He took the sugar bowl, put some sugar into the cup and stirred it thoughtfully with a spoon.

"You've already added sugar!"

"Really?"

He took a sip.

"Oh, you're right, I put too much of it!" He smiled at his wife, then at all of us, but there was a hint of confusion in his smile, as if he was asking for forgiveness—everything seemed out of place.

"Please, take this away and pour me a fresh cup!" He strained himself, making an effort. He was overcoming his anxiety, pushing it away. He compelled himself to think about what had been said earlier. He returned to his previous line of thought.

"We say: the people," he noted. "Historians compile hefty volumes devoted to the history of the Ukrainian people. We respect their diligence. But do they know what the people and its history are?"

His words sounded forced and unnatural. Why was he repeating himself? Why retread what had already been said?

He took a sip of tea.

"You forgot to add sugar!"

"Thank you, I'll drink it without sugar."

He took another sip from his cup.

"Our esteemed historians talk about the presence of the people in history, about the movement of history. But I would like to ask you, should we not talk about the non-movement of the people outside of history?"

Wooden bowling balls rattled across the floorboards. Pins fell with a cracking sound. I pushed back my chair.

"It's late. Shouldn't we thank our dear hosts and let them rest?"

XLIII

That's when we parted our ways, heading into the fragrant night, saturated with the scents of blooming trees. Behind me, Ivan Vasylovych Hulia was walking, even though it was already late and we were headed in the opposite directions.

He had been moved. He walked, reciting and singing. He kept repeating—"I, all of us…We all love you, Rostyslav Mykhailovych! We love and respect you. We love that you are so approachable for each of us, that you are so direct and unwavering! We believe in you, Rostyslav Mykhailovych!" Hulia proclaimed pathetically.

I turned back to look at him. What was this Hulia babbling about? Did he even know what he was saying?

Hulia tried to embrace me, even though I was much taller and heftier than he. I had to take him by the hands, to tame him somehow.

"Honestly, my dear fellow, you're about to tear my jacket apart. Please, don't pull on it."

But it was useless to try and persuade Hulia, and after a while, having released his hands, he again tried to wrap his arms around my waist. Pulling on my jacket, he reiterated his love and respect for me, how proud he was to be my student, and recommenced discussing the further prospects of museum work at the Varangian Church, after it had become a branch of the Museum.

A mischievous desire to tease him awakened in me— I wanted to introduce some discomfort into Hulia's certainty, to disrupt his elation, to destroy his sensitivity. I turned my whole body towards him.

"Please do tell, Ivan Vasylovych, are you a religious person?"

"How do you mean?"

"Well, it's very simple—are you a religious person or not?"

He fidgeted, feeling awkward. He couldn't understand why he was being asked that, and didn't know how to respond. I smiled.

"Obviously, you follow Ostap Vyshnia's dictum: At home, I am religious, but at work—I'm not?"[130]

Hulia waved his hands hesitantly.

"Well," I continued, "that's not the point! It's not about that, it's about something else: can you understand the feelings of a religious person?"

Hulia looked slightly offended that he was even asked that.

"Of course! Of course, I can!"

"Well, okay then. You can understand the situation, right? So, you sought to, you were the initiator—or rather, one of the initiators of converting the Varangian Church into a cultural and artistic reserve, instead of taking it away from the parish council and transferring it to the commune."

He couldn't understand why I was saying all this.

"Indeed, I was. Why? What did I do?"

"No, nothing! I'm just interested in some details."

"Details?" Hulia repeated.

He had too much to drink, our Hulia. He was already wobbling and his speech was slightly slurred; his thoughts were somewhat tangled, jittery.

"Details, okay! I see it!" he said.

"Let's say, one of these days you'd be appointed head of the branch. That's a possibility, right?"

---

[130] Ostap Vyshnia, *Vyshnevi usmishky krymski* (Vyshnia's Crimean Merriment), 1925.

Hulia laughed happily. It was his dream. He was hoping for this. He would like for this to happen.

"Well, that's great! So, if you're appointed to this position, your first task would be to open the royal doors, so that visitors could enter the altar and admire Lynnyk's mosaics. Correct?"

Hulia agreed,

"Yes!"

"As you well know, in accordance with canonical regulations, a layperson should neither open the royal doors nor pass through them. Nevertheless, you open the altar curtain and the holy doors, you pass through them, even though it's an apparent blasphemy!"

Hulia's throat became dry. He spasmodically swallowed saliva.

"Yes," he agreed obediently, "it's blasphemy!"

"Will you have the resolve, following the church rules, to write a proclamation and post it at the entrance to the altar, 'Women and those of non-Christian faith are prohibited from entering the altar'?"

"Rostyslav Mykhailovych!" he pleaded, "Rostyslav Mykhailovych, why are you doing this?"

But I was relentless. I put my hand on Hulia's shoulder, looking him in the eyes.

"Let's be honest, at least with ourselves. Let's finish this discussion. Let's abandon our intellectual habit of always stopping halfway and never reaching the end. We're used to walking on all paths because every path seems just as good to us as the one we walked before. Have the courage to acknowledge that there are no half-truths. There is only one truth, and it is absolute."

Hulia laughed in confusion, trying to cover his dismay,

"What do you want from me?"

"Me? From you? Nothing, my friend! Absolutely nothing! Nothing except clarity. Nothing except for you to acknowledge that a tax collector from the commune, who will close the church for the faithful and fill it with barrels of gas, oil, and herring, would be far more consistent than each of us is, than we are, than *you* are when, having transformed the Church into a Museum, you'd say, 'Glory to You, O Lord, that I am not like that tax collector!'"

Hulia tried to defend himself.

"But, Rostyslav Mykhailovych, you forget about the artistic value of the Varangian Church, about the aesthetic value of Lynnyk's mosaics. We are saving them from destruction, preserving them for future generations. This is our duty. I don't understand you, Rostyslav Mykhailovych, how can you say all this? Are you joking?"

"Not at all, dear Ivan Vasylovych, I am not joking! There are no aesthetic values in themselves. Lynnyk built a church, not an exhibition hall. This purely aesthetic interest in religious matters is a blasphemous denial of their metaphysical essence!"

I left Hulia completely bewildered in front of the hotel. He muttered helplessly:

"How can this be? It's impossible! What kind of jokes are these! Why? I am authorized by the Committee for the Protection of Monuments. That is my duty."

He fussed and hopped around. I didn't listen to him. I shook his hand and entered the dimly lit foyer.

I walked past rows of palm trees in barrels, reflected in the wall-mounted chandeliers, increasingly over-whelmed with rage. I was angry with myself: Why had I started this conversation with Hulia? Who needed it, and for what? Why had I disturbed the peace of a confident man, respectful to himself and others? I had agitated his conscience, and why? On a whim? What an idiot I was! Why did I have to interfere in matters that didn't concern me at all? I felt a staggering sense of disgust.

I collected the key on a large wire ring and a pile of letters and notes from the receptionist. Without looking, I shoved them into my pocket and walked up the wide staircase covered with soft carpet.

I opened the door, turned on the lights, and immediately saw a bouquet of flowers on the table. The roses, sprinkled with water, looked majestically lush and fresh. Their blooming beauty moved me. My dear girl! Today was the first evening since our meeting that we had spent apart. Wouldn't it have been better to skip lunch at the Vytvytskyis' and spend the evening with Larysa instead?

With gratitude, I brought my lips closer to the rose petals. What splendor of bloom! What grandeur of abundance! What luxury of color! I was filled with exuberance, which was followed, as always, by the sensation of pain.

I loosened my tie, sat on a chair, took off my shoes, and put on my slippers. Freshen up and get ready to sleep! I grabbed the towel, already anticipating the cold tickling of streams that would flow over my body.

The day was over. I was enveloped by calm. A pleasant sleep would come and bring the bliss of forgetfulness. With joyful anticipation, I gazed at the fresh bedding prepared for rest.

And then I heard a cautious knock on the door. I was surprised: What's going on? So late? Who could it be?

And suddenly, it occurred to me that it could be Larysa. Was it really her? Could she have been sitting downstairs on a boulevard bench, waiting for the light to come on in my window?

Insane, unbearable joy shook me. It propelled me to the door. Blood rushed to my face. Petals of roses blazed before my eyes like tongues of flame. Colors exploded. Thousands of meteors flared up, whirling around and within me.

I swung the door open. A triumphant cry— "Larysa!"—was about to burst out from my lungs.

In the corridor, Hulia stood before me with a guilty expression on his face.

He asked for forgiveness, disturbing me at such a late hour after we had already said goodbye, but he hoped for my understanding. After what I said to him, he couldn't just go home. He requested that I clarify something for him.

I put on a friendly face. I forced myself to smile. I did so with gentle kindness. I invited him into the room. I pulled out a chair. I offered him a seat. I asked him to be as comfortable as possible. I behaved as the most courteous host. Couldn't he see how glad I was that he had come to visit me? I made sure to offer him refreshments. I pressed the bell button. I sat in the chair opposite him.

"What are you drinking, my friend? What do you prefer: vodka, cognac, liqueur?"

He gave me a bewildered look. He didn't understand me.

"Drink? How do you mean, drink?"

"Well, as usual! You were kind enough to visit me. I am very pleased. I want to treat you. Let's have a drink!"

"But..."

He alluded to the late hour.

"No 'buts'! Exactly because it's late, let's drink!"

He hesitated.

"No, it's not about that, but so that you could clarify something for me…"

I interrupted him. I felt no remorse. I stated categorically,

"We *will* drink! The only option for you is to choose your poison: vodka, cognac, or liqueur?"

He listened to me with unspeakable horror. To drink again after so much had already been consumed? But Hulia's respect for me prevailed. He didn't dare refuse. No, this Hulia clearly lacked the audacity.

He sought salvation for himself, settling on liqueur.

"You prefer liqueur? Fine, liqueur it is!"

Hulia made a mistake. In his place, being a victim as he was, I would have chosen cognac! It would be much safer than the nasty sweet produce of the Spirits Trust. Cognac, at least, is more natural, especially if it is an expensive brand without any additives. But the lot had been cast. Today, my good man, you will have to cross your Rubicon, and the only difference from Caesar would be that he had not a single hair on his head, while you boast a thick mane. I placed an order with the waiter who appeared at my call.

"A bottle of Benedictine! And would you please give us tumblers, not glasses!"

Hulia had to drink. After each sip, he pushed the tumbler aside. He refused each one of my demands, trying to resume the conversation, to justify himself to me, to save himself. His conscience was affected, but I kept interrupting him,

"No philosophy. No dark, Dostoievskian soul-searching. I am no Stavrogin, and you are no Alyosha or Prince Myshkin. I am not a fan of gut-wrenching dramas."

I didn't let him speak. I forced him to drink. Eventually, he felt unwell, fainted, and fell asleep.

I called for a maid, and we moved Hulia to the couch.

Was I cruel to him? Perhaps. But wasn't it even more cruel on his part to disturb one's peace, late at night, when one ought to be sleeping, demanding answers to those questions that have no psychological motivation—that actually have no rationale whatsoever?

XLIV

Officially, I left the following day; in reality, I stayed.

The whirlwind that had risen from the abyss swept me away with it. The stormy gusts brought chaos, and nothing could be done about it.

Days and nights lost their boundaries. We plunged into the abyss of the primordial flow. In a motorboat, we traveled downstream, towards the rapids. We stood on the shore and listened to the roar of the restless river.

The river screamed, howled like a shaggy, wounded beast. Blue blood flowed from its wound. The turbulent flow crushed the blue expanse. The river's frenzy enticed us with its menace. Rushing from the rocks, the foamy stream surged downwards. The grayish foam went mad with pain.

I tried to shout over the river's roar.

"Fear has its charms, Larysa! Aren't you afraid?"

She shook her head. No, she wasn't afraid.

Primal rocks emerged from the water. Black cliffs protruded through the halo of foam. We were transported back millennia. We took the breaths of our Paleolithic ancestors. The barren shore resembled a Scandinavian fjord. Larysa's blond hair was the gold of that northern Solveig. What dangers did our love conceal?

The next day, we sailed up the Dnipro to Kamyanske.[131] There we disembarked at the pier to catch the next steamer coming from upriver to make our way back. I suggested taking the boat and crossing to the other side.

"The steamer won't be here for a while. We still have time."

We crossed to the other side, pulled the boat onto the sand. It was a gray, overcast day. Specks of soot littered the sand. The bitter smell of willow saturated the air. The water sloshed against the bottom of the boat. Larysa sat, not removing her dress, holding the billowing fabric on her knees.

"Don't you want to take off your clothes?"

---

[131] Kamyanske: a city near present-day Dnipro, where a major steelwork plan had been based.

In response, I heard an emphatic "No!"

"Are you cold?" I was getting slightly concerned. I glanced at the overcast sky,

"It's a bit cloudy today!"

"Oh, who cares!"

I looked at her, surprised.

"Are you unhappy about something?"

"No!"

"What's the matter?"

"Nothing, really. Oh, wait—I wanted to know why you never said 'I love you.'"

"I think," I replied without any pretense, "it's because I am shy!"

My words made her explode with laughter. She laughed uncontrollably, to tears, to hysteria. She stroked my head, saying,

"Oh, my dear, innocent boy!"

I kissed her hand.

"What can I do, Larysa?" I said to her somewhat melancholically. "Believe me, I would never dare say 'My sunshine!' to a woman I love."

"I didn't expect you to start reciting Oles's poetry to me!"

"You're right, the poets of our generation don't write lyrical poems. Their love poetry is anti-lyrical. Our generation is not only against all feelings, it is also against psychology!"

"Don't you think women are missing out on a lot because of that?"

"I've thought about that," I confirmed. "I suppose it is true. Maybe future generations will cultivate sensitivities again, and men will once again tell women about their feelings, and women will enjoy listening to their sensitive, sentimental words. But perhaps these future generations will live in a world of constant negation and denial. One ought to admit that there are no comforts in a state of decay!"

Larysa looked at me inquisitively and remarked pensively,

"Flaubert wrote a novel called *Sentimental Education*."

"Yes, *L'Éducation sentimentale*," I echoed her. "That was back then. He was a friend of Turgenev, and Turgenev was friends with Marko Vovchok.[132] Dear me, how the world has changed since then. We don't cultivate any feelings in ourselves or others. We're just slaves to our instincts. Look around—the sand of this beach is dusted with factory smoke. Slag floats in the river water, released from the open-hearth furnaces."

"I know," Larysa responded, "You're going to talk about the decline of the landscape, the ruining of pristine nature, the devastation of the land by modern technology. You've said it already!"

I agreed.

"You don't want me to talk about technology—fine, I'll talk about art. Take Lynnyk, for instance. He dreamed of founding a new era in art. He wasn't attracted to the psychological profiles of the people he painted. He didn't seek to convey the emotional states

---

[132] Marko Vovchok (real name Mariya Vilinska, 1834–1907): Ukrainian writer of Russian descent, who worked in the style of realism and ethnographic romanticism.

of suffering or joy. He didn't give weight to the individual nuances of inner experiences. Sentimentality escaped
his imagination."

The wind rocked the boat as it sat ashore. The waves
lapped. Somewhere a motor hummed. In the middle of
the river, on a black coffin of a boat, a man sat motionless, hunched over his fishing rods. Past the far
shore, strips of smoke from factory chimneys stretched
across the cloudy sky. Above the black silhouettes of
industrial structures along the shore, gloomy yellow or
bluish-gray flames flickered.

I took out a *Golden Label*[133] chocolate bar from the
bag and offered it to Larysa. I continued talking as we
chewed.

"We are talking about the crisis of realistic and individualistic art as we have known it until now. And that's
understandable. The focus of our time has shifted from
the individual to society. The state, the people, the nation, the class, and the party are the actors. When the
state is in action, when organized masses are in action,
can the actions of an individual remain psychologically
motivated? The individual, internal, personal motivation
for action disappears."

"And nothing comes in its place?"

"Instead, one develops a feeling of submersion. You
walk in file, one among many; you must walk like your
comrades do, like the thousands around you. By touching

[133] A high-quality chocolate produced by *MosSelProm* (the Moscow Cooperative Administration) in the 1920s-1930s, especially popular among
the party elites and intelligentsia.

your comrade's elbow, you must feel his presence. With this touch of the elbow, you confirm his presence."

I said this while looking at Larysa, who was sitting with her hands clasped around her knees, her shoulder propped against me. I felt the oval shape of her body and inhaled the scent of her hair. I was thinking that our love was not tinted with sentimentality, similar to the bliss of saints and the suffering of sinners in medieval frescoes and mosaics. I broke off a piece of chocolate and offered it to Larysa.

"Please!"

I sensed her hesitation.

"Try it, this is not *Mignon*! [134] I deliberately chose *Golden Label* because it's bitter, and I was certain you would prefer it."

Larysa took a piece, "Thank you!" And then,

"Feeling my neighbor's elbow... I don't want to walk in any kind of file. I prefer to go my own way!" she declared with heroic pathos.

I squinted. I looked at her mockingly.

"Oh, really! You reminisce about your great-grandmother's cookies, but in the meantime, you prefer the stamped taste of factory chocolate. I have not the slightest hope that you'll be pulling out the cookies or pies that you baked yesterday from your suitcase."

"Aren't you cheeky!" Larysa laughed. "I didn't have a single free minute yesterday to fiddle with the dough."

"That's exactly the point. The point is that you don't make any dough, you don't bake any pies. We're getting

---

[134] A bitter chocolate produced by *MosSelProm* in the 1930s.

used to coloring our actions and desires with the isolation of personal experience. We grow out of the habit of acting, feeling, and thinking in accordance with our own initiative. We're getting used to acting, thinking, and living according to common prescriptions that apply to millions and are mandatory for everyone."

Slowly, Larysa turned her face toward me. She had full, expressive lips that protruded slightly forward—two thick stripes of red paint.

She repeated,

"Actions, feelings, thoughts..." And then she asked, "And love?"

She stretched her lips, outlined in carmine, toward me.

"And love!" I replied.

The empty river. The solitary figure of the fisherman. The bitter scent of willow.

A distant horn, echoing down the river, reminded us of the need to be on our way. Larysa stood up, adjusted her dress, shook the sand off her boots, took out a mirror from her bag, and adjusted her wind-blown hair.

Waiting for the steamboat, we stood on the dock, leaning against the railing. Before us stretched the wide expanse of the river. It smelled of resin, bast, and wood. With a rumble, moored boats bumped against the shore. Bright reflections from the water wandered along the dark wall of the dock like tangled cobwebs.

We didn't go up on the deck of the steamboat. We settled on the bow in the restaurant lounge. Behind the wide, glassy windows, the banks drifted by, changing colors. The day faded. The engine rumbled.

I ordered food.

Larysa and I raised our glasses. The steep cliffs of the right bank lit up with an orange flame. And as the steamboat passed along the shore, in the tranquility of the evening air, the idyllic chirping of birds and the sweet smell of grass reached us.

A cold sip of liquid, bitter and tangy, we felt as the apotheosis of immediate liberation.

"You know how to enjoy a good drink, Larysa!" I said enthusiastically.

"Am I not good-looking, too?" she asked defiantly.

"You are!" I agreed.

"Well, then let's drink to my beauty!" she suggested.

And we clinked our glasses again.

And with that sip of vodka, everything around us immediately unraveled, became transparent. Every impression unexpectedly gained clarity and finality: the outline of the fork in her hand; the straight contour of her brow; the bend of the window's angle; and on the river, beyond the window frame, the wedge of a sandy foreland, sharp and pink like a flamingo's wing.

And then, returning to the theme of our conversation, she said,

"You were saying that love..."

"Yes, I was saying that in our time, love has become anti-psychological. We no longer say 'I love you!' but even if we do, we don't endow those words with any emotional content. Such is the style of our era, which rejects the psychological, personal characterization of action. We have become restrained in expressing our feelings. We renounce sensitivity. We assert a love devoid of compassion. We avoid defining our feelings for a woman as love, because we do not want to admit to any inaccuracies. Writers of our time have become stricter in their choice of words and more demanding toward the form. Our poetry does not cultivate lyricism. It scorns the subjectivity of lyricism and strives for mandatory norms, material that would be mandatory for everyone."

"You're a cynic, Rostyslav Mykhailovych, even though you prattle about modesty."

"That's clearly an unfair accusation on your part, Larysa Pavlivna! Firstly, I have always considered myself a highly moral and deeply principled person. And secondly, in my dealings with such a striking and beautiful woman as you, Larysa, I would never allow myself to be cynical, let alone even the slightest bit immodest."

Larysa looked at me skeptically.

I caught her gaze. "You're forcing me to appeal to you directly. What inappropriate or offensive behavior could you accuse me of in my treatment of you from the first day of our acquaintance?"

Larysa hastened to reassure me.

"Of course, nothing, Rostyslav Mykhailovych! Absolutely nothing! Throughout our entire acquaintance, starting from our first meeting, your behavior towards me has been impeccably proper."

Larysa was too much a woman of our time to attach any significance to words or assessments, perhaps even to actions and obvious facts.

XLV

Days rushed by in a blaze of sun-soaked madness.

After the days spent on the river and out in the sun, my skin looked like a Moor's.

I should have returned home long ago, but I lacked the resolve to tell myself that I was leaving. I kept postponing my departure day after day. I was dragging my feet. I couldn't rely on myself. I wasn't sure that once I said, "Larysa, I'm leaving!" I wouldn't do something completely unexpected or wouldn't take the most absurd, totally unforeseen step.

And yet, in the end, full of hesitation and uncertainty, I said,

"Larysa, I'm leaving tomorrow!"

I said it and was struck by how softly and gently the words sounded. Nothing catastrophic had occurred.

As always, both now and then, the hardest part was making the decision. Once made, the decision brought clarity. Now I faced a definite fact and acted within the confines it created.

Larysa persuaded me to postpone my departure by one more day because she wanted to arrange a small reception for me.

"A strictly intimate evening. I'll sing for you."

It was a small gathering with only a few people. In addition to the hosts and myself, there was Larysa's accompanist—a pale person of indeterminate age with long, bony, spider-like fingers and large feet in narrow shoes, and another family, neighbors, whose apartment was located opposite Larysa's, on the same landing.

The man was a professor of physics, a doctor, and a corresponding member of the Academy of Sciences. He was tall, slender, lean, with a narrow, sharply outlined nose and a thin slit of lips on his tanned face. I recognized him—we had met before. One summer, we had been together at *Buyurnus*, a resort for scientists in Hurzuf. At that time, he had given the impression of a very young man; now, though he retained his youthful appearance, his temples had already turned gray, and there was a yellowish tint to his tanned complexion. Over the years, he had quickly risen as a leading figure in the field of physics. I often came across his name or his presentations in the newspaper reports on academic congresses and conferences while flipping through the pages of the *Proceedings of the Academy of Sciences.*

His wife was still a relatively young woman, tall and full-bodied, with rosy cheeks and a round, fair-skinned face. The soft plumpness of her figure attested to her tendency to gain weight.

At first, Larysa sang standing in front of the grand piano. A striking woman with a face made for a concert stage. She wore a black dress in the fashion of the seventeenth century, with a narrow, cinched waist; a wide skirt; a deep rectangular neckline framed with white lace revealing rounded breasts; her head atop her high neck rose like a flower above the billowing black sleeves.

She sang love ballads with her deep voice, showcasing a flexible vocal range. I was filled with an odd feeling, as if I had been transported to a completely different world, unlike anything I was familiar with. Everything that had happened occurred in this altered world, where everything was the same and yet different. This altered world was reflected in the mirror of her voice.

I sat on a silk-upholstered chair, leaning against the back, feeling absorbed in Larysa's voice, gazing at the clear profile of the young scientist, at his high, narrow forehead with hair slicked back on his temples, and... I felt jealous. Yes, I *was* jealous. I knew nothing about Larysa's relationship with this physicist, but the venomous sting of jealousy sucked at my heart.

I thought about my departure the next day, about leaving Larysa here, and my brain was troubled by poisonous fantasies and thoughts. Every moment, I was on the verge of bursting forth in all the blindness of inflamed, unfulfilled passion. I wasn't sure of myself. Who knew what I was capable of?

Meanwhile, Larysa's voice rang out triumphant, mighty, boundless in its despotic power. Her voice spoke of love, and the lyrics of her songs were addressed to each and everyone. I felt envy, pain, fatigue, and unsatisfied desire.

I thought about everything that had happened over the past few days, about the sunlit chaos into which I had plunged, about Larysa, about Chaikovskii, whose romances she had performed. I thought about the strange, awful duality of Chaikovskii's life and creative work, about his tragic love, about his incredible romance with Mrs. von Meck, which spanned decades but didn't actually exist.

I was suffocating. I languished. I plunged into the abyss. I was destroyed. But it was all just an illusion. The reality was a small rectangle of brown paperboard, a train ticket lying in the pocket of my vest. It proclaimed that tomorrow I would depart.

Later, we dined. We drank. The host, Larysa's husband, complained incessantly about his ailing liver, but that didn't stop him from drinking more than any of us. Dinner was plentiful and tastefully served. Larysa, tilting her head to the side, said,

"Unfortunately, Rostyslav Mykhailovych, I didn't make any pies today either!"

"What is there to do?" I shrugged.

Stepping out onto the balcony, I kissed Larysa. The next day I departed. The trees had already started dropping their bloom; the wind carried white acacia blossoms that had begun to wilt along the sun-warmed pavement of the avenue. The heat blazed in the bright air.

Spring was ending. The southern summer was coming into its own. Larysa escorted me to the train station. We walked along the platform, holding hands, pressing tightly against each other. I promised to come back in the summer. She promised to come on tour to Kharkiv in the fall. I squeezed her delicate fingers.

The bell rang. I kissed the palm of Larysa's hand. I entered the train car, went to my compartment, lowered the window frame, and as the train began to move, leaned out the window and kissed the tips of her fingers one last time. Larysa was walking along the platform. Through the noise of the moving train and the clattering of the wheels, I heard,

"Admit that everything that happened was just a coincidence!"

I shouted back,

"No, it was a necessity!"

I didn't know if she heard me. The train accelerated. She waved her colorful, light parasol.

I sank into the soft sofa and shut my eyes wearily. In the swirl of fiery spots before me flashed the white, sun-drenched Varangian Church, the black triangles of the old women on the front steps, the gray cobblestones of the street below the hillside, the tram tracks, the narrow linen skirt, the high heels of the boots, Larysa.

The conductor pushed open the compartment door and said,

"Citizens, close the windows! We're approaching the bridge!"

I opened my eyes. From the azure abyss the un-bearably white shimmer of the Dnipro burst forth.